MARRIED TO THE DON

A DARK RUSSIAN MAFIA ROMANCE (KORNILOV BRATVA DUET BOOK 1)

NICOLE FOX

ALSO BY NICOLE FOX

De Maggio Mafia Duet
Devil in a Suit (Book 1)

Devil at the Altar (Book 2)

Kornilov Bratva Duet
Married to the Don (Book 1)

Til Death Do Us Part (Book 2)

Volkov Bratva
Broken Vows (Book 1)

Broken Hope (Book 2)

Broken Sins *(standalone)*

Heirs to the Bratva Empire
*Can be read in any order

Kostya

Maksim

Andrei

Tsezar Bratva
Nightfall (Book 1)

Daybreak (Book 2)

Russian Crime Brotherhood
*Can be read in any order

Owned by the Mob Boss

Unprotected with the Mob Boss

Knocked Up by the Mob Boss

Sold to the Mob Boss

Stolen by the Mob Boss

Trapped with the Mob Boss

Other Standalones

Vin: A Mafia Romance

Box Sets

Bratva Mob Bosses (Russian Crime Brotherhood Books 1-6)

Tsezar Bratva (Tsezar Bratva Duet Books 1-2)

MAILING LIST

Sign up to my mailing list!
New subscribers receive a FREE steamy bad boy romance novel.

Click the link below to join.
http://bit.ly/NicoleFoxNewsletter

MARRIED TO THE DON

My baby's father wants me dead.

I didn't ask to carry a mobster's baby.

But he never gave me a choice.

The man who gave me my son stole my innocence in return.

And now, his Bratva brother is coming to finish what he started.

Viktor Kornilov is a cold-blooded beast.

His name alone makes my blood run cold.

But his cruel touch makes my heart beat faster and faster.

We're trapped in a high-stakes game of lies and violence.

One wrong move, and he'll take my son away.

So when he gives me his sinful offer

—become his fake wife or become his latest victim—

The only answer I can give is yes.

1
VIKTOR

The neon signs from the store window wash my dashboard in red light. When I look over at the entrance, I see the husk of a beer can lying discarded on the steps. Most of the other stores on Bundt Street have closed for the night. But the liquor store is still open. The owner has been glancing out at me once every thirty seconds. My windows are too tinted for him to see inside, but I can see him. He looks nervous.

My phone is pressed to my ear, waiting for Fedor to continue.

"I only have another couple minutes," Fedor says, his voice growing quiet as he turns away from the phone. He's probably looking to see where the guards are. Maybe the guy in line behind him is bugging him to get off the phone so he can get a chance. Phone time in prison is a precious commodity. "I tried to get someone else's phone time this week, but no dice. Even the guys who don't give a shit about their kids are trying to call them up for the holidays. Christmas turns everyone into a fucking saint, apparently."

"I have to go anyway," I say, looking up as the only customer who'd been lingering in the store exits. He's a big man with a dusty pair of overalls on, probably a construction worker. He tosses his six-pack into the passenger seat of his lifted truck and rumbles out of the nearly empty parking lot. The only cars left are mine and the owner's.

"What's on your schedule tonight?" Fedor asks. Then, he sighs before I can answer. "God, I miss going out with you. Beating people down. Taking what's ours. We fucking ruled the streets."

More accurately, *I* ruled the streets. Fedor mostly got himself arrested. Time and time again.

My rap sheet is almost spotless, except for a small bar fight I got into when I was seventeen. The police nabbed me for public intoxication, battery, and possession of alcohol as a minor. I spent a few weeks in juvie. That was more than enough lock-up time for me. Since then, I've steered clear of obvious shows of criminal activity. But Fedor didn't learn from his older brother's mistakes.

"How do you know I'm working?" I ask.

He snorts. "You're always working."

Fair enough. "I just have to deal with someone who wronged me."

"There are plenty of people like that. Who is it?"

"No one you know," I say.

I hear a guard in the back shout that his time is almost up, and Fedor growls. "I'm missing everything in here. When are you going to get me the fuck out?"

Our conversations always go like this. Fedor wants me to tell him what I'm doing, but when I do, he starts to miss the lifestyle he had and then gets angry that he's locked up and wants me to break him out. When I try to spare his feelings and don't tell him what's going on in the Bratva, he gets angry because he's missing it and still wants me to break him out. No matter what, the conversation ends with him wanting me to save him.

Like I always have.

"Kent is trying to get the charges lowered from second-degree murder to involuntary manslaughter," I explain for what feels like the hundredth time. "If he can, then you'll be out a lot sooner, especially if you don't cause any trouble. But we don't know yet."

"Pay someone off," he says, loud and clear into the phone. "You control this entire city. Open up your wallet and help your baby brother."

The suggestion that he's in prison because I'm not generous enough makes me grip the phone even tighter, my knuckles going white. I take a deep breath. "We're going to get you out the right way."

I emphasize the last two words heavily, trying to remind Fedor that our conversation is being monitored. I've explained to him too many times to count that we can't talk business on this line, but he doesn't care.

"Fuck that!" Fedor yells. I'm sure he would have said more, but before he can, the line goes dead and the call is over.

I slide my cell phone into my pocket and lean back against the headrest.

Fedor has always been impulsive and reckless. He has the charm of our mother with the impulse control of our father, which is a deadly combination. Fedor can draw you in, make you love him, and then he detonates a bomb in your face. He threatens to ruin your entire life, but as soon as you get mad at him, he says something to remind you of all the good times, the better times. He looks at you like you're his only hope, and you just can't help but help him.

At least, I can't.

Ever since our mom died, I've looked out for my brother. Dad was too busy running the Bratva and killing people to come home to his kids, so I cooked and got Fedor dressed and gave him baths. Now, I'm twenty-eight and running the Bratva my father left behind, while still taking care of my twenty-five-year-old brother as though he's five. Because in my eyes, he will always be five.

Five and crying next to our mother's open casket.

The mortician put her in an uncharacteristic long-sleeved dress to hide the track marks on her arms. She looked thinner, but I hadn't seen her in almost two months. Dad had put her in a rehab facility, trying to clean her up enough so that she could take care of us, but as soon as she got out, she bought from a sleazy street dealer who, unlike my father's dealers, hadn't been instructed not to sell to her. The drug was laced with a synthetic she didn't know about, and she died in an alleyway.

I shake off the memory, pat my hip for the feel of my Glock, and pull my hood up. Fedor isn't five anymore. He isn't a helpless little kid. He's a grown man, and I can't clean up his messes forever. But it seems I will keep doing it for just a little bit longer.

I get out of the car and keep my face tilted downward as I walk up to the liquor store entrance. I stay that way as the bell above my head rings to announce my presence.

"Hey there," the owner says, greeting me in a gruff voice.

I tip my head without looking at him and head to the back wall of refrigerators, pretending to scan the shelves of cheap beer. I stay there for no more than a minute, just long enough to register how many cameras are in the store. By the looks of them and the rest of the shabby shop, it's a self-monitored security system. It won't be hard to erase the footage of my visit.

When I'm ready to do what I came to do, I shove my hands deep into my hoodie pockets and shuffle back towards the door with my head still down.

"Nothing for you today?" the owner asks.

I don't respond, lowering my head even further, and just like I hoped, he comes out from behind the counter and meets me at the door. His hand lands on my shoulder, jerking me back.

"I'm talking to you," he growls in the voice he has no doubt scared countless teenagers with. Liquor store owners have to be tough. They have to be ready to confront shoplifters and underage thieves.

But even all of that experience hasn't prepared him for the likes of me.

"No," I say, pulling the gun from my hip and pressing it into his side. "*I'm* talking to you."

The owner is middle-aged with a gut made rotund by beer and pretzels, but he still feels the pressure in his side. Confusion flickers across his face, followed by realization and then horror. His eyes go wide, and his face pales. He lifts his hands.

"On your stomach," I order.

He drops to the floor in a second. I keep my eyes on him as I walk backwards towards the door and flip the switch to turn off the neon "OPEN" sign, then slide the deadbolt into place.

"Crawl between the aisles," I say, walking towards him, gesturing with my gun for him to get out of view of the door.

As he scoots backwards on his stomach, I flip the light switches next to the counter until only the light in the far back of the store is left flickering.

"The cash register is full," he babbles. "Take it. Take it all."

I turn my head to the side, studying him. "Generous, but no thank you."

He glances up at me, brow furrowed. Something about my expression must unnerve him because he looks back down, his nose touching the dirty tile floor. "Then what do you want?"

"I know who you are." I pause, letting the words sit between us. "George McDougall."

He flinches when I say his name, realizing my vendetta is personal. This isn't about money; it's about revenge.

"Who are you?" he asks.

I drop to one knee in front of him, my gun arm resting across my leg, the barrel pointed at his head. "I think you already know."

He shakes his head, still looking down at the floor, but I can tell by the lowering of his shoulders that he knows exactly who I am. The nervous glancing out the front window before I even walked inside confirmed that he was nervous. He had every right to be.

"It's been weeks," he says in a near-whisper.

"Yeah, well, without my brother around to help out, I've been a little behind. Trust me, I would have come here sooner if I could have."

"Damien was my friend," George says. "I had to do what I could to make sure he got justice."

"My brother delivered his justice."

George glances up at me, and I feel the urge to look away. We both know that isn't true. Still, I hold his gaze, narrowing my eyes until he looks away. George is a brave man, but he's smart, too. He knows I hold his life in my hands right now.

He had to be brave to take the stand he did against the Kornilov Bratva. Anyone who has even considered it in the past received a visit from some of our enforcers. They all changed their minds pretty quickly. The only reason George slipped through the cracks was because the prosecution kept his identity anonymous until the very last minute. We didn't know he'd take the stand until he was being sworn in. By then, it was too late to do anything about it.

I'm angry with George for putting my brother in jail, but completely separate from that, he made me look weak. It was under my leadership that a witness finally dared to come forward and testify. No one would ever have considered doing such a thing when my father was in charge. That's part of the reason I'm holding a gun to his head.

The other reason is that the most important and difficult tasks should always be handled by the leader. My father would disagree—he disagreed with me on many different points—but I learned a lot from watching him lead. He delegated everything, sending his men around the city to do his business. They feared him, but they didn't respect him. I want their fear and their respect alike.

If I'm not willing to get my hands dirty, then how can I ask anyone else to do it for me? So, in this matter that intimately involves my brother, I want to be the one to pull the trigger. I want to show my men that I'm not above them, but with them. For my Bratva. For my family.

"I have a family," George says, his voice shaking. "A wife and children."

"I don't care."

George looks up at me, his eyes wide. His face is wrinkled, and he looks tired. "My wife wanted to leave town as soon as I testified. She wanted to change our names, but I told her I wanted to stay."

"That was your mistake," I say coldly.

"Was it?" he asks. "If your father had still been in charge, I never would have dared."

Just as I thought. I ready my finger on the trigger. Enough people have told me I'm too weak to be a boss; I don't want to hear it from an overweight liquor store owner too. I'll kill him before he gets the chance.

"But you're fair," he says, surprising me.

I let the gun slip slightly as he talks.

"At least, I believed you to be a fair man," he says. "It's the only reason I kept my family here. Because I didn't think you would kill me for telling the truth."

He meets my eyes for another second before looking back down at the floor, and I'm glad. I don't want him to see what I'm going to do next.

As I walk back into the parking lot, a man is idling in front of the store, squinting towards the store hours. That sign says it should be open, but the neon one is dark. He rolls down his window. "Are you open?"

If he'd gotten out and tried the door, he would have found it unlocked, but he didn't. He asked me. So, I shake my head. "Nope."

The man curses under his breath. "Update your hours!" he yells as he screeches out of the parking lot, in search of another place to quench his late-night thirst.

I just cost George some business, but he isn't in any state to care.

2

MOLLY

I bend over and wrap the towel around my hair. The towel is still damp from drying my son off after his shower, but it should help dry my hair a little bit before we have to head out into the cold. Walking around with frozen, crunchy hair all morning is not my idea of a good start to the day. Though, neither is showering in a gym locker room, when I really think about it.

My jeans feel sticky against my skin, and I make a mental note to set aside some of my tip money to make a laundromat run. My shirt also sticks to my skin, but that's because the towel was too wet to do much good drying me off. I pinch the thin material and try to pull it away from my breasts, but when I let go, it resumes clinging to my every curve.

I look up and scan the shower area again. There are no partitions or even curtains. Just one long row of showerheads protruding from a white tile wall. Even though we've been coming to this same gym for months, I can't seem to grow comfortable with the arrangement. I always feel like I'm being watched. It's why Theo and I shower so early in the mornings. The first arrivals of the day are still in the middle of their workouts when we show up. It gives us fifteen or so uninterrupted minutes to shower before any of the other members can complain to the front desk about a child being in the showers.

If they're so worried about children seeing a bunch of naked adults, perhaps they should spring for stalls, I think to myself. That would probably require a higher membership fee, however, which we don't have the money for. And showering in full view of other women beats smelling like body odor and diner grease, so I'll take what I can get. Though, I'll have to find another solution before Theo gets much older. At this age, he's too busy playing to pay any mind, but that won't last much longer.

Theo makes a loud roaring sound, pulling me from my thoughts. I turn around just in time to see his little face squished in fury as he squeezes a bottle with all his might, squirting shampoo up into the air in a tall arc.

"No, no, no!" I blurt out, rushing forward to yank the bottle out of his hands. I squeeze the sides of the bottle lightly, trying to assess how much shampoo we lost. I'd be annoyed even if it was the cheap dollar store shampoo, but I found this bottle in one of the showers last week. It's a salon-grade shampoo, way out of our price range and probably left behind by one of the stay-at-home moms after a private Pilates class. Probably one of the same moms who glower whenever they see me waiting in the lobby with Theo for the bus. I didn't mind taking the bottle because whoever left it probably wouldn't even notice. Things like shampoo are easy enough for them to come by that they don't worry much about it.

"It's a volcano," Theo says playfully, rounding his lips around the final "O," emphasizing it in a way that makes it hard to be angry. The little sucker is cute when he wants to be.

"This volcano is dormant from now on," I say, tucking the bottle into my stained duffel bag. "We can't afford to waste shampoo right now, buddy."

He frowns, both because he got in trouble and because he doesn't understand why. Theo makes that face whenever I talk about our finances.

I kneel in front of him and pat his clean hair. Even in the terrible fluorescent bathroom lighting, I can see the gold streaks in it, the lightness that didn't come from my mostly Dominican roots. The shape of his face isn't like mine either. His is sharp—always has been, even when he had a layer of baby fat covering his cheeks—whereas mine is oval. I run my hand from his hair, down his cheek, and lift his chin until we're looking into each other's matching brown eyes.

"That was a cool volcano, though."

His eyebrows rise, and he smiles. "Really?"

"Really. I loved it, but next time, you need to ask Mama if it's okay, okay?"

"Okay," he repeats, still smiling at my compliment.

I Velcro his shoes on, pressing my thumb down over his toes to see how much longer this pair will last before I need to buy new ones. They fit for now, but he grew out of the last pair almost overnight, so I know I'll need to allocate the money sooner or later.

Then, I slip into my white sneakers, stained with oil splatters, and pull on my coat. Theo is proud of himself for putting his on without my assistance, but he still needs help with the zipper. I zip it up to his neck and then kiss his cheek. He pretends to be grossed out, but when I hold my arms out, he wraps his skinny legs around my waist and hugs me, forcing me to carry him out of the bathroom and into the hall. It doesn't take much convincing. I've been working a lot of overtime lately, and we don't get as much time together as I'd like. I'm happy to make the most of every minute I can.

I see a figure in a gym employee's uniform dart around the corner ahead of us towards the front desk and thank my lucky stars they weren't standing just outside the door as I came out. Kids aren't allowed in the locker rooms. If you do bring a child, you either need to skip your post-workout shower or check them into the in-house gym day care. It costs five dollars per hour, which I can't afford. Plus, Theo needs to bathe. Early-morning showers mean everyone who might care is usually still waking up for the day and too tired to pay attention to me or whatever rules I might be breaking. I pray our luck in that department continues.

When we get into the lobby, Theo wriggles out of my hold and runs across the lobby to press his face against the steamy gym windows. He likes drawing pictures in the condensation, and I spend so much time telling him "no" for other things that I can't bear to take this little pleasure away from him.

Our bus still hasn't arrived, but Shonda drives on Monday mornings, and she usually runs ten minutes later than the other drivers, so I figure we have another five minutes before she shows up.

I'm walking towards the tables and chairs closest to the doors to wait when my path is suddenly blocked. I pull up short, surprised. "I'm sorry," I say out of instinct.

"Apology not necessary," the front desk employee says. "I cut you off."

I smile and glance at his name tag—Ted. When I look back up at his face, his eyes are scanning my chest as though also looking for a name tag. Except, I don't have one. What I do have, however, is a thin T-shirt clinging to a slightly damp chest, and I have a gross feeling Ted is admiring the view. I cross my arms. "Why?"

He looks up like he's just remembered boobs are usually attached to a human being and pulls one side of his mouth up into a confident smirk. "I've seen you coming in here pretty regularly the last few months."

"I have a membership," I say, reaching into my pocket to pull out the membership card. If he reads it closely, he'll see it's a solo membership, not a family membership. The solo membership is cheaper, and the woman who usually mans the desk and scans my card as we enter either hasn't noticed Theo isn't on my plan or she's guessed at our situation and takes pity on us. Whichever one it is, I don't want to ruin a good thing, but I also don't want to be kicked out by an employee who is okay with openly ogling women's bodies while on duty.

Ted waves his hand. "I know. I'm just saying … I've seen you."

I slide my hand deeper into my pocket, clutching the membership card even though he doesn't want to see it. Something in the way he says the words sends a chill down my back like some innate instinct from long ago, warning me of a predator. I look over towards Theo. He's drawing the outline of a Christmas tree in the glass, oblivious to our conversation.

"Oh," I say, trying to sound casual. "Yeah, I've seen you too. Working at the desk."

"Is that your son?" he asks, nodding towards Theo.

"Yes." I don't know why, but I feel like my answers are very important. Like I'm in a job interview.

Ted's eyes narrow and then drift down my body again. "You look too young to have a kid that old."

I cross my arms tighter, covering my chest. He's probably thinking exactly what everyone else thinks when they find out I have a four-year-old son. *Teen mom, slut, another statistic.* I've heard it all before, and I'm not about to hear it from Ted the Gym Pervert.

"Well, I'm not," I say coldly.

I try to walk past him, but he steps to the side, blocking my path again.

"Listen," I say, holding up a hand to warn him to keep his distance. "Whatever this is, I'm not interested in—"

"I see you come in every day, but you don't workout." He glances behind him to check that the desk is still empty and his fellow employee hasn't joined him yet. "You just come in, go straight to the showers, and leave."

I swear his pupils are larger than they were a second ago. His face is familiar in the way all predators seem familiar. There is hunger there, and I resist the urge to turn and run in the opposite direction. I stand taller, broadening my shoulders to look as big as possible, as though I'm trying to scare away a bear. "There are no rules against that."

He raises a brow, surprised by my fight, perhaps. Then, he nods towards where Theo is drawing a misshapen snowman. "There are rules against him, though. He isn't supposed to be in the showers with you."

I respond without glancing back. "He wasn't."

Ted's smile widens, and his white teeth glimmer in the yellow lighting. "Don't lie. Remember? *I've seen you.*"

The same cold-egg-yolk-moving-down-my-spine feeling I had in the shower this morning returns, and I suddenly know without a doubt that Ted has been watching me bathe.

I've had the same feeling every time I've showered in the gym, and I thought it was just my own self-consciousness at being in the open, but now I realize my instincts picked up on the presence of a predator.

Suddenly, I remember all the footsteps I've heard over the months we've been coming here. There were times where the locker room door would beep like someone had opened the door, but then no one ever came in. Only, now I realize, they did. *He* did. And he watched me—naked and vulnerable—without my consent.

My stomach turns. I know this feeling all too well. The violation. I want to throw up, and when Ted's eyes assess me again, I know he doesn't need me to take off my coat to get an idea of what I'm hiding under it. He has already seen it.

"What do you want?" I ask, my voice low and icy. I glance back towards the doors and see the bus pulling into the parking lot. Theo sees it too.

"The bus is here," he calls, dragging his coat sleeve through his condensation drawing to erase it and moving towards the doors. "Come on, Mama."

"Nothing," Ted says with an innocent shrug that I recognize as a farce. Then, his face sharpens, and he looks down at me over the long slope of his nose. "I just thought maybe you could reward me for keeping your secret."

"I don't have any money."

He shakes his head and looks down the length of my body, his tongue darting out over his lower lip like a snake. "I don't want your money."

I fight back a shiver.

Ted leans in, whispering, "I'll pay the five dollars for the day care. No one will ever have to know."

He lays a hand on my shoulder, dragging it down my arm. "It's your choice, Molly."

He knows my name, and something about that feels like the worst thing of all. That this man knows me and has seen me. That he's threatening me, blackmailing me with the ability to shower for sex. It's repulsive, and I clench my fingers into a fist, prepared to break his nose and make a run for the bus. I don't give a damn if I'm banned from the gym for life.

Before I can follow through with my plan, Ted moves away from me suddenly and heads back for the desk. He looks back over his shoulder one more time, smiling wickedly. "You better go. You don't want to miss your bus."

Theo asks once on the ride to his day care who I was talking to at the gym, but when I distract him by pointing out the Dalmatian being walked down the sidewalk, he forgets about the incident entirely. I wish I could do the same.

We get off at our stop and have to jog three blocks to Theo's daycare provider's house. Krista lives on the second floor of an apartment building that is way nicer than anything I could ever afford, but would still be considered lower class by many standards. She has a box of dead flowers hanging from her narrow balcony, and I can see paper snowflakes and snowmen taped to the window, made by Theo and the other kids she watches.

Her daycare is not official. I tried to find a place registered with the state, but they were all too expensive. Krista seems nice. Her place is clean, Theo always tells me he has fun at her house, and I have no other options. So, I take Theo to her every day, hoping she takes care of him and doesn't eventually get shut down by her apartment complex or the city.

Krista lets us in when we buzz and has the door open when we walk up the stairs. Two other kids, both younger than Theo, are sitting at a table eating oatmeal. Krista's hair is pinned back with a clip at the base of her neck, and she is in a pair of sweatpants and an oversized sweatshirt. Theo gives me a quick hug and darts past Krista to take his place at the table.

"We'll probably go to the park down the block, if that's okay?" she asks.

"Yeah, that's fine. Have fun." I wave to Theo. "I'm running behind, so I better get going. Thanks again, Krista."

"Molly?" she says, moving towards the door. Her lips are pressed in a nervous line.

"Yeah?" I prepare myself for bad news. Devastating news. Years of life kicking me while I'm down has taught me to keep my expectations low. If I imagine the worst possibility, I can't be caught off guard.

"You're behind in payments," she says, voice low so Theo won't hear. "You said you'd pay me last week, but—"

"Shit." I squeeze my eyes shut for a second and shake my head. "Theo got a cold, and I had to take him to the urgent care center. The appointment cost almost one hundred dollars, and I just—"

"I can manage for another week," she says, sympathy written in the lines of her face. "But beyond that, I can't make any promises. He's a growing boy, and he eats a lot. Twice what the other kids do. I just—"

"I understand," I say, holding up a hand to stop her. "I'll get you the money. Thanks for being patient."

Krista gives me a tight smile, and I run down the stairs and jog five blocks to the diner where I will slave away for eight hours, making only enough money to wake up and scrape by all over again.

3

VIKTOR

Petr kicks his feet up on the corner of my desk and leans back in his chair, arms behind his head. If he was anyone else, I'd kick his feet off the table and threaten to break his kneecaps. As it is, he's not only my consigliere; he's mine and Fedor's only living cousin. I trust him more than almost anyone else in the world.

"You never checked in last night," he says accusingly. "I had to call the maid to make sure you came home."

"Since when do I answer to you?" I ask, the words harsher than my tone.

"Since you decided to go on solo missions and handle shit your enforcers should be taking care of." Petr raises a brow, meeting my gaze without fear.

I can hear my father's warning in my ear—*Don't let anyone challenge your authority. It's weakness.*—but I ignore it as I so often do. "The guy was middle-aged, fat, and alone. If I can't handle him on my own, I don't deserve to be the head of the Bratva."

Petr laughs, showing off the front tooth he chipped in a wrestling match gone wrong with Fedor when they were teenagers. "That's true."

I lean forward, hands folded on the desk. "But I guess you're here to tell me that certain people don't think I deserve to be head of the Bratva, anyway."

"Don't worry. I'll tell them about the fat old man you killed. That will change their minds," he says in a teasing voice as he drops his feet to the floor and sits up. Petr has a hard time being serious about serious things. But then his smile fades. "People are upset."

"When aren't people upset?" I growl. "I swear, half of my job is making sure people's feelings aren't hurt."

"Fedor is in prison, and they worry who's going to be next. It's a legitimate concern."

"No, it's really not." I stand up and run a hand through my hair. When I turn back to face Petr, he's looking at me like I'm an animal he's afraid will jump the barrier and escape the enclosure. "Fedor put himself in prison."

I don't often speak the truth about my brother. Definitely not to the Bratva. I don't want people to look at Fedor and feel sorry for him. Or roll their eyes at him. I don't want people to think he's a complete joke. Even now, I'm trying to protect the reputation he has spent most of his life trying to destroy. "Fedor acted recklessly, didn't cover his tracks, and refused to leave the city when I ordered him to. He was arrested because of his own arrogance," I say. "As long as no one else behaves that way, they won't be arrested. I'll protect them."

Petr nods. "I know, but—"

"But what?" My voice is loud and sharp, and Petr flinches.

"The witness," he says, meeting my eyes and then looking back at the floor. "A witness stood on the stand and identified him. That has never happened before and—"

"And I took care of it last night."

"That's too late," Petr says, quickly adding, "according to a lot of people, anyway. He should have been taken out before the trial."

"I didn't know his fucking name before the trial." I flop back down in my chair and swivel back and forth, full to bursting with nervous energy.

"I know."

The words leave an unspoken echo in the room. *Your father would have known his name.*

That's what everyone thinks, no matter how much I've done for the Bratva. We have strengthened our ties to the Mazzeo family, something my father worked hard to establish and I've worked even harder to maintain. Though, I admit our alliance with the Mazzeos might be on shaky ground.

There are whispers that the head of the family wants me to marry his beautiful, vivacious, and out-of-control daughter, Maria. As attractive as she is, I can't imagine marrying her. I can't imagine marrying *any* woman.

I have doubled the Bratva's profits and fostered a sense of respect and partnership with our various business associates. Yet, I fear I will never be as good as my father in the eyes of my men.

My father was feared. He called it respect, but to him, the words were interchangeable. As long as people cowered and gave him what he wanted, he was pleased.

I want more than that.

I want to live a life where I'm not constantly looking over my shoulder, waiting to be taken out by a rival or one of my own men. I want my men to be loyal to me because they respect me, not because I'll kill them if they aren't—though I certainly will do that if I'm betrayed. When I took over after my father's death, I wanted to build an actual family, and maybe I have done that. My father always said families were nothing but heartache. The Bratva has certainly been that and then some.

"Maybe it wouldn't hurt to meet them in the middle," Petr suggests.

I raise a brow. "What does that mean?"

"Half of your men are uncertain of the future of the Bratva. They need to be reminded that you're on their side. Let them cut loose. Have some fun. Terrorize some people."

I snort. "We aren't boogeymen. I'm not just going to let them run free on the streets. That's exactly what got Fedor locked up. We only strike when provoked."

Petr nods, and I can tell by the tension in his shoulders that he disagrees.

"What is it?" I groan. "Just say it."

He folds his hands, thumbs tapping together. "Your father scared people so they knew what to expect if they crossed him. Perhaps, under your style of leadership, people are forgetting what those consequences look like. Perhaps," he continues, "it would work better if you reminded them every so often."

I've spent the last five years of my life thinking only about the Bratva. Focusing solely on what would be best for this criminal family of mine. Everything seemed to be trending towards the positive... until Fedor got himself locked up. Suddenly, doubts are creeping in. At the first sign of trouble, my men want to return to the lifestyle that nearly got all of them killed.

Maybe I should remind them of that, of what my father's style of leadership almost led to.

"Sorry," Petr says. "I mean no disrespect."

I wave away his concern. Maybe I should be angry, but I'm not. I'm tired. I'm tired of fighting to keep hold of a Bratva that seems reluctant support me, and I'm damn tired of cleaning up the messes of a brother who refuses to see the error of his ways.

Speaking of Fedor, my phone buzzes, alerting me to my next meeting. "Shit," I mumble, grabbing my phone and dismissing the alarm. "I need to go."

Petr nods and holds open my office door for me. He walks next to me down the hall and out to the driveway. Before ducking into his own car, he lifts a hand and calls out, "Tell Fedor hi for me."

I give him a nod and get into my car. The prison is twenty minutes away and my weekly hour-long visit starts in fifteen. Fedor won't be pleased I'm late, but then again, after the twenty-four hours I've had, Fedor can fuck off.

"You're late." Fedor is already sitting at a table, hands folded in front of him, his wrists shackled. Beneath the table, his ankles are shackled, too.

The first time I came to see him, he was unshackled, and he jumped over the table and ran for the door when another inmate's wife and kids opened the door to come into the visitation room. He didn't even make it halfway across the room before three guards were on him, screaming and pinning him to the floor. Hence, the shackles.

"You had only to walk down a hallway to get here," I say, scraping the metal chair legs across the concrete floor and sitting down. "Outside, there's such a thing as traffic. Do you remember it?"

Fedor lifts his middle finger, the metal chains jangling as he does so. "Did you bring me any money?"

"I sent it last week. It should be in your account by now."

"Good. Commissary is tomorrow, and I need a new pair of shower shoes."

It's strange to hear my brother talk about prison life as though it's the weather. To hear how normal it has become for him. "Didn't your lawyer mention you finding a job in here?"

Fedor's face darkens. "You can't be fucking serious."

I shrug. "Too busy with your other extracurricular activities?"

He snorts, top lip pulled back in a sneer. "I may not have my freedom, but I have my dignity."

"And if you had a job, you'd have money," I argue.

"That's what you're for." He leans back in his chair, crosses his arms, and smiles.

Fedor has never had a job. Not once in his entire life. My father pushed me to get a job as soon as I turned sixteen. Even though the plan was always for me to take over the family business, he wanted me to know what it meant to work. Fedor never got those same lessons.

By the time Fedor was sixteen, I was already working for the Bratva, and my father knew I'd take over after him. So, why waste time with Fedor?

That was his thought, anyway. His children were solely to be used for his own personal gain. So long as we could help him, we mattered. Fedor, unfortunately, didn't have much to offer Dad, so Dad didn't have much to offer him either.

Maybe that's why I have always been the closest thing he has had to a father figure. Maybe it's why I'm still the one taking care of him to this day. God knows Dad would not have visited him in prison and given him a monthly allowance for shower slippers and snacks.

"How are things?" I ask, trying to change the subject.

"Amazing," he says. "Better than ever. I'm having the time of my life."

I roll my eyes. "If you're looking for sympathy, you aren't going to find it here."

He flips me off again, but this time when he looks away, there's a sadness there. A loneliness that brings me back to the dark days after Mom's funeral. Fedor would look up at me every morning like he was afraid I was going to disappear too. I see that same kind of desperation in his expression now, and I feel bad for being harsh with him.

"Sorry." The word is clumsy, dusty from disuse.

Fedor glances up and then shrugs. "What about you?" he asks. "What are the guys up to?"

Planning my overthrow, I think.

"Causing trouble," I say instead. A generic answer. "The usual."

"When is Petr going to get out here to see me?" he asks. "I haven't seen him at all since I got locked up."

"You know how he is about prisons."

Fedor nods and then glances around the room as though only now remembering he should be nervous.

Both of Petr's older brothers died in prison. They were killed by rivals in a prison attack. It's one of the many reasons he's able to sympathize with the men doubting my leadership. He's just as afraid of going to prison as they are.

"I don't have any rivals in here," Fedor says. "Not since you cleared out the Magnani Mafia. Anyone who was loyal to them isn't anymore. I could probably do some recruiting if you want."

More members with the same penchant for being arrested as my brother? No thank you. Besides, more bodies mean more men to keep loyal. I'm having a hard enough time with that as it is.

"Nice offer, but no thanks."

"What? Inmates aren't good enough for you?" His brows are furrowed, his tone argumentative.

I'm spared having to answer by the arrival of Fedor's lawyer. Kent worked for my father and has been our family's legal representative for as long as I can remember. He brought us full-size candy bars on Halloween and attended our birthday parties, always in a black suit as though he was perpetually on his way to a funeral. Considering how many criminals he works for, that wouldn't be surprising.

I stand up and hug him. "Good to see you."

"You too," he says, patting me on the back. Over his bald head, I see the guard against the wall eyeballing us. Physical contact between visitors and inmates is forbidden, but any contact at all is met with scrutiny. The guards are looking for signs that anything illegal is being smuggled in.

"Fedor," Kent says with a nod of his head. "Good to see you, too."

"It would be better to see you if it wasn't across this table," Fedor says, getting right to the point. "When am I getting out of here?"

"Working on it, working on it," Kent says in a tone that is impossible to read. There's a reason he has been our lawyer for so many years. Then he turns to me. "How have things been going on your end?"

"The witness. George McWhateverTheFuck," Fedor suddenly says, remembering something.

Kent lifts a discreet finger to his lips, but Fedor rolls his eyes and turns back to me.

"Did you take care of that issue?" Kent asks.

"He did," Fedor says before I can answer. "Didn't you? That's what you were doing when I talked to you last night."

"You two talked?" Kent asks, eyes narrowed.

"On the phone," Fedor explains.

Kent shakes his head. "No, no. Limit those conversations. They're all recorded." Then his face goes even more pale than usual. "Did you say anything about George?"

"No, I'm not a fucking idiot."

"Agree to disagree," Fedor snorts, biting back a laugh.

I level him with a glare.

"But you took care of him?" Kent asks quietly, glancing towards the guard who has diverted his attention from our table to an amorous couple in front of us who look seconds away from tossing all rules aside and pounding it out on the table. "He's already given his testimony, but he could be brought back if we get the charges dropped to involuntary manslaughter."

Fedor growls, clearly displeased with any charges at all, and then turns to me, eyebrows raised. "Well?"

"Yes," I snap. "I fucking did it, okay? I'm the responsible one, remember?"

Surprise flickers across Fedor's face, but he masks it with a scowl.

Kent just nods, ignoring our brotherly bickering. "Good. That's good news. One less person for you to worry about."

We both turn to Kent at the same time. "What does that mean?" Fedor asks. I was about to propose the same question.

Kent takes a deep breath, folds his hands in front of him, and looks Fedor directly in the eye in a somber kind of way. "Unfortunately, there's another witness."

Fedor blinks, and I run a frustrated hand through my hair. "*Another* witness? Did you kill the man in front of an audience?"

"Fuck off."

"A witness to a different crime," Kent says. He glances at Fedor and then looks away, the tops of his cheeks going red. "She was witness to a slightly more *intimate* crime."

"She?" Fedor says, sounding stunned.

"Who is she?"

"It doesn't fucking matter," Fedor says, almost shouting. His shock from a moment before has turned into something frantic. The guard's attention is back on us, and I lean forward to grab his arm and calm him before I remember it's not allowed. I curl my fingers to fight the urge.

"She's a waitress. The police know of an evening she and Fedor may have spent together a few years ago."

"Years? Surely that isn't relevant anymore."

"It sure as fuck isn't," Fedor says, pounding a fist on the table. "Are they also going to bring my second-grade teacher to the stands? I gave my seatmate a wet willy when I was eight. Next you're gonna tell me that's a chargeable offense. Goddamn it, this is bullshit!"

"It will be fine," I say, holding out a hand to ease him back down. "We've handled witnesses before. If Kent knows who she is, I can scare her out of testifying for whatever it is."

"Kill her," Fedor says, much too loudly.

I lean away from him, trying to distance myself from the word.

Kent laughs nervously and matches Fedor's volume. "You can't make jokes like that in a place like this."

"Lower your voice," I grit out between clenched teeth. "Calm down."

Fedor's head is rapidly shaking back and forth, almost vibrating, and all the blood in his face has drained out. He looks like he's wearing white stage makeup. "If you two can't get me out of here, I'm going to kill myself. I can't stay in here. I can't live like this. Not trapped in these walls with these damn guards telling me where to go and who to touch and—" His voice cuts off, and he drops his face into his hands, his shoulders shaking.

Kent looks at me nervously, but I don't know what to say. Partly because I'm too angry. Anything I say to Fedor right now would only make things worse. I take a deep breath and turn to Kent.

"Whatever she has to say, it can't be worse than murder," I whisper. "Right, Kent?"

"My best guess is that the district attorney only added the witness to scare Fedor into a confession. They want to hit him with everything they can to prove he's a danger, but I'm sure this won't stick. Still, things would certainly be easier if she wasn't part of the picture at all."

I tip my head back and pinch the bridge of my nose. I've lost years of my life trying to control Fedor, but every time I turn around, there's a new fire flaring up. It feels hopeless, like trying to bail out a ship with a teaspoon. "How many times am I going to have to clean up the same mess?"

"At least you're free and able to do it," Fedor bites out with shocking venom. "I'd give anything to be able to clean up your messes."

I press my palms against the table and lean forward. "The difference between the two of us is that I don't have messes for you to worry about. I take care of my own messes. Like an adult."

Fedor rolls his eyes, only highlighting my point. He is still a child in so many ways. "I'm sorry our family is such a burden to you, *brother*."

I know Fedor well enough to know he's masking his pain. As angry as I am with him, I don't want to be another person he thinks sees him as a burden. Our parents made him feel that way plenty without me piling on.

"I'll take care of it."

"No, please," Fedor says, waving a hand and leaning back in his seat. "Don't do anything on my account. I'll just rot away in this fucking prison, thank you very much!"

This time, the guard claps his hands at Fedor's outburst. When we look over, he shakes his head in warning.

"I'll take care of it," I say again, afraid of what Fedor will do if I don't calm down. He'll get himself put in solitary or whatever the fuck kind of punishments they dole out in prison—whatever might be worse than already being in prison. "Okay? It's a done deal. Just give me the information, Kent, and I'll deal with it."

Fedor is too proud to show gratitude. He slouches further in his seat, his top lip pulled back in a scowl. He maintains the same expression as the guard announces visitation is over and everyone begins saying their goodbyes.

"I'll talk to you soon." Fedor shrugs and shuffles back down the hallway, the chains around his ankles dragging on the floor with every step.

When we get outside to the parking lot, Kent pulls a manila envelope out of the glove compartment of his car and hands it to me. "Everything you need to know is inside."

"You really think I need to kill her?" I ask. "If she's just being used as a threat, then there doesn't seem much point."

"Fedor's freedom is the point," Kent says sharply. He has always had a soft spot for Fedor. As a lawyer, Kent likes to control situations and people. Fedor, for all his erratic behavior, relies on the advice of those around him to make the big decisions. Kent likes to be the one to offer that advice.

I open the manila envelope and Kent hisses, "Not here."

I ignore him and slide the picture partially out of the envelope. Then

I sigh and drop it back inside without looking. "This feels unnecessary."

"Let me be the judge of that," he says, slamming the car door and walking around to the other side. He opens the driver's side door and looks at me over the roof of his car. "All of her regular haunts are in the folder, but she was last seen at the homeless shelter. I'd start there."

Before I can say anything, he ducks into the car and slams the door. A few seconds later, he squeals out of the parking lot like he's the lead in a street-racing movie.

4

MOLLY

When I get back to Krista's, Theo is the only kid left. He's sitting on the floor in front of the television while Krista makes dinner for her own family, who are gathered around the table.

"I'm so sorry," I say as soon as she opens the door.

She has an apron on and waves me inside with the spatula while she goes back to tend to the chicken cooking on the stove. "It's fine. It happens."

I pull out a wad of bills from my pocket, my tips for the day, and hand them over. Krista takes them, looking slightly guilty about it.

"I'll pay you the full amount soon," I say. "I get paid at the end of the week, and I'll cover last week and the overtime. I got asked to stay for another few hours because someone skipped their shift and—"

"And it's fine," Krista says firmly. "He's just been playing by himself. Aside from one mess involving a shampoo bottle in the bathroom, he's been great."

I wince, wondering if I should have come down on him harder for the shampoo volcano this morning, but it's too late for that now.

"But like I said this morning, I can't do this much longer."

"I know. I hear you, and I'll take care of it." I mean it. Truly. I just hope I can follow through.

Work was so crazy I almost didn't have time to call Krista about being late. I didn't get to call her until five minutes after I was supposed to have picked Theo up. I know things can't go on like this. I can't continue working crazy hours at the diner and leaving Theo with another family for twelve hours a day. But what other option do I have? I don't have a degree or any useful skills. I don't even have a bed.

Knowing I'm letting Theo down is a weight I always carry, but it feels especially heavy today.

Theo finally notices I'm there and runs across the room, hugging my legs. I pat his back and kiss the top of his head. When he sees the chicken Krista is making, he touches his belly. "I'm hungry. What are we having?"

Some days I can snag a wrong order from the kitchen on my way out and split it with Theo, but when Bob is the manager on duty, everyone is extra careful not to make any slipups, so I didn't get lucky today.

"We'll talk about it later," I say, smiling at Krista, hoping she can't see the desperation in my face. The shelter has been bursting at the seams since the weather turned cold, and I'm running later than normal. I slip Theo into his coat and hurry out the door.

Halfway there, I pick Theo up and run the rest of the way, but the shelter is full by the time we arrive.

The volunteers are always sympathetic, but there is only so much they can do. I look at the line of people being let inside, hoping someone will see Theo and take pity on us, but so many of them have families, too. I recognize some of them who've given up their own spots for Theo and me previous times. I can't ask them to do such a thing again.

"Are we going inside?" Theo asks, looking up at the stone church building. He squints up at the dark sky and then buries his face in my shoulder when a cold wind picks up.

"Not today," I say, my voice breaking. I clear my throat. I don't want him to see me cry.

It's cold and growing colder by the second. I have enough money in my pocket for dinner but not a place to stay. Not even the cheapest hotel rooms are in our price range since I handed my tips over to Krista.

Krista. I could go back there, see if she could take Theo for the night.

As if reading my mind, Theo wraps his legs around my middle and his arms around my neck. "Where are we going, Mama?"

I squeeze him back, knowing I can't impose upon Krista any further. I'm his mom. I'm the one who's supposed to take care of him and keep him warm and fed. I'm the one who's supposed to comfort him when he has a bad dream.

"I'm not sure," I say, walking away from the church. "But Mama will figure it out."

Despite the incident this morning, the gym is the first place I think of. It's open twenty-four hours, and if we find a quiet corner, we might be able to go unnoticed all night. That doesn't solve the problem of what we'll eat, but we won't freeze, and that seems like a good start.

As soon as I pull open the front doors, however, I see the same man from early this morning coming around from the desk and walking towards us, his eyes pinned on me.

I didn't think he'd still be at the gym, but maybe he had to work a double as well. Regardless, his expression this morning was predatory, but now it's disgusted.

"Back so soon?" Ted asks, blocking the door with his body. "Have you thought about my offer?"

Theo dozed off on the bus ride over and is still asleep. I can feel his drool pooling on my shoulder.

My stomach clenches as I nod. "I have."

"And?" he asks, biting his lower lip in a way that makes me shiver with disgust.

"I'll do it." I feel like I have to be a violent shade of green. I've never felt more disgusting in all my life, but if five miserable minutes with this man is what it takes to keep my son from spending a night on the sidewalk, then so be it. I will do anything for Theo.

Ted tilts his head to the side, a smug smile pulling across his face, and then he suddenly frowns. His lower lip pouts out. "I'm sorry, but that offer has expired."

A cold wind blows through the door and freezes my back. Theo cuddles into me harder in his sleep, and I feel frozen in every way that is humanly possible.

"What?"

"Limited time only," he says, clearly enjoying his power trip. "If you come in here tonight, I'll make sure you're banned from the gym for life."

"But—" I'm stunned and ashamed. Am I really going to beg him to let me sleep with him? That is what he wants, after all. It's obvious how much pleasure he gets from ripping the rug out from under my feet.

"Maybe try again in the morning," he says, stepping away from the door and letting it close. "I'll see you in the showers."

I walk away from the gym like I'm walking on stumps. The day has shit on me in every way possible. I'm not sure how much more I can take.

I clutch Theo to my chest and walk down a street in the small business district. I could try to find a big box store that's open all night, but if we're found sleeping in there, we'll be kicked out. Theo needs sleep. We both do.

By the end of the block, most of the businesses are dark and closed. I'm beyond hopeless. The wind feels like sharp needles of ice all over my skin, and I have to get Theo inside somewhere. Anywhere.

Then, a rundown motel called the Twin Chandeliers shines its yellow light down on us.

I've stayed there in the past until we were kicked out for missing a payment. I even tried to get hired on as a maid, but they didn't have any open positions.

I don't like to beg, but tonight, there is no other choice.

The lobby smells like cigarette smoke, even though there's a yellowed "no smoking" sign hanging behind the clerk's greasy head. He closes his laptop when I open the door and looks up at me. I don't want to imagine what he was doing on there.

"How can I help you?"

"Hi," I say, not entirely sure how to start. Asking for help never gets any easier.

The man looks from Theo sleeping on my shoulder to me, eyes narrowed. He stands at the counter and crosses his arms over his chest. "What can I do for you?"

"I need a room."

The man nods and starts grabbing for a room key from under the counter.

"But I can't pay for it right this moment," I finish, speaking the words so quickly they jumble together.

He freezes, half-bent down with his arm still under the counter. "What?"

"I will set up a payment plan," I say. "Half today and half tomorrow. I'll have tips. I can come back and pay you—"

He scowls and shakes his head, sighing as he stands to his full height again. "Yeah, sure, and this place is a five-star resort."

Another wave of disappointment washes over me, and I can feel tears burning the backs of my eyes. "Please. I will pay you. I swear it. I've never stolen anything in my life. It's just that I don't have the money right now and the shelter is full and it's so cold outside."

"And this is a business," he says. "If we took in every cold person desperate for a bed, we'd be bankrupt in a day."

"I *will* pay you," I say again. "Just not right now. We'll even stay in a break room. Or a closet. I'll take whatever you have."

The thought of tucking Theo in for bed in a cleaning closet brings fresh tears to my eyes, but at least he would be warm.

The man looks bored with me, but I see the moment the idea comes into his eyes. Like a rabbit who has learned to notice the presence of hawks overhead, I recognize the gleam in his eyes. The way his expression switches from annoyed to assessing. He looks me up and down and then leans forward on the counter, resting on his elbows.

"Whatever I have?"

At that moment, Theo wakes up suddenly. He lifts his head and looks around. When he sees the man behind the counter, he frowns.

"Where are we?" he asks groggily.

I set him on the floor and bend down to look into his face. "Can you go sit in that chair over there? I'm trying to see if this nice man has any rooms available for us."

He blinks at me sleepily and then shuffles over to a timeworn chair next to a card table covered with a spread of snacks so dismal even my empty stomach isn't interested.

"As I was saying," the man says, coming around from behind the counter. He leans his hip against the edge of the laminate top, and I can see where his shirt is riding up across his hairy stomach. I stare at his shoulder. "You'll take whatever you can get?"

I swallow and nod.

He takes a step closer to me, moving into my personal space. When his hand touches my arm, I flinch, but that doesn't stop him from dragging his index finger across my coat and beneath the opening. He traces the curve of my ribs, and I can feel where he has touched me like the trail is covered in slime, cold and disgusting. "What can you offer me in return?"

"Maybe a payment plan," I start, my voice high-pitched and meeker than I'd like.

He shakes his head. "All payment must be up front. Company policy."

I open my mouth and close it several times, trying to find the words. "I could work for it. Clean or—" I look around the room, trying to think of another job I could do. It's obvious the place isn't busy enough to need another worker at the front desk, and I'm not handy enough to even begin to know how to fix the wood panels peeling up from the counter.

The path of his finger shifts upward, moving up the center of my body towards my breasts. I'm frozen for a second, too horrified to move, but just before he reaches his target, I jerk back and pull my coat closed.

The smirk on his face falls, and he looks over at Theo. "Hey, those are for customers, kid."

Theo is reaching for a cracker on the table, and at the sound of the man's voice, he sinks down into his seat, pulling his hands in close. I want to punch the man in the nose for talking to my son like that.

"You two better go before I call security," he snarls.

I highly doubt the motel has its own security, but the man's meaning is clear: *do what I say or you're out of here.*

Wasn't I just willing to do the same thing with Ted at the gym? And that was for a corner in the locker room. This time, it would be for a bed. A tub. Theo could take a bath like a normal four-year-old. He could watch cartoons in the morning while I got ready for work rather than sit on the cold floor of a communal shower.

One moment of sacrifice for one semi-normal night.

"But we're customers," I say, trying to sound alluring even though my voice is shaking.

The man studies me and slowly, realization seeps into his thick Neanderthal brain. He moves closer to me, his thigh brushing the outside of my leg, his hand moving to my hip.

I hold up a hand, pressing it against his fleshy chest.

He knocks my hand aside and backs me against the wall.

I push harder on his chest, but he doesn't move away, and I can feel a primal kind of panic rising up inside of me.

"Not here," I gasp quietly, hoping Theo will remain oblivious to all of it. "Let me put him in a room first. Let me take care of him."

"Up-front payment," he repeats, swiping his hand beneath my coat and grabbing at my breast through my shirt.

I whimper and try to go limp, sinking towards the floor to escape him, but he pins me to the wall with his hips.

"It'll be quick," he growls. "No one will see."

I pinch my legs closed and shove at his chest, but I can feel how useless it is. He's too big and too strong, and even if I do fight him off, I have nowhere to go.

Shame slides through me like a snake, tangling itself around my limbs and my mind and my heart. Shame holds me still and keeps me quiet as the nameless clerk's sweaty hands slide under my shirt towards my chest.

I squeeze my eyes shut and pray for it to be over soon.

"*Bol'she ne nado!*"

The clerk and I both freeze at the sound of the deep foreign voice. Then, slowly, the clerk turns around and his face goes white.

Suddenly, he can't get his hands off me fast enough.

5

VIKTOR

"Enough!" I repeat, this time in English.

The man behind the desk is some mindless idiot we hired to check people in and take their money, but even he has enough brain cells to recognize who I am and know to listen to me. He steps away from the woman with his hands raised, but the image of him sliding those hands over her body is still fresh in my mind.

She looks from me to the clerk and then towards the corner of the room. I follow her gaze and see a small boy holding a cracker—stale, no doubt—his eyes wide and confused.

My vision goes red around the edges. The piece of shit clerk was going to assault a woman in front of a child. I could kill him. I gesture to the boy. "Who is that?"

The woman—Molly, I remember from the dossier Kent handed me—seems to come alive at the mention of the child. She straightens her shirt and moves past the clerk, keeping as much distance between them as possible. The little boy runs to her and hugs her leg.

No one said anything about a child. He wasn't mentioned in the folder or by anyone at the homeless shelter when I asked about her.

One of the volunteers looked at the picture I showed her. She must have assumed I was a bounty hunter or some kind of private investigator because she told me exactly what I needed to know. "Molly usually comes here, but we were full tonight. The Twin Chandeliers is nearby and a lot of our overflow clients head there if they can afford it."

"Is he yours?" I ask her now.

Molly lays her hand protectively on the boy's shoulder and levels cold eyes at me. "Yes." Her cheeks are red with embarrassment, but even after being found in the compromising position she was in, she manages to look dignified.

"Are we staying here?" the boy asks his mother, though he's staring at me.

Molly looks from me to the door where wind is whistling through the cracks. Her face goes pale, and I can practically see the gears in her head turning. She was turned away from the homeless shelter and now the motel is proving to be a bust. She has nowhere to go.

"Yes," I answer before she can.

Molly snaps her attention to me, eyes narrowed. "No, we aren't."

I smile, though it doesn't reach my eyes. "You can eat whatever you want from the table over there and your room will be ready in a few minutes."

The boy's eyes light up, and he spins away from his mom and hurries over to the table, grabbing one handful of crackers and another of salted mixed nuts. She holds out a half-hearted hand to stop him, but he's eating something, and it's obvious that's a weight off her mind.

"Who are you?" she asks, looking from me to the clerk. "Do you two know each other?"

She thinks there's a possibility I'm associated with the asshole whose belly is hanging out of the bottom of his shirt. I spin around and face the clerk. "What's your name?"

He looks like he hoped we'd forget about him entirely, and when I address him, he flinches but does his best to hide it. "Greg."

"Well, *Greg*," I say, wishing I could wrap his stained T-shirt around his neck and strangle him with it, but knowing I can't because it would only traumatize the child more, "I'd like you to prepare a room for this woman and her son."

"She doesn't have any money."

I stare at the fat oaf until he realizes I have no need for his commentary and begins the process of getting their room ready.

"Name on the room?" he asks.

"Use mine," I say before Molly can say anything. I'm here for a purpose, after all. Better not to leave a paper trail. "And make sure the room is clean."

"The maids cleaned everything earlier today."

"And they do a shit job," I say. "Do it again."

"Me?" he asks. "But the front desk …"

"Then call another employee," I command. "Get them here. Now. You don't seem capable of running the desk in an appropriate manner anyway. Perhaps you'd be better served in another role. As a matter of fact, I'll watch the desk while you clean her room. Now, go."

Several more questions and comments no doubt sludge through the wiring of Greg's brain, but he has enough intelligence to keep them to himself as he rolls a cleaning cart from the back room and out through the front door, leaving me alone with Molly and her son.

Fedor's son.

That's who the boy is, after all. Right?

The folder Kent gave me said that Molly was a woman Fedor assaulted. She'd gone to the police years before and filed a report, but it was never followed up on. It could be followed up on this time around, though, now that the D.A. is desperate to keep Fedor behind bars.

But there was no mention of a pregnancy. Of a fucking *child*. Does Kent know? Does Fedor?

With his dark hair and pointed chin, the boy is Fedor's twin. His hazel eyes are not as vividly green as Fedor's, but I can still see the flecks of his father in them.

"Do you want a drink?" I ask the kid, pointing to the rattling mini fridge under the table. "Take a water."

Molly rushes over, cracking open a small bottle of water and helping him take a drink. Water sloshes down his chin, and she wipes it away with the sleeve of her shirt. Then she fixes him a small plate of cherry tomatoes, crackers, cheese slices, and a small bunch of grapes that she cuts in half with a plastic fork. He sits down in a chair in the waiting room. I turn the television hanging in the corner to a random cartoon. The volume on the TV is broken, but the kid doesn't seem to mind.

With the boy occupied, Molly slowly makes her way towards me, her face lowered to the floor. "Are you the manager or something?"

"No." I shake my head. "The owner, you could say."

The Twin Chandeliers is one of many different motels the Bratva operates from around the city. They are little more than fronts for our other businesses. I rarely do any kind of oversight, but apparently, I need to start. Greg is a piece of shit.

"You didn't have to give us a room. He wasn't lying when he said I can't pay."

"After the way he treated you, you shouldn't have to."

Plus, I might kill you before the morning. The thought is acid in my stomach. I try to ignore it for the time being.

"What's your son's name?"

She hesitates a long time before deciding to answer. "Theo."

"I'm Viktor."

She looks up at me, and some of her defenses have lowered, though not all of them. Molly doesn't seem like the kind of woman who is ever entirely defenseless. Based on the way her life has gone thus far —a homeless single mother assaulted by the likes of my brother and Greg—she probably can't afford to. "I'm Molly."

"What brings you to my lavish motel tonight, Molly?"

She smiles faintly at the self-deprecating humor. "I needed a place to stay, but I wanted the aesthetic of a 1980s bowling alley, so this was the only place that fit the bill." The room is designed in dingy shades of orange, yellow, and green. She isn't wrong. "Sorry if that's rude," she murmurs. "But, I mean, you don't have to be an interior designer to know this place could use some work."

"Are you an interior designer?" I ask. If she was, surely she'd have a home of her own. That would be the irony of ironies.

"No. It's a dream, but not quite."

I can't be talking to Molly about her dreams. It's like naming a chicken you plan to eat. It only makes the slaughter more difficult. She tucks a strand of long dark hair behind her ear, and I see a beauty mark on her chin. She hugs her arms around her narrow waist and rolls from heel to toe and back again on a pair of worn sneakers.

This particular slaughter is going to be hard no matter what I do.

"Is it just the two of you?" I ask, unable to help myself. "You and Theo, I mean."

She looks over at Theo with a hint of sadness behind her eyes and nods. "Yeah, just the two of us."

I want to ask her for the whole story, but she probably wouldn't tell it. Even if she would, I'm not sure I want to hear. I know enough.

My brother ruined her life. Whatever plans she had for herself, it's safe to assume they didn't include becoming a single mother or being homeless. Her life has obviously been hard, and now, it will be short.

"I should say thanks," Molly says suddenly, looking at my shoes as she talks. "For stepping in and stopping him. I'm not sure what would have happened if you hadn't—well, actually, I *am* sure what would have happened." Her cheeks go pink.

I nod. "Happy to help."

She glances up at me, her golden eyes soft and warm. For the first time, she gives me a small smile.

Shit.

It isn't just that Molly is beautiful, which she is. I've killed beautiful people before. It's part of the job, and I don't mind doing what has to be done. It's the fact that Molly is innocent. She didn't do anything to deserve this. Any of it. And Theo certainly doesn't deserve to lose his mom. But what other choice do I have?

Let Fedor go to prison for life. That's the choice. If the DA can pin anything on him, they'll be able to present a case that he has a long history of criminal, often violent, crimes and shouldn't be able to walk free. My baby brother will be locked away forever, and it will be my fault.

"So," Molly says, moving over to lean against the check-in desk. "What is it like owning a motel?"

"Several motels, actually. I think there are seven or eight."

Her eyes go wide. "Wow. That's a lot to keep track of all by yourself."

"It's a family business."

Her pink lips form a silent "oh," and she nods. "That must be nice. Working with family."

I almost snort. "If you knew my brother, you'd change your mind." My blood goes cold. She does know my brother.

A sick feeling worms its way through my chest, but Molly just smiles. "I don't have any siblings, so I wouldn't know what that's like."

"Where are your parents?" I ask, shifting the conversation away from my family.

"Divorced, unhappy, and unconcerned," she says quickly. I can tell it's an answer she gives out often. "We don't talk."

"So it really is just you and Theo."

"It really is," she says, looking over at her son with a small smile. "He's amazing, though. More than enough family for me."

Shit, shit, shit.

I want Molly to be a terrible mother. I want her to be abusive and miserable and a thief. I want her to be someone it would be easy to kill. A woman I wouldn't mind taking away from her son.

Molly doesn't appear to be any of those things.

She's someone who life has happened to. Mostly without her consent, things happened, and she reacted, and here she is. Still standing, still fighting, still trying. And it is damn admirable.

"Mama." Theo is suddenly between us, his knees pinched together. "I have to potty."

"Oh." Molly's eyes dart around the room, and I point her to the employee bathroom in the back corner.

"It might not be very clean, but it's a toilet."

"Perfect." She nods at me in thanks and then rushes Theo off to the bathroom, his small hand firmly clasped in hers. I stand in place and wait.

When he's finished, Theo runs out of the bathroom ahead of Molly and stops in front of me. He tips his head all the way back to look at me and then smiles. It's a child's smile. An innocent smile. One given without expectation or reason, and when I look into his face, I see Fedor. Not just in looks, but in temperament.

I see Fedor before our mother died, before Dad clearly preferred me over him, before he fell by the wayside and found reckless ways to keep himself entertained. I see my baby brother when his heart was open and kind. I see my family.

That's what Theo is, after all. He's my nephew. My flesh and blood.

Would Fedor want me to kill Molly if he knew she was raising his son?

More importantly, can I do it?

Molly pats Theo on the head, mussing his dark hair—hair only a shade darker than my own—and then bends down to kiss his forehead. Theo wrinkles his nose but wraps his arm around his mom's leg, hugging her close.

It's almost like they know what I'm planning. Like they're trying to show me how much they don't deserve to be separated. Trying to show me they're good people.

But Fedor could be a good person. If he could get out of prison and get his head on straight, he could start over. He could have a position in the Bratva that would keep him busy and out of trouble. He could maybe find someone to balance him out and have a family of his own. If his genes could make a kid like Theo, he could have a whole brood of wide-eyed, lopsided-smiling kids. Fedor could have a life.

But only if I take Molly's.

Greg arrives back with the cleaning cart, his forehead sweaty from the exertion of cleaning the room. "It's ready," he wheezes. "Should I show you to your room?"

"No," I answer a bit too quickly.

Greg doesn't ever need to be alone with Molly again. He hands her the card, disdain obvious in his eyes, and then retreats behind the desk.

"I could show you," I offer. "If you want."

The room number—thirteen—is printed on the back of the card, and Molly holds it up, her hand wrapping around Theo's. "I'm sure we can manage. Thank you, though. For everything."

Room number thirteen. Unlucky. An omen, perhaps.

"Of course," I say, my smile tight and false. "Be sure to order room service. A snack tray isn't a good enough dinner for either of you."

"Um," Greg says behind me. "We don't have room service."

I spin around, eyes narrowed, and growl the words between clenched teeth. "You do now. Our list of amenities just got an upgrade. Get her whatever she wants. Make sure someone else delivers it, though. You will be keeping your distance from her."

When Molly and Theo walk away, I wonder what the next time I see them will be like.

I came to the motel to find her and kill her. And now?

Now, I really don't know.

6

MOLLY

Apparently, the snack table was enough for Theo because, a few minutes after getting into the room, he burrows under the scratchy blankets and falls asleep. The mattress is bad by most standards, but it's better than the thin pads we usually get at the shelter, so Theo probably feels like he's sleeping on a cloud.

The room was probably redecorated at the same time the lobby was—no more recently than the late eighties—but it's clean. I'm hesitant to give Gropey Greg from the front desk any credit at all, but the room smells lemony fresh and every surface is shining. Clearly, he had the fear of God put into him by Viktor.

The thought of Viktor makes my frazzled mind nearly short circuit, so I quickly shove him aside and focus on the basics.

I'm hungry.

I've never ordered room service, but even if I had, I don't think that experience would be of much use considering the motel doesn't actually offer room service. So, I call the front desk and try to remember which restaurants I saw nearby. Greg has been replaced by the other employee Viktor told him to call in, and he takes my order of a cheeseburger and large French fry from the burger place next door as though it's something they do for all the guests.

When I hang up, I pace across the floor and then look back at Theo. He's still sleeping soundly, and I'm not sure what to do. Usually, when I find any small amount of free time, I flip through some of the interior design books I've picked up from garage sales and donation bins over the years. They aren't exactly textbooks like what I would have had if I had gone to school, but I can still learn from them. Unfortunately, I forgot them in my gym locker. After everything that happened this morning, I'm not sure I'll be allowed in to get them back.

With nothing else to do, I pad into the bathroom and close the door.

I can't remember the last time I showered without an audience. The showers at the shelter are always overcrowded, with lukewarm water at best, which is why I take Theo to the gym. *Took* him there, I suppose, since I doubt we'll be able to do that anymore.

I close my eyes and take a deep breath. That's a worry for tomorrow. For right now, I have a sleeping boy in the other room and a clean, hot shower to luxuriate in.

The water is almost too hot, but I don't mind. It washes over my achy muscles as I finally let myself think about Viktor.

He saved me, yes. If he hadn't shown up, Greg would have taken advantage of me and probably kicked me out without even giving us a room. So, I owe Viktor for the bed and the shower and the food.

But why would he do it?

If he owns motels like this one all over the city, then he has to know unsavory things are happening on the premises. Most people coming to these places are renting by the hour, and everyone knows it. He wouldn't be worried about someone as inconsequential as me running off to tell people what the clerk had done to me. The reputation of his business wasn't in jeopardy. So, there was no need for him to be kind to me, to make amends. Why did he?

Pity is the first option that pops into my mind, but men like him—powerful, wealthy, and incredibly handsome—rarely ever have a concern for the less fortunate. I've met enough of them to know that they believe they got to where they are because of hard work and that I got to where I am because of a lack of it. If I could only work more hours, spend my money more responsibly, and open a savings account, then things would turn around for me. As though I haven't been trying that for the last four fucking years.

I feel latent anger rising up inside of me, and I tip my head back into the spray and remind myself that Viktor didn't say any of that. He was nice to me. And Theo.

He was also handsome.

I know that shouldn't have a bearing on the situation, but how could it not? One minute, I was desperate and sandwiched between a dirty wall and an even dirtier man. The next, I was looking up at a square-jawed, blue-eyed savior. My prejudices aside, Viktor has been nothing but a saint to me, and I have no reason not to trust him.

So, why don't I?

I towel off, and slip back into my jeans and T-shirt. Is this one-night stay just a taste of what Viktor can offer before he, like most men I've known in my life, expects something in return? Or is he really as kind as he seems?

I quickly do the math of how long it would take staying in the free room before I could save up enough for a deposit on an apartment. I'd need first and last month's rent plus the fees, but once I had that, I could make the monthly rent fine.

I don't know how much Viktor is willing to give, but when there is a knock at the door, I know that right now, he's at least willing to give me one night and a meal. I plan to take it.

"Your food," a young red-haired man says. His nose is covered in freckles. He looks like he can't be older than twenty.

I step into the breezeway and pull the door partially closed behind me so I don't wake up Theo. "Sorry, I wish I had a tip or something, but I really don't have anything to—"

"Viktor told me not to accept anything if you did offer it," he says, waving away my concerns. "So don't worry about it."

I nod and take the food. Grease is leaking from the bottom of the bag, and I think I probably should have ordered a salad, but I didn't want to make my free meal rabbit food. I wanted it to be indulgent.

The man smiles and turns to leave.

"Wait."

He turns back, eyebrows raised. "Do you need something else?"

"Um, well. Actually, I just wanted to know who Viktor is."

"Viktor?" he asks as though I might be mentally slow. "The owner. The man who gave you the room."

"I know who he is," I explain. "But I'd like to know *who* he is."

The kid frowns and shrugs. "I mean, I'm not sure how to answer that. To be honest, I don't know him very well. This is the most time he's ever spent around this motel. I know he owns a few of them, but I probably can't say much more than that."

I tilt my head to the side. "You can't? What does that mean?"

"It means you should probably enjoy the room and the food and leave it alone." He smiles. "I don't mean that to sound rude. It's just the truth."

"I'm not good at leaving things alone." I check my front pocket for the room key and then pull the door all the way closed. "If my kid is sleeping here, I want to know who I'm dealing with."

The kid steps forward and drops his voice. "Listen, I'm just trying to pay my way through community college. This job works with my schedule, and I'm not looking to get fired."

"And I'm not looking to get you fired," I say. "Just tell me his name at least."

"That I can tell you," he says, letting out a short sigh of relief. "His name is Viktor Kornilov."

It's a miracle I don't drop the bag of food.

It's a miracle I manage to smile and thank the redheaded kid and make it inside without my knees giving way.

I know that name.

Kornilov.

A name I've remembered and feared and avoided as though it was the boogeyman. As though saying it in a mirror three times would bring out a ghoul or a monster to hurt me. Because he did hurt me.

Not Viktor, but his brother.

I see the family resemblance now. Viktor is broad and menacing where Fedor is lean and charming. But they have the same golden coloring and the same mouths that turn down at the corners. The same mouth Theo has.

I want to grab Theo and run. But I can't.

For the first time in weeks—maybe months—Theo is getting a solid night of sleep. I can't take that away from him.

Robotically, I take my food to the small table at the back of the room and unwrap it. It seemed appetizing when I ordered it, but now the thought of it turns my stomach. I can't imagine eating anything.

I push away from the table, lean forward, and cradle my head in my hands.

Fedor saved me once, too.

I was at a concert a few weeks before I was supposed to head off for college. A man kept grinding against me and wouldn't take no for an answer. When he got especially rough, Fedor appeared. He was smaller than the man, but something about his presence was menacing, and the creep held up his hands and left. I thanked him, we talked, and he bought me a drink.

Just like Viktor, I thought Fedor was handsome.

How lucky am I? I thought when he asked if he could buy me a drink.

I had one and then another and about the time I tried to cut myself off, Fedor offered me another. "Last one!" he said. "Just one more."

I agreed and then everything went fuzzy.

Part of me is glad I don't remember, though I've always wondered how it happened. When. Where.

I woke up the next morning in an unfamiliar apartment, alone, confused, and *sore*. He was asleep next to me as though this was normal. As though I'd wanted this to happen.

At eighteen, I'd only ever slept with one guy before. I never would have gone home with someone right after meeting them, and I *never* would have agreed to sex.

I snuck out as quietly as I could and tried to forget the entire thing. I didn't want anything to derail my dreams of college and becoming a designer and making a life for myself. I had wanted to get away from my parents' fighting and disappointment, and I had a job lined up to help me pay for tuition. I couldn't let this one event change my entire life.

Then I missed my period and got sick, and everything turned upside down.

I talked to a few people and an officer about the incident and eventually found out about Fedor's connections. I left the police station knowing I could never tell anyone he was the father. It would put me and the baby in too much danger—because even then, I knew I would keep it.

Now, four years later, here we are again. In danger.

Viktor asked our names. There is no way he doesn't know who we are, and if he knows, there is no way he doesn't want something from me. Maybe even Theo.

The thought sends a chill down my spine.

7

VIKTOR

Greg takes the hint and stays out of my sight for the rest of the night. I reschedule a few of my meetings to take place at the Twin Chandeliers. I don't want to get too far from Molly. Not until I know what my next move is.

The motels are a perfect front for backdoor firearm sales. The police come sniffing around every so often in search of traffickers or prostitution, but they don't expect to find guns and ammunition in the bulk toilet paper boxes. The operation works because we're hiding in plain sight.

"I didn't ask for any of these," I say, gesturing lazily to a crate of handguns.

"They're a bonus," the man says, his Russian accent thick, though I know he has been living in the city for over ten years. He sold weapons to my father as well.

"They're extra, you mean. You're trying to give me your scraps and make a pretty penny while you're at it."

He opens and closes his mouth, trying to dispute my claims, but he can't.

I hold up a hand to silence him before he can even try to lie. "I don't care that you're trying to unload your leftovers on me, but I do care that you're charging me full price for them."

"They're all good guns. Shoot straight, no serials. Completely scrubbed."

"And they'll be completely useless to you unless you bring the price down by half."

The man grinds his back teeth together, jaw clicking back and forth, thinking. He's annoyed at the deal, but he knows I won't give him any better. Some of my men claim I'm too lenient because I'd rather compromise than smash someone's face in. But they don't see the business side of things. They don't see how much money I save the Bratva, how many business relationships I foster by being firm but fair.

Well, not entirely fair. The weapons are worth their full price, but I don't want anyone to think the Kornilov Bratva picks up scraps like a street dog. The man is losing money because he didn't show me and my operation the proper respect, so this is a kind of fairness. In a way.

"Fine," the man agrees, looking longingly at the box next to him. "I'll take half."

I thank him for his business and instruct him and another of my men to carry the box to the storage room. There, the guns will be discreetly packaged and shipped to our other motels across the city to be sold and distributed.

The kid who replaced Greg at the front desk comes in to tell me Molly ordered a value meal from the hamburger place next door. She could have ordered an entire lobster dinner if she wanted, and I wouldn't have cared. But she probably didn't even think to do anything that lavish. Considering she'd planned for the snack tray in the lobby to be her dinner, the hamburger probably is a five-star meal compared to what she's used to.

Still, I'm glad she ordered something. It means she's getting comfortable here.

I plan to do the same.

"Give her whatever she wants for the rest of the night," I say as I grab my leather jacket from the back of my chair and shrug it on. "I'm going to bed."

"You want me to stay all night?" he asks with a smile, though I notice the way he glances at the clock. It's already almost midnight.

"I'll pay you double your hourly wage."

His eyes widen like he's won the lottery, and he gives me a thumbs-up. "Aye, aye."

"Don't do that."

He smiles sheepishly and asks if there is anything else he can do for me. "Your suite has been readied to your specifications."

"Then no, I don't need anything else."

He nods, and I turn off the lights and take the maintenance elevator up to the fourth floor.

The space just above the lobby is reserved for two floors of offices and then a suite on the top floor. It isn't a luxurious suite by any means. It shares the same dingy vibe as the rest of the motel, but it's spacious, has a mattress that was purchased within the last five years, and a Jacuzzi in the bathroom. I don't use the space much because I'd rather just sleep at home, but I don't want to give Molly the chance to disappear.

The door is unlocked when I get there, and when I open it, I realize why.

Your suite has been readied to your specifications.

My specifications—as written by me three years prior—are to have a woman waiting for me at the end of every deal. And there she is, sprawled across the bed.

"Hello," she purrs, curling her fingers in a wave.

She has thin strips of black fabric barely covering her breasts. They join together over her midsection and then slip between her legs. Her body is brown and curvy and beautiful and any other day of the year I'd be thrilled to find someone like her in my bed.

Usually, I like a release after making deals. Even when things go perfectly, there is a lot of adrenaline involved in negotiating. Or some other chemical. I'm not sure; I'm not exactly a scientist. Whatever it is, it builds up inside of me, and I like having a beautiful woman nearby to channel it into.

But today, the sight of her feels like a burden.

"I've been waiting for you," she says, standing up and moving towards me, one foot in front of the other.

"Sorry about that, but I'm actually not—"

She slides her body across mine like a cat marking her territory. I know she's gorgeous and that I should be almost popping out of my pants with excitement, but I'm not. I step away from her and open the door slightly. She looks out the door as though expecting to see someone else waiting to come in.

"Don't you want…?" she asks, gesturing to herself.

I shake my head. "Not tonight."

Immediately, her shoulders slouch and the seductive tone in her voice goes flat. "They told me you'd pay me."

I unfold my wallet and slip a few bills into her hands. She's about to argue, but then she realizes the denomination and smiles. "Pleasure doing business with you."

She throws on a coat and leaves without argument.

Left alone in the empty room, there is nowhere for my restless energy to go, so I have no choice but to think about my brother. And given the choice between fucking a beautiful woman and thinking about my fuck-up of a brother, only a madman would send the woman away. Apparently, I'm a madman.

I wash my face with cold water and wonder if Molly is finding the room comfortable. I wonder if Theo is sleeping okay.

I wonder if Fedor knows about Theo.

I don't see how he could. If he did, he would have blurted the information out ages ago, probably by accident. Plus, family is everything to us. Our dad may not have been like the warm and fuzzy dads on television, but he taught us the importance of family and loyalty. It's why I've spent so many years bending over backwards for Fedor. And that's why I know he would do anything to protect his own flesh and blood.

Right?

I run my hands down my face and sit on the edge of the bed. I don't know anymore. I wouldn't have assumed Fedor would drug and hurt a woman, so maybe I don't know him as well as I think I do. Maybe I still see him too much as a kid rather than the man he has become. I'd hope the two wouldn't be a far cry from one another, but since when does hope equate with reality?

Sleep seems impossible. I lie back with my eyes closed for minutes that seem to stretch on and on, but I never get drowsy. I don't even slip into the place between consciousness and dreaming where your thoughts turn liquid and flow from one to the next without effort. I am fully awake, aware of every second, and desperate to take my mind off Fedor and Molly and Theo for even a second.

I roll out of bed and slip into my shoes. I could call down to the front desk for a drink to be sent up. Though the Twin Chandeliers really doesn't have room service, it has always been available to me. But I'd rather get it myself. There is a bar next door that my men are known to frequent. Maybe a haze of alcohol would help me forget about my problems for a minute.

The elevator is slower than the stairs, but just because I'm not sleeping doesn't mean I'm not tired. It has been a long day, and I don't want to walk. So, I press the button and wait for the rattling elevator to arrive and open.

The chances of me getting trapped inside it seem marginally greater than me making it all the way to the first floor unscathed, but I take the risk.

I pass the third floor without issue, but then the lift shakes to a stop on the second floor. I groan and reach to push the emergency button when suddenly, the doors open. For a second, I think there is no one standing there. But then, I see the small figure standing barefoot in front of the doors.

"Theo?"

His hair is mussed from sleep, his cheek creased from the pillowcase, but when he sees me, he grins and jumps into the elevator.

"Hello."

"Hi," I respond, looking around for Molly or anyone with any knowledge of what to do with a rogue four-year-old. "Where's your mom?"

"Sleeping." He reaches up and pushes all the buttons on the elevator and the doors close.

"Does she know you aren't in the room?" It's a stupid question. I don't know Molly well, but I saw enough of her parenting style earlier to know there is no way she would let her four-year-old traipse around the motel. Especially with men like Greg lurking around.

Theo shrugs, as though this point hardly matters, and pulls faces at his reflection in the chrome button panel.

For someone living on the street, I'd expect Theo to be nervous around strangers. The fact that he's perfectly comfortable in his environment means that Molly has done a better job than most at protecting him from the realities of the world around him. In this case, that is both a blessing and a curse.

Neither of them knows, but my sole purpose in coming to the motel was to separate them forever. Theo should be more afraid of me than anyone in the world, and yet, he's making faces and giggling at his own reflection. I shake my head, the corner of my mouth turning up in amusement despite my efforts to hide it.

"I think we should take you back to your mom, bud," I say, easing him away from the elevator buttons by grabbing the collar of his shirt and pulling him slowly backward. He resists for a second before giving in to my authority.

"The room is boring, and I'm not sleepy."

"It is—" I check my watch. "After midnight. You should definitely be asleep."

He groans. "I'm thirsty."

Thanks to Theo's button mashing, the elevator is set to stop at every floor in the hotel, so it takes us to the ground level. There, we get out, and I grab him another water from the mini fridge.

If the kid working the desk thinks it's strange I'm with a little kid instead of the sex worker he had sent up to my room, he doesn't make his feelings known. He smiles at us both and then continues wiping down the surfaces of the lobby with a bleach wipe.

Theo and I have to wait a few minutes for the rickety, empty elevator to make it all the way up to the fourth floor and then back to the ground floor, but when it does, we hop inside and return to the second floor. I make sure to keep Theo's active fingers away from the button panel this time.

Theo races down the hallway, probably annoying the other guests in the motel, but I dare one of them to come out and say anything about it. I'll have them thrown out on their asses before they even know what happened.

The kid spins around and smiles at me as he clumsily runs backwards, and a surge of protectiveness rushes through me. It's the same sensation I've always had with Fedor. The same instinctual need to make sure nothing bad ever happens to him.

I know it's probably only happening because Theo and Fedor might as well be twins. It's probably just a nostalgic or biologic response to seeing a human who shares my genetics. It shouldn't override logic and common sense.

Except, I fear it might.

I know Molly needs to be out of the picture if there is any hope of Fedor being free. And I damn well know my hands are full enough trying to keep Fedor out of trouble that I don't have the energy or resources to add two more people to that list. And yet …

Theo runs back to me, his little chest rising and falling like he has just run a marathon.

"I'm the fastest kid at day care," he says with pride. "Some of the kids are babies, but some are big like me. I'm still the fastest."

"Is that so?"

He hums a confirmation. "Krista doesn't let us run around the apartment, but when we go to the park, I run as fast as I can, and she can't even catch me."

An image of Fedor running around the playground with one arm extended in a fist, pretending to be a superhero while I gave mock chase behind him, rushes into my mind. I shake my head to clear the image, but it refuses to budge.

I protected Fedor then and still do now because he's family, and that is the one useful thing my father ever taught me: family over everything.

And now, Theo is family. Whether Fedor knows it or cares, this kid is my family, and I have to protect him, too.

I just have to figure out how to do that.

8

MOLLY

The knocking invades my dreams before I finally rouse. It has been so long since I've been in a truly deep sleep that I'm confused for a minute. Sleeping in the shelters means waking once an hour to someone coughing, going to the bathroom, or begging their kids to stay in bed. It has rarely ever been so quiet.

The knocks happen again, propelling me out of bed. They are soft, not violent or threatening, but my adrenaline spikes, and I fling an arm out across the bed to hide Theo.

If Viktor knows about my connection to Fedor, he might be here to claim his family. Men like him are all about their family. He won't want his flesh and blood living on the streets with a waitress. They'll take Theo away, raise him away from me, and I won't have any means of stopping them. No one will listen to the cries of a homeless woman who lost her child. They'll probably rejoice that he's finally being taken care of.

Except, when I reach out across the bed, the small lump I expect to find there is missing. Instead, the covers have been thrown back haphazardly, leaving the bed cold.

Dread drops into my stomach like an anchor, nearly bringing me to my knees.

Theo is gone.

There is more knocking on the door, but I barely even hear it over the sound of blood pumping in my ears. Theo is gone, and I have no idea where he is, and *oh my God, I think I might die.*

One time when Theo was two, he ducked underneath a clothing rack in a thrift store and disappeared. When I ran to the other side of the aisle, I couldn't find him. He was out of my sight for maybe a total of forty-five seconds, but it felt like an hour of running from aisle to aisle, trying to find him, looking for his little dark-haired head. Another shopper caught him when she saw me frantically looking and brought him back to me, but the feeling of him being out of my sight—being lost—never left me. And now I'm feeling it again but a thousand times worse.

We are in a hotel owned by the family of his father—the family of the man who attacked me. And they know. Maybe they've taken him. They could have drugged me just like Fedor did all those years ago. What time is it? I can't find the alarm clock in my panic.

This time, I register the knocking, and I stumble to the door in a blind panic, my vision blurry as tears begin to crowd in.

As soon as I throw it open, I see there is a man there, but before I know who, my eyes snag on the little head at his side. Theo is smiling up at me kind of lazily, like this reunion isn't special. Like I should have known he'd be right back.

A relieved sob bursts out of me, and I hold out my arms to grab him before I remember the man next to him. I look over and every despicable theory floating around in my head is confirmed. *Viktor.*

I reach out and grab Theo's hand. He jerks forward with a groan of annoyance and as soon as he's out of Viktor's grip, I draw my leg back and then lunge forward, driving my knee up as hard as I can—directly into Viktor's groin.

His eyes go wide, and then he doubles over, letting out a string of curses not at all suitable for Theo's ears. Though, seeing his mother knee a man in the crotch also isn't very suitable.

Before Viktor can rally, I squeeze Theo's hand and drag him down the hallway behind me.

Theo is crying, I'm barefoot, and neither of us has our coats, but I know this is a matter of life and death. If we stay in this motel, Viktor will have us killed. The only reason I got the best of him this time is because he didn't know I'd figured it out. But I have, and I won't go back into that room willingly.

"Molly, wait," Viktor wheezes behind me, but I ignore him as I sprint past the elevator and take the stairs. Theo is still fighting, trying to pry his fingers from my grip, so I scoop him up in my arms more deftly than I've ever done before and keep running.

A plan is formulating in my mind. We aren't far from the shelter. There may not be a place to sleep, but they can't turn me away if they know I'll freeze to death on the streets. They'll have to give me a pair of shoes and give us both coats or blankets, at least. Then I'll use the ten-dollar bill in my back pocket to take the bus to a box store somewhere. It was my last choice earlier in the night, but now, it will be our salvation.

I burst through the door into the lobby more ferociously than intended and between my panting and Theo's crying, we draw some attention. The kid who delivered my food looks up from his laptop and frowns.

"Is everything okay?"

I try to calm my breathing and nod, moving towards the door.

"Do you need something?" he asks.

I shake my head, still too out of breath to speak. I don't want him to know I'm running away. He seems nice, but he could be in on the plan with Viktor. He might try to stop me from leaving if he knows that's what I'm doing. I'm not safe until I get away from the motel.

I'm halfway across the lobby when a distant roar winds its way down the stairwell and into the lobby. The kid perks up and tilts his head to the door, and I walk faster, trying to pretend I didn't hear it.

"What is going on?" he asks just as Viktor's voice becomes clearer.

"She grabbed the kid and ran. I don't know where she's going, but she doesn't even have shoes on."

His voice is as clear as though it was in the room.

No time for playing it cool. I have to run. *Now.*

Theo is limp in my arms and getting heavier by the second, but I hug him to me and lower my head to make a break for it… when suddenly, there is a dark shadow in front of me. I look up to see the human equivalent of a brick wall. He is tall, dark, and solid. He lays a hand on my shoulder and pins me in place with the sheer weight of it.

I was so focused on the kid behind the counter and Viktor giving chase that I didn't notice the man standing guard in the corner. Perhaps he's the security the pervy clerk mentioned earlier. I assumed he was making it up, but apparently not.

"Where are you off to?" he asks, his voice a deep rumble that seems to shake the building.

"Stop her before she does something stupid."

Viktor's voice sounds extremely close now, and I realize it's because it's coming out of a small headset in the security guard's ear.

"Why are you running?" he asks, looking from me to Theo. "Have you stolen something?"

"Just let me go." I try to twist out of his grip, but he holds onto my arm and spins me around just as the stairwell door opens and Viktor walks into the room.

His face is red, either from recently being hit in the balls or from running—or both—and his eyes are narrowed in frustration. He growls as he stomps across the floor, takes my arm from the guard, and walks me towards the door I was just running towards. The door to the outside.

"Where are we going?" I ask, suddenly wishing we'd go back inside. When I ran out, it seemed like a good idea, but now, walking into the cold and dark seems ominous.

Theo seems to calm in Viktor's presence which only makes me more frantic. What did Viktor say to him during their time alone? Could he really have brainwashed my own child against me in that short of a time? It's the only thing I can think of which would explain why Theo trusts Viktor and not me. Why he calms in the presence of a relative stranger and cries in the arms of his mother.

The security guard is walking behind us, and Viktor holds out a hand to tell the man to stay back. I suppose that's a good sign, though I'm not convinced. Nothing about this situation seems good.

"Why are you running?" he asks, his voice deep and even, though I can tell it is taut and strained like a wire cable about to snap. There is a deep vein of fury running just below the surface.

"Don't hurt us," I plead, pressing Theo's face to my chest and covering his ears with my hands. "Please."

I don't want to scare him. I don't like that he seems comfortable around Viktor, but I also don't want him to be traumatized.

"Just let us go. You'll never see us again. I swear. Just let us go." I'm only half-aware of what I'm saying. My clearheaded adrenaline of a few minutes ago is shifting into a caged kind of panic. I feel boxed in, claustrophobic, and I'll do anything to get out.

"I'm not going to hurt you if you just cooperate," Viktor says. He lets go of my arm when we reach a black car in the back of the parking lot. He nods for me to get inside.

I hold Theo more tightly until I can feel him squirming with discomfort, and look around for a path of escape. Viktor steps into my line of sight again, shakes his head, and pulls back his leather jacket to reveal a gun on his hip.

"I'm not going to hurt you if you cooperate," he repeats. "Put Theo in the car."

Lost. Hopeless. Desperate.

My will to live is draining, and now I'm focused only on saving Theo.

"Let Theo go. He's innocent. He doesn't deserve this. Please, let him go. Take me, but leave him."

"I'm not going to hurt him," Viktor says, his patience growing thin. He sounds frustrated, but yet, I believe him. I don't think he wants to hurt Theo. "Now get in the car."

When it becomes clear I'm not going to move, Viktor pries Theo out of my grip. I want to cling to him and scream, but I don't want to do anything that will scare him. If he starts to scream and cry, will Viktor change his mind? Would he hurt him just to try and make him quiet?

The thought is acid in my stomach, so I fall back against the car as soon as Theo is taken out of my arms and sag down to the ground as Viktor buckles him into the back seat. Seconds later, he's in front of me, hand extended.

"Why are you doing this?" I ask. "Why now? It's been years."

Viktor says nothing, but reaches down, grabs my hand, and hauls me onto shaky legs.

"Get in." He opens the driver's side door for himself and nods for me to walk around the car and get in the passenger seat.

Once I get in the car, I don't know what will happen. I don't know where he'll take me or what he'll do. Maybe he's taking us to Fedor. Maybe he's going to give Theo to the man who attacked me and then dispose of my body.

Tears burn the backs of my eyes, and I know this is my last chance at getting away. If I let myself be driven away from the motel, I might never be seen again.

So, I walk around the front of the car and reach for the passenger side door. Then, as fast as I can, I lunge forward, wrench the door open, and throw myself across the back seat.

Theo had just started to calm down, but he gasps in surprise as I fumble with his seat belt and try to drag him across the leather seat to me.

Just as I'm about to pull him through the door and run, I hear a mechanical *thunk*. When I look up, I expect to see Viktor with his gun pointed at me, but I'm still unprepared for the rush of fear that tears through me when that expectation is confirmed. My arms go slack, and I drop Theo back onto the seat.

Viktor hides the gun behind the car seat so Theo won't see it—something I'm grateful for, as absurd as it sounds—and shakes his head at me.

"Get in the car."

That was it. My big escape attempt. Foiled in under five seconds.

I buckle Theo into his seat, kiss his forehead, and get into the front seat. Viktor waits until I'm buckled in before he puts the gun away.

"My aim is perfect," he says quietly as he pulls out of the lot. "If I were you, I wouldn't test it."

9

VIKTOR

Proof that kids can adapt to anything, Theo miraculously falls asleep in the back seat. Molly is rigid and shaking next to me, refusing to look in my direction, and as much as I want to comfort her, I decide her being afraid of me isn't the worst thing that could happen. Maybe she won't try to run anymore.

Why now? It's been years.

When she said that back in the parking lot, it all made sense. She figured it out. Somehow, Molly figured out who I am, how I'm related to Fedor, and must have guessed why I found her at the motel and offered her a free room.

I can't even imagine how terrified she must have been to wake up and find Theo missing. She probably thinks I took him from the room, but if that was the case, why would I have returned him to her? Perhaps as a show of my power over her, I guess. Though Molly didn't seem to be thinking rationally enough to make that kind of logical leap. She was acting on pure instinct. So much so that she and Theo were going to leave the motel barefoot and coatless.

They are still barefoot and coatless, and I'm not going to let them wander around on the streets that way, no matter how much Molly fights.

"Just let him go," Molly whispers, breaking me out of my thoughts. She glances into the back seat to be sure Theo is asleep and then relaxes back against the headrest. "Whatever this is about, Theo has no part in it. He doesn't know anything. He's too young to hear the details."

The details of her assault. Of how he was conceived. I'm twenty-eight, and I think *I* might be too young. Nothing could ever prepare me to hear how my baby brother hurt an innocent woman.

"Don't hurt him," she continues, her hands folded nervously in her lap. "Make sure he's taken care of. That he has everything he needs. And please …" Her voice breaks, and she clears her throat. "Please don't speak badly about me. Please let him know how much I loved him."

My hands tighten on the wheel, my knuckles going white. I don't respond or make any move that I've heard her, but Molly must feel moderately better just getting it all off her chest because she sits back and doesn't say anything else the rest of the drive.

∼

When we pull up to the house, I call for one of the full-time guards to come out and carry Theo inside. Molly tenses up when he grabs Theo, but the boy is so fast asleep that he doesn't even stir.

"You'll only scare him if you throw a fit," I say, grabbing her arm.

She glares at me and wrenches her arm away, but she must agree because she stays quiet. She watches through the tinted windows until Theo is carried up the stairs and through the front door.

"Why aren't we going inside?" She's trying to sound tough but the fear is obvious in her voice.

"Because I need to talk to you first."

When she turns to me, her golden eyes are glassy with tears, but none of them leak down across her cheeks. She's trying hard to be strong.

"About what?"

"Your living arrangements."

Confusion flickers across her face. "Living arrangements?"

I nod.

"So, you aren't going to kill me?"

"We'll get to that in a minute." I reach across her and point to the stairs at the corner of the building. "That is my home. You and Theo will be staying there with me for the foreseeable future."

Molly's mouth falls open in surprise, and her outward expression mirrors my inward one. I hadn't fully made the decision until the very second the words came out of my mouth. And now, it seems, I'll have two houseguests when I've previously had zero. Ever.

The idea has merit, though. I'll be able to keep a close eye on both of them if they are in my house. I have guards who can monitor them when I'm not around, and I can guarantee that they are safer here than in the motel. No one on my staff would dare hurt either one of them, but the same can't be said of the workers at the motel.

Molly leans down to get a better look at the building. It's three stories tall and takes up most of the city block. The brick has been whitewashed and flowers stand outside large windows restored from when the building was once a warehouse. It's an eclectic mix of industrial and homey that looks nothing like where anyone would expect the head of the Bratva to live. That is part of the reason I chose it. The other reason was because of the private entrance.

"My penthouse takes up the first two floors on this half of the building."

"Maisonette."

I frown. "What?"

"It's a maisonette," she says. "A penthouse is an apartment on the top floor of a building, but yours is on the first and second. Plus, you have a private entrance. That makes it a maisonette."

I remember the realtor saying that word often when I was buying the place, but I hardly cared about the terminology. I liked the location relative to my office downtown and where I do business. And the private entrance and belowground parking garage meant I wouldn't ever have to try and smuggle things or people through a crowded lobby and up an elevator without being noticed.

"Either way, you'll have a roof over your head, food on the table, and you won't have to pay a thing," I say. "I'm going to take care of you."

Molly's normally dark complexion has gone an ashy gray color, and I'm not sure if it's from the streetlights or the situation. More likely than not, it's from both. She looks like she's about to be sick.

I feel about the same.

I don't like that I want her and Theo near to me. I've never wanted people nearby. Even with Fedor, I've kept him at arm's length. I care for him in all the ways I can, but I've never wanted to share a space with him. I like coming home and having the quiet. I've always liked being alone.

Except now, mere hours after being introduced to Molly and Theo, I want to protect them. I want to keep them safe from any men Fedor may get to work for him. If he finds out I'm not taking out the people he thinks I'm taking out, he might decide to take matters into his own hands. Or, considering his hands are shackled, the hands of men more loyal to him than to me.

I will deal with that when the time comes, but for now, I'll keep them nearby until I can figure out what to do. Until I figure out what I have to do.

"Has it been a minute?" Molly asks. "Because I'd like to talk about whether or not you're going to kill me."

She turns to me, her eyes clear and her jaw set. I admire her fire, regardless of how inconvenient it might be for me over the next several days or weeks.

"I don't want to kill you," I admit.

"But you might have to?" she asks after a long pause.

"Perhaps."

She nods, absorbing the information. "Is there anything I can do to change your mind?"

The question is dangerous. She has already done more than she could ever know to change my mind. The way she cares for Theo, the way she was hesitant to accept my offer despite her desperation, and the way she has continued to strive in the face of obstacle after obstacle have all gone a long way to make me admire Molly more than I ought to. Certainly more than I've ever admired anyone else I've ever killed.

If I tell Molly any of this, however, it will show weakness. A crack in the armor she could use to manipulate me. And I can't afford to be manipulated.

"I want to see Theo."

I need to exert some kind of control over the situation. I need her to know she should defer to my commands. That regardless of my temporary kindness, I am the one in charge.

So, I walk around the car and open her door, but I keep a firm grip on her arm as we walk up the stairs and into the entryway.

Molly smells like citrus. Like summertime and sunshine, which is in complete opposition to the dark cold outside. I hold her at arm's length to get away from it, but there doesn't seem to be an escape.

"Where is he?" she asks as soon as we walk through the door. She pulls against my hold, but I grab her tighter.

"In a little bit," I say, ushering her into the sitting room just off the entryway. "Let me show you around."

"I don't care."

"You will when you can't find the bathroom in the middle of the night," I snap.

I can tell she wants to argue, but she presses her lips together and follows me through the house.

The building used to be an old warehouse, but extensive renovation and remodeling turned it into a large building with eight different luxury units. I can tell Molly is interested in the design of things as we move from one room to the next, but she doesn't say anything. She just observes every detail, looking from the ceiling to the floor and back again. I wonder what she's seeing.

When we get to the kitchen, I lean back against the counter and point to the coffee machine. "Why don't you make us both some coffee? I suspect neither of us will be getting much sleep tonight."

Molly raises an eyebrow at me in challenge and crosses her arms over her chest. "I spend all goddamn day making coffee for money. I'm not going to make it for you for free."

"You work at a diner."

She rolls her eyes. "What else do you know about me?"

"Less than I'd like to." The admission catches me by surprise. I didn't mean to say it. I'm usually not forthcoming with anyone about my thoughts or feelings. Especially with women. But something about

Molly puts me out of sorts. Something about her makes me unsteady, like I'm standing on the edge of a tall building, trying to keep my balance before I go toppling off the ledge.

Molly looks like she doesn't know whether to be frightened or flattered. Her face is getting some color back, and maybe it's the nervous flush in her cheeks or the way she's chewing on her full lower lip, but I don't want to scare her again. So, I start pulling out the necessary equipment to make the coffee.

"Damn," she says softly. "Even if I'd wanted to make coffee, I couldn't have. It looks like you're building a rocket ship."

"It's just a grinder, an electric kettle, and a Chemex."

"At the diner, we have a coffee pot." She keeps her distance as I grind the beans, heat up the water, and pour it slowly over the grounds. Making coffee is one of the few things I find pleasure in doing myself. I've never liked to cook and nobody likes to clean, but making coffee is calming.

"Are you hungry?"

"If I say I am, are you going to ask me to cook?" she asks.

I shrug. "That depends. Can you cook?"

"Let's just say I take food to customers, but I don't make it," she says. "If you make me cook, you're likely to end up poisoned."

I pour the coffee into two mugs and hand her one. "Would that be a purposeful or accidental poisoning?"

Molly takes the mug from me, careful not to let her fingers touch mine in any way. When she takes a sip, she scrunches her nose, either because it's hot or she doesn't like it, and looks at me over the top of the rim of the cup. Her eyes are wide and serious. "Do you want to let me cook and find out?"

Despite the underlying threat, I can't help but laugh. "You win. You don't have to cook."

She lifts her cup in a sarcastic toast of victory, and I hate how much I like her. She's funny and brave and a hard worker. It certainly doesn't help that she's effortlessly sexy. Even in jeans and a sweater, there is something magnetic about her. Something that draws you in and refuses to let go. As disgusting as Fedor's crime was, I can see why he chose Molly.

"You could almost be bearable if you weren't thinking about killing me," Molly says.

Again, the words are tough, but her voice is wavering. There is still fear there. Still uncertainty.

"We can't all be perfect." I set my mug down and walk around the island so I'm standing just across from her. When I lean back against the countertop, my knee brushes hers. This time, Molly doesn't flinch away from my touch. She looks down at where our legs are touching, like there's a snake in the grass, and she isn't sure whether she should run or remain still.

"What does that mean?"

"What?"

"We can't all be perfect," she repeats. "Do you think I'm perfect?"

Did I mention smart? Molly is smart. I hadn't even realized what I said. Hadn't even realized what information I let slip out in my attempt at humor. But there it is between us. My initial feelings about Molly are on display for her to see, and now I have to decide whether I'm going to take it all back or whether I'm going to, for once in my life, tell the truth.

I'm tired. More tired than I've been in a long time. But here I am, standing in the kitchen with this woman. A woman who should be trembling in fear before me, but is instead quizzing me on my feelings about her. And I have to admit to myself that I do find Molly rather perfect.

Her good qualities as a human and a mother have been playing through my head all night, but now I'm looking at her, studying her as she watches me, and I realize she's perfect all over.

Her eyes are wide and warm. When she blinks, dark lashes fan out like they're moving in slow motion. The shadows brush across her cheeks, which, in the white light of the kitchen, I can see are marked with a light constellation of freckles that cluster at the corner of her eyes. Earlier, I thought it was makeup, but I'm no longer sure she has any on at all.

She pinches her lower lip between her teeth, drawing it into her mouth and then letting it pop out, shining with moisture. Her mouth is the color of overripe fruit, and before I realize what I'm doing, I'm moving forward for a bite.

Fear sparks in her eyes, and her lips fall open in surprise. I bend low, wrapping an arm around her lower back and bringing her to me. Molly is too shocked to resist. Her body presses against mine, meeting me point for point, and when I finally press my mouth against hers, I taste the bitterness of coffee mixed with the same hint of citrus I smelled before. A smell I can now only attribute to her for its unique mixture of warmth and sweetness and bite.

Her lips are soft and pliable, and I tilt my head to the side to taste her more deeply.

On some level, I know I'm not thinking clearly. I know this is a mistake, but as I just told Molly, we can't all be perfect. I'm as far from perfect as they come, and I want this regardless of what it means for the Bratva and my brother. I want Molly because she's soft and warm and beautiful. I want Molly because she has made this one of the most interesting nights of my life, and I'd like to see just how much more interesting it could be.

Apparently, Molly wants that too.

She should be pushing me away, but just when I think she's lifting her hand to slap me, she presses her palm against my cheek. She drags her hand down over my stubbled face and traces her fingertips over the muscles in my neck.

Molly's mouth opens, and her tongue slips into my mouth, and dear God, this woman really is perfect.

10

MOLLY

He smells like cedar.

Cedar and leather and coffee beans. He's the human equivalent to a hipster coffee shop. I haven't been in one since before I had Theo, but I can remember the smell.

Viktor curls a hand around my back, pressing me firmly against him, and his body feels good against mine. Solid and warm.

He is strong. Healthy. The kind of man that could throw me over his shoulder and carry me into a cave.

And I melt.

My body fuses with his, my hips pressing into his, my chest arching up as I grab his square jaw in my hands and open my mouth to let him in.

He tastes good, too. I hear someone moan—it might be me.

The men I've been with since having Theo have not been good experiences. Quick, anonymous, forgettable. Just physical encounters good for releasing some pent-up energy.

This is different though. Rather than releasing energy, I seem to be drawing it from Viktor.

I was tired a moment ago, but now, I've never felt more awake. My body is humming with electricity. I feel like a live wire.

Viktor sucks on my lower lip and swirls his tongue with mine, and I feel my entire body go weak. This should not feel this good. It's not normal for kissing to feel this good.

In the back of my head, my rational brain is fighting for control. It's kicking and screaming for me to push him away and run in the opposite direction, but I don't want to. As bad as Viktor is, I think I'm attracted to him.

I almost laugh out loud at my own naivete.

Of *course* I'm attracted to Viktor.

I found him handsome the first moment I saw him. His particular mix of wine-colored hair, chiseled jawline, and sculpted body is like catnip for women. He is genetically predisposed to making women swoon. Which is probably the reason I accepted a shot from his brother at that concert five years ago.

Fedor.

His name is like a shot of clarity in a cloud of fog. I jolt back into my body, making me aware of what I'm doing for the first time in minutes —hours? I push on Viktor's chest until our bodies separate. Until I have enough distance to think clearly.

Fedor and Theo. Two very different yet very important reasons why I can't let this kiss continue.

Theo needs me to be alert, to stay strong and resilient. I can't let our attractive captor ensnare me in this trick. Because that's what it is—a trick. He's trying to lower my defenses and make sure I won't try to escape again.

And Fedor.

He's the reason I'm here in the first place. What he did to me changed the course of my life and sent his brother chasing after me. He's the reason Viktor cares at all about Theo. Fedor is the reason there is a chance my son will be taken away from me.

I can't let that happen.

Viktor's eyes are glazed over, but he blinks and tries to focus on me. His lips are red and swollen, and I'm sure I look just as disheveled as he does. The thought makes me self-conscious, and I smooth my hair down and run the back of my hand over my mouth.

The air between us, once electric, feels stagnant. It feels heavy and full, like a rain cloud threatening a downpour. I'm not sure what to say.

Viktor just stares at me.

"I'm sorry," I blurt, and immediately feel stupid for doing so. I'm mostly just sorry that I allowed myself to get so caught up in my physical attraction to Viktor that I could forget what his family is doing to me. I'm sorry that I lost control and gave him the impression that I am a moony girl who will fall over backwards because his blue eyes smolder when he's frustrated.

He clears his throat and grabs his coffee, taking a sip. We stand there in an uncomfortable silence for another second before Viktor breaks it, surprising me further.

"What kinds of toys does Theo like?"

"What?"

"Toys," he says, as though I might not know what the word means. "What does he like to play with?"

I blink at him, confused why this would matter.

"If he's going to be staying here, I should make him a room. I have a few guest rooms upstairs. You can each have one."

The more he talks, the more it feels like he's speaking in another language.

Theo has never had his own room. He had his own bed before we lost the apartment, but since then, we've been making do with the shelter and the kindness of what few friends I have left. When you are living that way, toys don't enter into the equation. I feel like a terrible mother for admitting it, but I'm not even sure what he likes. Viktor must see this realization on my face because he shrugs.

"I'll just have one of my guys buy him a bit of everything. Kids are easy to please, right?"

I nod. "Especially Theo."

Viktor's mouth pulls up at the corners. "He seems like a good kid."

Something cold runs through me. I shouldn't be talking Theo up. I should be trying to convince Viktor that he's a terror. That he throws temper tantrums that rattle the walls and burst eardrums. I should be trying to convince him that Theo is not a kid he wants to raise.

"What about you?" Viktor asks, interrupting my thoughts. "What do you need?"

My mouth flops open like a fish.

"Clothes?" he asks. "If there are any foods or snacks you prefer, you can leave a list on the counter and the chef will pick them up when she delivers meals in the morning."

Foods? Snacks? I've been struggling so long to simply get food of any kind that I'm not sure I even snack anymore. There have been a few meals that have been mostly things I could buy from a vending machine, which has honestly put me off the idea of snacks altogether. I'd rather have a pot roast with mashed potatoes and gravy. I wonder if I can put that on the list.

Then I chastise myself.

Again, Viktor is drawing me in with special treatment. He couldn't get me to submit with his body, so now he's putting on the charm. It's all a trick.

Or is it?

He turns his head to the side, watching me think, and I can't help but feel like he's being genuine. Like he actually cares what I eat.

I haven't had anyone care about me in so long that even this distorted kind of concern feels good.

"Why would you care what I want?" I ask. "You're going to kill me, right?"

It feels surreal to say the words so casually. To somehow both feel safe in the moment, but also recognize that Viktor could decide to end my life any second. I have no way to explain the dichotomy other than exhaustion. At this moment, I think I could fall asleep standing up.

"That remains to be seen," Viktor says, looking down into his now empty coffee cup. He curls his large hands around the mug, drumming his fingers on the ceramic. "How long have you and Theo been homeless?"

"A couple years."

"Where is your family?"

I shrug. "Around, but they don't care about me. Sex before marriage is not something they support."

"They let you raise a kid on your own?"

"They let me raise myself on my own." I don't talk about my parents. With anyone. I don't talk about my shitty childhood because I know there are people out there who grew up the way Theo is now. People who had no homes, skipped meals, and wore clothes that were too small. They won't give a shit about my parents being cold while they still fed and clothed me.

"How old were you when you had Theo?"

"Nineteen. Eighteen when I got pregnant."

Something resembling pity crosses his face, and he won't look me in the eye.

"Did you know?"

Viktor looks up at me. His blue eyes are bloodshot but piercing. He watches me for several seconds, weighing whether or not to answer the question. Just when I think he's going to ignore me, he blinks and then shakes his head slowly. "No."

"About me or about Theo?" I clarify.

"I didn't know about either of you until this afternoon." He sighs and looks away, running a hand through his dark hair, sending it sticking straight up. "Fedor's lawyer told me about you."

"About me? Not about Theo?"

He doesn't answer, but I can see in his face that Theo was a surprise. Which changes things.

When I meet men, they are often surprised to find out that I have a four-year-old son—apparently homeless women with children aren't a big turn on—so Viktor's surprise at the motel seemed normal to me. But as soon as I found out who Viktor really was, I assumed it had all been an act and that he was there to take Theo from me. Now I know he didn't even realize Theo existed.

"So why did you take Theo from my room earlier? What did you say to him?"

"I found him wandering in the hallway," he explains. "He woke up and snuck out without you realizing it."

After the food was delivered, I was so shocked to learn whose motel I was sleeping in that I didn't lock the door. I remember now. When I was woken up by the knocking and stumbled to the door, I didn't have to unlock the deadbolt first. That's how Theo was able to get out without waking me up.

"You thought I kidnapped him," Viktor says.

I nod. There's no sense denying it.

"That explains the knee to the groin." He winces from the memory, and I can't help but smile. "It wasn't funny."

"Agree to disagree."

I could be mistaken, but I think I see a ghost of a smile on his face too. Then it disappears and a deep line appears between his eyebrows. "I didn't come for Theo. I came for you. To keep you from testifying."

Now it's my turn to frown. "Testifying? About what?"

He raises a brow, waiting for me to catch up, and I do.

"Oh." The assault.

"Did the police approach you to testify? You can tell me the truth."

"I don't have to lie," I say. "Nobody has approached me at all. I haven't thought about your brother in a very long time. Not until I found out who you were."

He clenches his teeth, his jaw working at the corners, flexing in a way that makes me think of the way his lips felt on mine. I look away and push the thought out of my mind. Or, if not all the way out, at least to the back. To unpack later.

"Will you testify if they ask you to?"

"Not if it endangers Theo." The moment I found out who Fedor was all those years ago, I dropped the pursuit of any charges. Getting some kind of settlement could have gone a long way to helping keep me and Theo off the streets these last few years, but the money wouldn't be worth the risk of either of us being hurt. It didn't take much searching to figure out what happens to anyone who dares testify against the Kornilovs.

Viktor is quiet for a minute. Then he takes my empty mug from me, puts it in the sink, and pulls out his phone. I don't know who he's calling or if it has anything to do with me. My heartbeat quickens as I contemplate whether I should stay put or run. Then, Viktor begins ordering someone to get to a store in the morning and buy blocks, toy cars, puzzles, and stuffed animals. He also tells them to buy pajamas and warm clothes for a four-year-old, and then turns to me.

"You're a small, right?"

"I can't pay for this," I say. "For any of it."

He squints in my direction. "You look like a small."

He tells the person on the other end to buy pajamas, underwear, socks, leggings, and T-shirts for a small woman.

When he hangs up, he slides his phone back into his pocket. "I'm sure you'll want to pick out your own jeans and bras." His eyes flick to my chest at the mention of my undergarments, and I feel my neck warm.

"What do you want?" I ask. "I can't pay for this. I won't be able to pay you back. So what is in it for you?"

"You'll live here," he says simply. "I just need you to stay here for a while and not turn my nephew against me. Or try to escape."

His voice turns menacing on the final word, but I'm growing tired of being scared of him. Besides, I can't help but focus on another point.

"Your nephew?"

"That's what he is," Viktor says defensively.

I know it's true, but I hadn't really thought about it until this moment.

Theo has an uncle. A family. For his entire life, it has just been the two of us. Now, suddenly, he has this whole other part of himself.

The trouble is that I'm not sure it's a part I want him to learn about.

Viktor leads me from the kitchen and continues the tour. Now that I'm ever so slightly more comfortable, I can take in the design of the room.

It was clearly once some kind of industrial building. Exposed pipes run across the ceiling and the windows are large reclaimed warehouse windows. Juxtaposed with that, however, are modern touches. Shiny hardwood floors in the living and dining room, white marble in the kitchen, and granite countertops so smooth they make me want to spread out on them and lie down.

The furniture, too, is surprising. I'd expect a man like Viktor to buy nothing but leather and wood, but the furniture is deep and plush, perfect for cuddling into and sitting by the fire. I wonder if Viktor has ever had someone to cuddle. He doesn't strike me as the type.

The first floor is mostly open space—a kitchen looking into a dining room and a large living room. The second floor, however, is for private use.

The rooms all branch off a main hallway. He passes by one door on the right, which he identifies as his room, though he doesn't open the door to show it to me. As he passes the next door, he presses his finger to the wood. "My office."

"Do I not get to see it? I thought this was a tour."

He looks over his shoulder, amusement lifting his brow. "You'd do well to stay out of there or else risk overhearing something you'd rather not know."

I want to ask if he'd kill me for knowing too much, but decide I don't want to know the answer. In this instance, ignorance probably is bliss.

The third door opens onto a bathroom. It's a blinding white with tiles that cover the entire floor. The only thing separating the rest of the room from the shower is a single drain positioned towards the back wall and a large circular showerhead hanging directly above it. In the back corner is a claw-foot tub with a fluffy white towel draped over the side.

"Your bathroom," he says. "And Theo's. I have my own off my room."

This bathroom is nicer than any house I've ever lived in. It's one of the nicest rooms I've ever even been in, but I try to hide the spark of excitement that rushes through me at the idea that it could be mine.

Because it isn't mine.

This is all Viktor's.

Everything I'm seeing belongs to him, and I only have access to it as long as he decides to keep me around. Like so much else in my life, this can all be taken away in an instant. It would be to my benefit not to forget that.

Before opening the next door, Viktor holds a finger to his lips, and I only understand his meaning when I see a small shape in the middle of a large bed.

Theo is lying on his side facing us. His mouth is open, his tiny body rising and falling with the deep, innocent sleep of a little kid. He looks perfectly at home in the room.

The walls are a bright blue with navy blue curtains and cream-colored carpet. It's a room nicer than I ever would have imagined for him. A room nicer than anything I could ever give him. The sight of it leaves a bittersweet taste in my mouth. I'm so grateful he's comfortable and sleeping, and so sad that this isn't the life I've given him.

Viktor pulls the door closed. "That will be his room since it's right next to yours."

Without pausing, he moves to the next door and pushes it open.

I stand in the doorway, too stunned to move, only stepping inside when Viktor presses a hand into the middle of my back.

"Make yourself at home. Feel free to rearrange the furniture or redecorate however you want. I never use this room, so I really don't care."

The room is perfect.

I don't say so out loud, but it is. Absolutely perfect.

The walls are concrete with a built-in wooden headboard stretching from floor to ceiling behind the bed. One wall is floor-to-ceiling windows covered in white curtains thick enough to keep out most of the light while still letting a bit filter through. It makes the room look like it's bathed in starlight.

The bed is covered in a light gray comforter with more pillows than I even know what to do with. A white throw blanket is thrown over the end of the bed, casually but also purposefully, like it was staged for an interior design magazine photoshoot.

The closet has glass doors that allow a view of the wooden shelving inside. Usually closets are closed away, hidden rooms to hide your junk, but here, the closet is another feature of the room. It's beautiful. Metal pipes hold up the shelves and light comes from above each of the shelves as though putting the clothes inside on display like they're works of art.

I don't have nice enough clothes to showcase like that.

"The clothes are mine right now," Viktor says, seeing where my gaze has landed. "I'll get rid of them tomorrow and have your things put in there. For now, you can borrow whatever you want to sleep in. It will probably be too big on you, but …"

I look over when he stops talking and realize his eyes are trailing down my body. He swallows and looks away.

"I'm sure you'll make do."

Make do. I almost laugh at the absurdity of the idea. That anyone would ever *make do* in a room like this.

I've 'made do' at the shelter and the gym showers. I've 'made do' with vending machine meals and scraps from the diner.

Living in this room is not 'making do.' It's luxury. It's beyond my wildest dreams.

Viktor puts his hands in his pockets, and I finally let myself admire him.

Before, the features that stuck out to me most were the ones he shared with Fedor. Now, however, in his own home, I can admire the things that set him apart.

The broadness of his shoulders and the fullness of his face. It's almost hard to imagine them as brothers at all now. Fedor looks like a sick ghost of Viktor. Like the unhealthy runt of the litter compared with Viktor's muscle and mass.

Viktor also looks kind.

Despite the gun he pulled on me earlier. Despite the threat in his voice when he told me not to escape. Despite everything, I can see that Viktor is torn. That he isn't sure what to do with me because he didn't expect this situation. He didn't expect Theo. And yet, he has treated him so well.

"Thank you—" I clear my throat to break through the raspiness in my voice. "Thank you for taking care of Theo. For the toys and the clothes and … the room."

It feels strange to thank him for such a thing, especially considering we're being held hostage here, but he could have left us chained in a closet somewhere. Instead, a closet will be filled with clothes for me in the morning.

Viktor nods like it's nothing and shrugs, his shoulders curling up to his ears. Then he looks at me, and his jaw tightens. His lips part like he's going to say something, but no words come out, and the thought I shoved aside before of his lips on mine comes racing back to the forefront of my mind.

Almost as if he can read my mind, Viktor slips his hands from his pockets and takes a step towards me.

I let out a harsh breath, and he takes it as an invitation. Viktor crosses the distance between us in an instant, wraps his thick arms around my body, and pulls me against him.

Like a buoy caught in a storm, tethered to the ocean floor but swirling with the waves, I rise up to meet him and press my lips to his. Immediately, I'm lost in the current.

11

MOLLY

I've never been able to let my guard down. My lifestyle doesn't allow it. I am constantly on my toes, ready for the next disaster to come around the corner. Ready for whatever life has to throw at me.

But with Viktor's arms wrapped around my body, my defenses are disabled.

I can't think about anything except the warmth of his body on mine. I can't focus on a single thought beyond the way his hands move through my hair and the way his strong thigh presses between my legs.

I open up to him, spreading my legs for him, and he fills the space I make for him and then some. He drags his hands from my hair to my waist and lower until his hands are curled around my legs. He lifts me up, and I wrap my legs around his middle, drawing him close.

His mouth is commanding. He flicks his tongue across my lower lip, coaxing me into a deeper kiss, and the moment I respond, Viktor takes. He claims.

Considering it's a first kiss—not counting the one in the kitchen earlier—I expect it to be a fumble of teeth and tongues as we learn the rhythm of each other, but this feels natural. It feels like what kissing is supposed to be. A give and take of sucking and probing and licking. A symphony of breaths and pants and small moans that could be coming from me, but also might be coming from Viktor.

I dig my fingers into the deep muscle of his back, holding onto his shoulder blades like handholds, and Viktor presses me against the wall.

There is a vague thought in the back of my mind that I was in this position earlier in the day. With Greg the grabby clerk. Except, then, I felt trapped and terrified and disgusting. Now, I feel like I'm liquid fire. Like my body is burning from the inside out and Viktor is fanning the flames.

He pins me to the wall with his hips and hooks his fingers under my shirt. He tugs up on it sharply and the threadbare fabric rips in an instant. I'm too turned on to care that it's my only shirt now that the rest of my things are stuck in the locker at the gym.

Viktor follows the rip up my center and uses both hands to tear the collar of the shirt. Then he slides the material off my shoulders and explores the newly exposed skin with his lips.

His mouth follows the dips of my collarbone and the smooth plane of my sternum until he's buried between my breasts. I tip my head back and sigh as he pushes the cotton material of my bra aside with his mouth and kisses the skin hidden underneath.

I clench my legs more tightly around him, circling my hips against his, and it's Viktor's turn to sigh. His warm breath washes over my breasts, and I want more of it. So, I reach around to my back and unclasp the bra. When it falls on the floor with the ripped remains of my shirt, Viktor pulls back and looks at me.

His blue eyes are hazed over. If I didn't know better, I'd think he was drunk.

His lips are red and swollen, his eyes are black with need, and he's breathing heavily. He is raw and beautiful.

The man who has kidnapped me and locked me away in his luxurious home is absolutely gorgeous.

"I think you mean intimidating," he says, leaning down to flick his tongue over my nipple. I jump at the contact.

I must have spoken out loud, and I'm embarrassed for him to see me so out of sorts.

"I meant what I said."

His eyes spark with amusement and something else. Something I don't immediately recognize.

"Is that so?" he asks.

I grind my hips against the growing bulge at his front and nod.

Suddenly, he whips me around and heads towards the bed. Air rushes across my now-exposed back, and I flinch and curl into his chest even more tightly, but in another second, Viktor tosses me on the bed.

I bounce on the mattress, momentarily amazed by the softness before my attention is directed elsewhere. Namely to Viktor crawling over my body and unbuttoning my jeans.

His blue eyes pierce mine as he drags the denim down my body, exposing my boring cotton panties. For a second, I wish I was the kind of girl who could afford lacy undergarments that barely cover the necessities, but the thought is gone when it becomes clear Viktor couldn't care less.

Like he did with my shirt, he grabs a handful of the well-worn material and tugs. There is a ripping sound and then cool air moves over my now-exposed body.

"Good thing you're buying me new clothes," I say, hoping he doesn't notice the thick layer of lust in my voice.

His hands start at my ankles and press upwards over my knees and my thighs. Then he pushes my thighs apart and settles between them, his breath warm over my skin.

"Don't pretend you're thinking about your clothes right now," he whispers, sending shivers straight up my spine. I arch my back against them, and he smiles.

Then he buries his mouth in me.

If I thought his kiss was delicious, this is another level entirely.

Warmth spreads through me like honey. I rock my hips up to meet him, shameless in my desire for more and more. For everything he can possibly give me.

I feel the moment my thoughts flip from pleasure to need, and Viktor must feel it too. His movements become purposeful. He circles a thumb over my center, matching the rhythm of his mouth, and I curl my hands in his dark hair and tug.

My thighs clamp around his ears, and I arch my back, squeeze my eyes closed, and hold my breath as the axis of my world seems to shift.

When I release, it's as though my heart is beating in every atom of my body. Everything is ebbing and flowing with life and warmth, and it's only when I feel a hand cover my mouth that I realize how loudly I'm moaning.

Viktor crawls over my body, and when I open my eyes, I see him looking down at me, his eyes sparking with amusement and something resembling pride.

"If I pull my hand away, do you promise not to wake Theo?"

I feel too good to be annoyed by his cockiness. I lift my shaky legs and curl them around his body, hooking my ankles behind his back.

That's when I feel the stiffness between his legs.

"My turn," I say, unhooking my legs and pushing on his chest.

Viktor is more than capable of resisting my shove, but he allows me to push him onto his back and crawl over him.

There is no need to delay the inevitable. We're both ready for this, so I crawl off him and find his wallet in the back pocket of his jeans. Inside is a small foil packet. I tear it open with my teeth and slide the condom over him in one deft movement. He watches me with predator-like focus as I position him at my opening and sink down.

The amusement in his eyes fades. The small smile on his lips turns downward into determination as he grabs my hips and slides me over him.

I reach back to grab my hair with one hand, pulling it out of my face, and Viktor slides his hand from my hip to my breast. His palm is warm as he rolls it across my skin, pebbling the skin beneath it.

Goosebumps bloom over my body like a cold wave. I close my eyes and lean back, rolling across him.

He is so big. I feel my body stretching and stretching, and I keep waiting for it to stop but it doesn't.

"I didn't take you for a dirty talker," he grunts, gripping my hip with one hand and thrusting into me forcefully.

Again, I didn't realize I'd spoken out loud, but based on the way his pupils are blown wide, I don't suspect Viktor minds.

I push his hand away and lean forward, pressing kisses to his smooth chest and across his neck while he thrusts upwards shallowly. When I reach his mouth, I bite his lower lip between my teeth and tug.

"You don't know anything about me."

Viktor clamps his hands over my backside while he slides slowly in and then out. "I'd love to learn."

I lift myself up and drop back onto him, and his eyes close as he sighs. Then, before I can react, he has flipped us over so he's on top. His hands are pressed into the mattress on either side of my head, his face cast in shadow.

"For instance," he says, sliding out of me slowly. "Do you like it rough?"

At the same moment he speaks, he crashes into me with all his weight. My back arches against the intrusion, and then I adjust around him again. My heart is thundering in my chest and it feels like it might burst clean through my rib cage.

"Or gentle?" he asks, following the movement with a softer one.

I clamp my hand on his lower back, anchoring myself so I can rise up to meet him, and Viktor smiles.

"Rough, okay," he says, nodding. "See? I'm learning things already."

I'm tired of the games. Of the talking. I want him inside of me, falling apart because of how good it feels. I want him beside himself with pleasure.

I curl my hand around his neck and pull him down until our lips meet. His breath is warm, and I slip my tongue into his mouth, tasting him fully.

Viktor's hands glide over my breasts and tangle in my hair. He grips my waist and drives into me. He moans into my mouth and pulls away to catch his breath, his eyes closed. With every connection of our bodies, he seems to grow a bit wilder, his movement becoming harried and frantic.

This is exactly what I want. It's the side of him I want to see. I want to know that, at least for a second, I have the power to control him. That for even a single moment, I have the ability to slide under his skin and can make him bow to my whims.

Earlier, in the kitchen, his kiss felt like a trap. But now, if this is a trap, at least I know it's mutually assured destruction. This—the meeting of our bodies—means something to Viktor.

It isn't love. It's lust. Which, in many ways, is more powerful.

He groans, pulling me from my thoughts, and his body stiffens. For a second, he pulls back and looks into my eyes, the blue swallowed by the black of his pupils. Then he shakes and buries his face in my neck.

My second orgasm comes quickly. I shiver around him as he finishes, feeling a mixture of relief and shame as the haze of the act dissipates, leaving me with the reality of what we've done. Of what I've done.

Still, I can't ignore the attraction. Even as Viktor pulls away and slips his clothes back on, I watch the move of his muscles beneath his skin, the way his abs flex and clench as he pulls his shirt back on.

I like the way he looks, it's true, but Viktor wants me. And that's useful.

He clearly enjoys my body, and as long as I know that, I can use it to my advantage.

I just have to be careful I don't start wanting him too.

12

VIKTOR

Molly's fire runs deep. I experienced it in her fight, but also when we were in bed together. She doesn't yield control easily. She gives as well as she gets, and the admiration I feel towards her is dangerous.

It's why I do my best to stay away.

I planned to stay around the apartment for the first few days, to be present in case Molly tried to make an escape or in case she had any questions, but now I regret that decision.

The clothes the guard bought for her are killer. He told me he deferred to the knowledge of the saleswoman to pick things out, and she clearly had a preference for cleavage and lace. Everything is low-cut and tight and makes me wish my hands were on her hips rather than clenched into fists at my sides.

Theo is happy to play with his new toys, and Molly quits her job, so she's able to play with him. She resisted at first, but the hourly pay was so low it was criminal, and it didn't take much to convince her to quit and hang out with Theo. It's the most time the two of them have spent together in a long while. I know because Theo keeps being surprised Molly isn't leaving.

I hover on the periphery, trying to stay away.

Molly seems fine with the arrangement and doesn't make any attempt to talk to me other than polite conversation at the few meals we share together. Otherwise, I stay in my office and focus on work.

Theo came into my office on the first full day they were at the house, and Molly, following the order I gave her the night before, didn't follow him in. She told him she'd be in her room when he was done, but he was content to sit on the floor and color on printer paper with my blue and black pens. It has become a routine, and he has come to see me every afternoon all week.

When it's time for me to visit Fedor at the prison, I'm almost sad that I won't get my usual hour to talk with Theo. That probably means it's high time I got out of the house, though.

"Where is your head?"

I look up. Fedor is frowning at me. His cheeks look hollower than they did a week ago, and he has a swollen black eye and a fat lip. I try to ask him who hit him, but he refuses to say. Then I ask him if he is eating, and he dismisses that question too. Both mysteries can probably be solved by the same answer: he has found a dealer on the inside and is swapping out his meals for pills. He failed to pay and got his ass beat, which would also explain the tremor in his hands. Withdrawal.

"Right here," I say.

He snorts. "Then answer my question."

I try to replay the last few minutes of conversation but come up blank. I look to Kent for help, but he just shuffles through the papers in front of him and ignores us both.

"That's what I thought," Fedor says, shaking his head. He pounds his flat palm on the table. "Did you take care of my problem?"

"Which problem is that?" I ask, though we both know what he's talking about.

He lowers his chin and looks up at me from beneath his dark brows. The swollen eye is little more than a slit. "The girl."

The girl. Molly.

He doesn't know about the boy, who at this moment is probably watching a cartoon on the flat screen in the living room and eating animal crackers out of a plastic cup. Fedor doesn't know about him at all.

"I took care of it." My mind makes the joke that I *took care* of her all night long, but I can't say that. Because Fedor can't know that Molly is back at my place, sitting next to Theo and flipping through the interior design books I had delivered to the house for her.

I sent one of my guys to clear out her locker at the gym and bought some newer books for her, too. She didn't say anything when she came to the living room and saw them sitting on the coffee table, but she has spent every afternoon poring over the pages, studying each picture in detail.

Fedor sits back in his chair and lets out a sigh of relief, and I've never been so close to hitting my baby brother. I've never wanted to give him a matching black eye more in my life.

He is sighing about what he believes is the murder of an innocent woman. A woman he attacked, impregnated, and left to fend for herself.

Our lifestyle is a dark one. There are plenty of moral gray areas and unconscionable things we've each done, but hurting a girl like Molly and leaving her to live on the streets is unforgivable.

I bite my tongue and grip my knee under the table, my fingernails digging into my jeans.

"Good because I've got to get the fuck out of here," Fedor says, gesturing to his face. "People in here aren't so nice."

"Neither are people out here," I say before I can stop myself. No one knows that better than Molly.

"Yeah, but out there, I'm one of the not-so-nice people. That makes it a lot more fun." Fedor is joking, but I can barely muster a smile.

On the way home, I keep reflecting on the conversation. Fedor is locked up and can't hurt Molly and Theo, but that doesn't make them safe. Especially now that they're connected to me. As long as they stay in the apartment, they're protected, but out on the streets there are people like the clerk she told me about at the gym, Greg from the motel, and Fedor. Plus anyone who would seek to hurt me. My enemies might get the idea that Molly and Theo are important to me, which could put them in harm's way.

I want to keep her and Theo safe, but if I put a Bratva guard on her, that will make it seem even more like she's important to me. I need to have her covered by someone no one else would know or recognize—a civilian guard.

I'm almost home, but as soon as the idea crosses my mind, I turn the car around and head back towards the strip of bars and liquor stores I visited just over a week ago.

~

I get pulled into another meeting when I'm only two blocks from home. The call is from Petr.

"Discipline case for Geoff," he says.

Petr tells me Geoff had been hiding out in a halfway house with one of his ex-con friends. The man is guilty of stealing our profits. He was in charge of our books and had been skimming some off the top for years until one of my new guys—a young guy with an amazing head for numbers—noticed the discrepancies and came to me with his concerns. Geoff's actions cut into my men's paychecks. Any man willing to steal from his own family doesn't deserve to be part of the Bratva. Though he'd been evading us for a few days, he finally surfaced at the bar where a lot of the Bratva members hang out. They had him trussed-up in the back of an SUV within the hour.

I hang up and head towards the Bratva's unofficial headquarters. It's where I meet with actual suppliers for the motel business, but also where I keep an office. It has a large basement—with no windows—that doesn't appear on any of the city's blueprints. It's the perfect place to handle cases like this. Cases that might get a little ugly.

Petr's car is parked just outside the front doors right next to an SUV with deeply tinted windows.

I unlock the front door, walk down the long hallway, and enter the hidden door inside the maintenance closet that leads down to the basement. There are three secret doors in total. The basement is a secret, but I still wanted multiple points of exit.

I'm halfway down the stairs when I hear someone begging for mercy. Geoff, no doubt.

"Thank God you're here," Petr says, clapping me on the back. "He won't shut up."

Geoff is sweating, his face pale, eyes wide. He looks like an animal caught in a trap. But I see him for the spineless, opportunistic predator he really is.

One of the other soldiers reported Geoff's misdeeds to me as soon as he found out. There are many crimes I'll turn a blind eye to, but a few I won't. Don't hurt a woman. Don't talk to the cops.

And don't take my fucking money.

"Did you do it?" I ask as I approach, pulling back my leather jacket to reveal the gun I keep tucked underneath.

Geoff swallows, trying to decide how to answer—whether to be honest or not—and that is answer enough. An innocent man denies the crimes until his dying breath. Only a guilty man weighs whether an admission could lead to a better outcome.

Before he utters a word, I whip out my gun and pull the trigger.

～

By the time I make it home, it's well after dinner.

Molly's design books are scattered across the couch as I walk in and there are plastic blocks spread across the floor, under the coffee table, and all over the sofa cushions like shrapnel from some kind of toy bomb.

I curse under my breath and swipe some of the debris to the floor just as Molly walks into the room.

"Oh, sorry." She hurries past me, sets a steaming mug on the coffee table, and begins cleaning up Theo's toys. "I was just coming in here to clean these up while Theo is busy. Esmerelda volunteered to give him a bath tonight."

"The maid will get it later," I say, waving away her efforts to tidy up. "Sit down."

I regret the order as soon as she follows it.

She's wearing a pair of dark gray leggings with a white tunic that hugs her waist and hips. The neck scoops low across her chest, revealing a lacy maroon material that must be one of the new bras I paid for. I should have instructed she be clothed in oversized sweats. Maybe I can get an extra jumpsuit from the prison next time I'm there. Though Molly might even make orange look good.

She scoops up a stack of notecards and places two of the books in her lap. I can tell by the arrangement of the cushions that she was much more comfortable here before I arrived. Now, she's sitting with her back straight and her feet firmly on the floor.

"Don't let me interrupt."

"You're not," she says. "I mean, I wasn't doing anything. Just reading."

"And taking notes, apparently." I nod to the notecards.

She chews on her lower lip. "A bit. Just vocabulary. It's stupid, really. Pointless."

"You knew what a maisonette was. Doesn't seem pointless to me."

She smiles and shakes her head. "I guess so."

Theo suddenly comes tearing down the stairs in a new pair of dragon pajamas and matching slippers. He runs through the house like he owns the place, which, after a week of filling every room with his toys, he basically does. Molly tells him not to run, but I undo all her discipline the moment Theo kicks a soccer ball in my direction and asks me to play.

I turn the coffee table against the wall as a goal and then guard it diligently when Theo tries to make a goal. He gets past me every time, but not before I gently tackle him on the floor and tickle him behind the knees.

Molly eventually sits back on the couch, slips out of her shoes, and tucks her bare feet underneath her on the couch. She makes a few more notecards while I play with Theo, looking up and smiling in our direction a few times.

I can't get over how surreally natural the whole situation feels.

Being with Theo is like being ten years old again, taking care of Fedor and playing with him. It feels like just yesterday I was building blanket forts in the living room and making him macaroni and cheese on the stove.

And looking up at Molly—it's unlike anything I've ever experienced. I've only known her a week, but it feels like she has always been smiling up at me from the couch. It feels like we have always shared this space. Like she has always been with me.

But she hasn't been, and she won't be for much longer, I remind myself. This arrangement has an expiration date; I just don't know when it is.

When Theo goes to kick the ball in the goal, he catches it with his heel on the wind-up and ends up kicking it down the hallway. He chases after it, and I take the opportunity to watch Molly.

I think maybe she needs the reminder that this arrangement isn't permanent, too. She looks far too comfortable on my couch. She's absorbed in her book and sipping on a mug of tea, and I wonder how long it has been since her life has looked like this. Or if it has ever looked like this.

She must feel my gaze on her because she looks up from her book suddenly, her eyes searching until they land on me.

"Sorry, I haven't even been paying attention," she says, closing the book and laying it on the floor next to the couch. "Do you need something? Is Theo behaving?"

"He's great," I say, surprised by how much I mean it. I never imagined myself with a family, not after the way I was raised. I couldn't picture myself playing with a kid and being settled enough to fuck one woman for the rest of my life. Yet, we're the image of domesticated bliss right now. Anyone who didn't know us would look in on this moment, tilt their head to the side, and *aww* at our little family.

This isn't forever, I remind myself yet again, feeling a frustrated storm cloud settle over me. *They'll be gone soon. We aren't a family.*

"Do you always leave Theo to entertain himself?" The words are biting, and Molly tucks her chin in, clearly surprised by my tone.

I feel bad, but before I can rethink the words or apologize, Molly frowns and stands up, walking over until we're almost chest to chest.

"Why are you behaving like such an absolute asshat?" she asks, talking quietly so Theo won't overhear while also jabbing her finger into my chest.

Now it's my turn to be surprised.

Nobody ever stands up to me that way. As the leader of the Bratva, any pushback to my commands or critiques is done behind closed doors. Not even my soldiers are daring enough to say it to my face. And I've certainly never been called an asshat before.

The situation is ridiculous enough that I almost smile, the dark cloud that had gathered over my head dissipating slightly.

Before I can break, Theo runs back into the room. He's ready for another round of soccer, but Molly tells him it is time for bed. He begins to pout, but she fixes him with a glare, and he quickly bids me good night and runs up the stairs.

Apparently, she doesn't take any shit from anyone.

I pad into the kitchen while she's upstairs and rifle through the leftovers in the refrigerator. I have a chef make me a few days' worth of meals at a time since I eat at strange hours of the day and night. My schedule isn't regular enough to have a full-time chef or have my meals delivered. The fridge is more full than usual with meals for Molly and Theo as well.

I'm warming up a plate of teriyaki chicken with rice and broccoli when Molly comes back down the stairs. I'm prepared to let the conversation from before go, chalking the entire thing up to a flare of tempers, but when Molly rounds the corner, I can tell by the set of her jaw that she's back for round two.

"Sorry, I would have loved to stay and tell you what a conceited, power-hungry jerk-off you are, but I had to go put Theo to bed. You know, my son? The one I've taken care of day in and day out for years now?"

I hold up a hand to stop her, but she swats it away and keeps coming, pointer finger extended and ready to begin jabbing again.

"Excuse me if I sit down and take a break for a second. If I kick my feet up and read a book for ten fucking minutes." Her finger connects with my chest. "Excuse me if I thought you had some mild interest in playing with him since you've made such a big stink about being his uncle."

I grab her hand and twist it away from me, holding it over her head.

Molly's eyes go wide, and she strains against my hold. When she can't break free, she reaches for me with her other hand, but I grab that one as well.

Both of her hands are locked in mine, and her glare is fire and flames. She's beyond livid and thrashing in my hold like a fish caught in a line.

"You son of a bitch," she grunts. "Get your fucking hands off me before I—"

"Before you what?" I ask. "Before you bruise my pec with your finger? Before you insult my character?"

She sets her jaw, her eyes narrowed. "I'll do worse than that."

I raise a brow in challenge. Then I release her hands and step back. "Go ahead. I'd like to see it."

Truly, I would. Molly can hold her own in an argument and in the bedroom, so I would be fascinated to see how she would do in a fight. Especially considering I saved her from being assaulted in the motel lobby. If I hadn't shown up, would she have fought him off? I'm not so sure.

Her eyes flare, and she licks her pouty lower lip. "No, you wouldn't. You just want me to fight back so you'll have an excuse for killing me."

I don't say anything because her logic is so far removed from my current train of thought that it takes me a second to switch gears.

"Exactly what I thought," she says, stepping towards me, her socked foot brushing against my shoe. "Well, I'm not going to make it that easy for you."

I snort. "What a surprise. Up until this point, you've cooperated so well."

"Bastard," she growls.

I take a deep breath and put my hands on my hips. In the process, the front of my jacket pulls back slightly, revealing the gun on my hip. Molly doesn't miss this fact. She glances down at it and fear sparks in her eyes. Just for a moment.

Molly has no idea how much my plans have shifted. She has no inkling of the inner turmoil I've been going through trying to decide what in the fuck I'm going to do with her. I suppose that, once you threaten someone's life, they can never fully relinquish the possibility that you may one day do what you said you would. Even when it no longer seems possible. In fact, it seems ludicrous now that I'd ever been able to even entertain the idea. I can't kill her now. And I think she knows that.

But part of her will always fear it.

"You wouldn't know how to fight without your gun," she says softly, taking a step back. "It's the only reason you were able to get me in your car. If it hadn't been for your gun and your guards, Theo and I would still be free."

They'd still be on the streets, cold and shoeless, but I don't mention that. "You don't think I could handle you on my own?"

She shakes her head.

Holding her gaze, I slip my gun from my hip, not missing Molly's nervous swallow, and place it in the drawer behind me.

"Do you want to test that theory?" I ask.

Molly doesn't answer. She just stares up at me with her golden eyes blazing and her mouth puckered. She dares me to touch her by just existing. By wearing infuriatingly tight clothes and having infuriatingly soft hair and being flat-out infuriating.

When I move towards her, she flinches like she wants to round the island and put a countertop of space between us, but my hand catches her hip before she can. My fingers slip beneath the material of her top and graze the soft skin just above her leggings. The touch is soft, delicate, but this feels like a war between us.

Will she push me away or raise the white flag?

I take more ground, sliding my hand up her waist and around to her back where I find the clasp of her bra. She stands still, breathing heavily, as I unhook it with one hand.

Molly lifts her arms when I grab the bottom of her shirt and pull it over her head, but otherwise, she stays perfectly still.

I slip her bra straps down her tanned arms, exposing her full chest and the desire she has been trying to hide. But even she can't fight her own body. Even someone as fiery as Molly can't control desire.

I lean down and flick my tongue across her, and she hisses softly. When I take her breast in my mouth, she finally lifts her hand, curling her fingers in the hair at the back of my neck. She holds me to her, pressing me for more, and it's as close to a surrender as I'm liable to get.

I wrap my other arm around her waist and lift her onto the counter. She draws me in with her legs and grabs my face, bringing my lips to hers.

She swipes her tongue across my lower lip before nibbling it with her teeth. Things move quickly from there. We are nothing but roving hands and greedy mouths, sliding over one another as clothes pile on the floor at my feet.

How is this the easy part with Molly? We can't have a conversation without biting words and flared tempers, but this comes easily. The first night we met, I kidnapped her and her son, and we still found our way to bed. It's like we were made for this. Made to be wound up in one another. And wound up by one another, apparently.

Molly practically leaps off the counter and wraps her arms around my neck. "Take my pants off," she sighs.

I peel the material down her backside to her thighs, and she sits back down on the counter and extends her legs.

I'm not used to taking orders from a woman during sex, but I do as she says. I slide the leggings off, revealing her lean, toned legs. Then I grab the lacy panties she has on and pull them down, too.

While I'm admiring her soft skin and the warmth of her thighs, Molly unbuttons my jeans and, with little to no fanfare, pulls me free of my boxers.

I gasp when her hand wraps around me and stand there dumb as she pulls my wallet from my back pocket and slips the condom out.

"You replenished your supply after last time," she says, her eyes making some kind of assessment that I'm far too turned on to understand.

I put a new condom in my wallet the very night we used the previous one. Even as I told myself I had to stay away from her, I was planning to fuck Molly again.

Who am I becoming?

She rolls it onto my length with deft fingers and slides her naked body to the very edge of the counter. This started as a fight, but neither of us is resisting anymore. I slide into her in one movement, all the way to the hilt.

Molly throws her head back and moans, wrapping her legs around my back and hooking her ankles.

It's fast and hard, the sound of our bodies meeting echoing off the marble floor.

I still have staff in the house. Guards nearby who are probably listening in, but I can't be bothered. Certainly not enough to pull out of Molly and walk upstairs.

No, as much as I hate to admit it, I want this ... and I have no idea what that means.

I press my face into the soft crook of her neck and breathe in the sunshine scent of her. I bite the muscle there, nipping at her gently with bared teeth like the domesticated animal I am, pretending to be something more. Pretending there is a chance I'll still hurt her. Pretending this encounter doesn't mean something much more than sex.

I've had a lot of sex with a lot of women. It's not a fact I'm ashamed of. But it means I know what meaningless sex feels like. I know what fucking someone for the sheer pleasure of getting my rocks off feels like, and being inside Molly isn't anything like that.

When we part, her legs still shaking from her orgasm, my body shining with sweat, I don't feel relief. The fire inside of me seems to burn brighter. I want to tuck her under my arm and carry her naked up the stairs. I want to throw her down on my bed and pin her there with my body.

But I don't. I can't.

Molly pulls on her clothes and pads quietly up the stairs to check on Theo, and I go back to warming up my dinner, which has since gone cold in the microwave. I eat robotically, shoveling food in to replenish my energy, barely tasting it at all. Unable to focus on anything except the nagging feeling that I've gotten myself into a huge mess, and I have no fucking idea how to get out.

13

MOLLY

Weeks pass, and I start to forget this arrangement began as imprisonment. Even at the very start, it felt like being in a luxury prison. Like the places where they send the rich and famous when they neglect to pay their taxes. I can't really call it a prison when I spend an hour each evening soaking in a claw-foot tub with a glass of wine. And as the days pass, it feels more and more like home.

That word holds such mixed feelings for me.

Even as a kid, my home was tainted. Discolored by the fighting of my parents, by being placed in the middle of their arguments and used as a threat. They were constantly telling one another that they would never see me again if ... *fill in condition here*. After a while, I was surprised the threats worked at all since neither of them seemed to want me around even when I was.

So maybe I just don't know what a home feels like. Maybe I can never know because I've never had it, but being at Viktor's house feels comfortable.

There is food in the refrigerator, clothes in my closet, and toys for Theo.

When Viktor comes home for the day, he lies on the floor with Theo and plays games. Then, when Theo goes to bed, Viktor finds me. Usually in my room. Sometimes in the kitchen. Never in Viktor's room or his office. I still don't go in those rooms. Mixing that part of his life with what we have feels dangerous, and I don't want to break the illusion.

Because that's what it is, isn't it? An illusion.

I like to think otherwise, especially when Viktor is biting my neck and swirling his tongue over all the sensitive places of my body. When he's breathing between my legs and pushing into me, I like to think this could be forever. I like to think that I won't ever have to stand in line at the shelter again or deal with men trying to take advantage of my circumstances. When Viktor is hovering over me, wrapping me in the woodsy smell of him, I let myself believe that this could be the beginning of my new life. But it can't be. Viktor said as much.

This is temporary.

So, I decide to take advantage of it for as long as I can.

I relax and eat my fill and enjoy the hard lines of Viktor's body without guilt. I take solace in his warmth and the comfort he has provided for me and my son and vow not to waste a second.

Viktor brings in a nanny to take care of Theo part-time. The first time she came to take him to the park, I almost couldn't let him go.

What if she didn't bring him back? What if it was a trick?

But I pushed through my fear and let him go, pacing the living room until he returned safely ninety minutes later.

Since then, I've eased up slightly, growing more comfortable with our arrangement, trusting that Viktor isn't trying to steal Theo away and discard me like trash.

So, when Theo is busy with the nanny, I read through the interior design books that keep appearing in the living room. I know Viktor is behind it, but we don't discuss it. I'm afraid it will stop if I do.

I take notes and learn and try not to get lost in the pangs of sadness that overwhelm me when I think about what my life could have been if I'd gone to school and earned my degree.

I could have a job as a designer. I wouldn't live in a house like this one, but I could be paid to design them and that would be more than enough for me.

Though I also wouldn't have Theo. And that has always been the saving grace, the thing that brings me back from the edge of despair again and again. I would never trade a single minute with him for a degree or a job or a house. He is worth everything I've had to give up, though sometimes, I wish I hadn't been forced to choose. I wish I could have had both.

After we'd been living with Viktor for two weeks, he introduced me to his interior designer—a middle-aged woman with a sharp white bob haircut and dark-framed glasses.

"I thought Theo deserved a proper bedroom," Viktor said.

"But he has a bedroom." His bedroom is large with a full-size bed and a walk-in closet full of clothes and toys.

The designer clicked her tongue and shook her head. "A bed doesn't make it a bedroom just as hair doesn't make it a hairstyle. Artistry makes the difference."

She spoke in a clipped way, like she was in a hurry, but when she got to Theo's room, she took her time marking down the dimensions. She stood in the doorway and sketched out her ideas with an authoritative finger wagging through the air, outlining invisible furniture and lights I couldn't see.

"You're the mother." It was a statement, not a question.

"Yes," I said, stepping forward, hands folded behind my back.

"Then, you'll help me." Again, not a question.

So, I did. And ever since, I have been.

I eat up every second of time I spend with Matilda, not wasting a single second. I want to learn as much as I possibly can from her, hoping the experience will help me become a designer myself one day.

The room is nearly finished now. I replace the full-size bed with a more manageable twin, giving Theo room to play with blocks and puzzles in the middle of the room on a short orange and yellow rug.

We keep the walls blue, but add pops of colors in the details. A red lampshade, warm abstract art prints on the walls, and a yellow dresser.

I'm not sure whether Matilda really likes my ideas or whether Viktor has instructed her to default to me, but she writes down everything I suggest. I mention the idea of building a small hideaway in the corner of the room—a kind of clubhouse with a child-sized door and separate lighting inside—and she makes it happen. The day after I mention it, two men are in the apartment building it. Then, I paint it and seal it while Theo spends the afternoon at an indoor play gym with his nanny, and now it's a permanent fixture in the room. An idea I imagined, saw through, and now exists in the real world. It feels like an accomplishment.

At first, I run the ideas past Viktor, trying to ensure I'm not spending too much money, but it becomes apparent he doesn't care. Either because he has enough money he doesn't need to worry about a small remodel or because he trusts me. Truthfully, I think it's both.

Viktor has killed people and done horrible things. But unlike other men in power, he's fair and kind to those who are loyal. I've never heard Viktor raise his voice to his household staff or his guards unnecessarily. He treats the people around him with respect so long as they give him the same.

It makes me like him even more. Much more than I should.

On one of the last days of the bedroom remodel, I try to pull Matilda into a long conversation over a cup of coffee, but she says Viktor isn't paying her for chitchat. I can see why Viktor likes her. Matilda is straightforward and all business. She doesn't mince words, and I understand why Viktor has continued to rehire her for projects over the years.

"Will you be back tomorrow?" I ask.

"I'll have to speak with Viktor first," she says. "I've told him you will be fine to finish the project on your own."

I gape at her. "Why?"

"Because you've done most of the design work already. Though, don't tell Viktor that. I still expect my full paycheck at the end of this."

Finally, I gain the confidence to ask the question I've been wondering for days. "Did Viktor tell you to listen to my ideas?"

Matilda stares at me for a moment and then barks out a laugh. She pushes her glasses up on her nose. "I'm the designer. Viktor doesn't tell me what to do when it comes to the details. I listened to your ideas because they were good. I shouldn't be surprised though. Viktor bought most of my library of design books for you, which means you're learning from the absolute best."

"You gave him the books for me?"

She holds up a finger. "*Sold* him the books. But yes, they're mine. Keep studying the way you are, and you might be coming for my job."

I smile, taking it as a compliment, but then Matilda's eyes narrow for a second. Clearly, she's not the kind of woman who is comfortable with competition.

When she leaves, I'm restless. Theo is down for a nap and Viktor is at work, so I'm not sure what to do. I was so busy helping with the finishing touches of Theo's room and thinking about whether I could convince Viktor he needed to have something else remodeled if only to keep me busy that I only ate a few bites of the lunch that was delivered for us. Now I'm starved.

The refrigerator is full of prepared meals, things I simply need to throw in a pan or in the microwave and warm up, but I feel the strange urge to cook something. To make something for myself.

My mom played with the idea of teaching me to cook when I was a kid, but as soon as I made a mistake or asked a question, she would push me aside and take control. Then I was so busy trying to survive that I never had time to cook. Now, I have the time, and I'd like to be able to make something halfway edible.

I wasn't joking when I told Viktor he would end up poisoned if he expected me to cook for him.

That first night in his apartment feels like a long time ago. It feels more like a dream than anything else. The fear and uncertainty I felt is a distant memory compared to how comfortable I am now.

The thought flickers in my mind that it could all disappear in a second, that the plush, expensive rug could be pulled out from under my feet in an instant, but I push the thought aside and search the kitchen until I find a small stash of cookbooks.

Most of the spines are still perfectly intact and the books crack as I open them, showing Viktor has never once flipped through them.

I look at pictures of dishes that look like they belong on the menus of the nicest restaurants in the city. They're far beyond anything I'm capable of making.

Finally, I find a picture of a homestyle macaroni and cheese recipe with bread crumbs and herbs. I've made boxed macaroni and cheese. How much different could homemade mac and cheese be? Melting cheese? Easy.

I lay the book flat on the counter and move to the pantry, trying to find all the ingredients I need.

Flour—check, though I can't imagine what that would be for.

Milk, cheddar cheese, cream cheese, Dijon mustard.

I stack the ingredients on the island, trying to imagine how mustard belongs in macaroni and cheese, and wonder if I could make this meal for Viktor.

It would be a thank you of sorts. For his kindness.

If I could go back a few weeks and tell the past me that I would be grateful to the man who flashed a gun at me and locked me away in his apartment, I'd think I was going insane. But here I am, wanting to take care of him in a small way to thank him for taking care of me. Or mostly, for taking care of Theo.

I always thought Theo was playful. An outgoing, bright kid. But since living with Viktor, he has opened up in ways I never knew were possible. He likes to build and design things. Viktor bought him wooden blocks and then plastic LEGOs when those became boring. Now, the two of them are working on a LEGO recreation of a castle from a movie I've never seen, and I never would have thought Theo capable of something like that.

Having the necessities in life has given him the opportunity to branch out and explore his interests, and for the first time in a long while, I'm hopeful that he will be okay. I'm hopeful that he'll break the cycle of poverty I've dropped us into.

That deserves some fancy macaroni and cheese, at least.

When I hear a key in the front door, I assume it's Viktor home from work early.

Thoughts of food disappear when I realize he's home, Theo is sleeping, and I'm feeling especially warm towards him at the moment. Perhaps we could swipe the food onto the floor and make use of the counter the way we have several times before.

Warmth pools in my abdomen, and I have to bite back a smile as I pour him the last bit of coffee left over from the cup I shared with the designer earlier.

Apparently, I like fancy coffee now. Viktor taught me how to use the grinder and the Chemex, and while I still can't drink it black like he can, I don't need much more than a pinch of sugar and a glug of milk to make it drinkable.

Then I grab the mug and pad barefoot across the marble floor to greet him.

Because I was working with the designer, I opted for one of my more modest outfits—a pair of skinny jeans with a cream knit sweater—but the neckline still cuts low enough that I know Viktor will notice. He is a boob guy, after all.

When I turn the corner, however, Viktor is already there.

I hold the cup away from me to avoid the coffee splashing over the rim of the cup and yelp in surprise. "I didn't hear you," I gasp, laughing at my own clumsiness. "I was bringing you coffee, but I hope you like licking it off the floor." But then I make eye contact with him freeze.

"Excuse me?"

I can't respond. My words are trapped in my mouth.

My free hand is pressed to my chest, and I stare at the face of the man who is not Viktor.

It's Fedor.

14

VIKTOR

The man is pale and growing paler by the second at my feet, his blood pooling around his head. The gun is still warm when I tuck it into the waistband of my jeans, and when I turn around, my men are gathered and waiting in a semicircle.

I swore to them all when I took over for my father that I would not execute any one of them without a witness. I didn't want them to distrust me, to think I would kill them for minor offenses without any group oversight.

They all seem pleased with the outcome. Still, the idea nags at the back of my mind that they are unhappy with my performance. That they don't trust me.

These aren't just my insecurities talking. Petr has told me there are whispers of discontent. Those whispers are growing louder now that I've been spending more time at home. They all just think I'm growing lazy. Only a few choice people know about Molly and Theo, and if word gets out, those people know they'll be killed first for telling my secrets.

With Molly and Theo waiting for me at home, my work and home life have never felt more different. I'm the same person at work and at home, but here I kill men who betray me while at home, I build LEGO castles and play soccer in the living room. How can both be me?

"If any of you feel you are not being fairly paid, you are free to speak to me," I say, my voice echoing around the concrete basement. "But if you are caught stealing from me, this is the fate that awaits you."

A few of the men grunt in approval.

"I will not show mercy for anyone willing to cross our family. For anyone willing to lie to us for their own gain."

Molly's face looms in my mind. I lied to Fedor about her every week for a month. He thinks she's dead. Not only is she not dead; she's remodeling a guest room in my fucking house. If she asked, I'd let her remodel the whole damn house.

"Dispose of the body," I say, nodding to two younger soldiers near the far edge of the group.

The cluster of men begins to break up, some of them leaving to take care of other work, others chipping in to help with mopping and wrapping the body in a tarp. I turn to Petr and call him over to me.

"I want a full review of our finances," I say. "Assign a few men you trust to make sure everyone is receiving pay equal to their status and seniority. If they aren't, have them run it past me, and then fix it."

Petr nods and turns to leave, but I stop him. "I need you to be ready to leave with me in five."

I haven't told Petr where we're going, but he nods in agreement and hurries towards the business offices upstairs to carry out my orders.

I want my men to fear my wrath, but I also want them to be happy. Unhappy soldiers who feel they aren't valued turn against you, and I can't afford that. Not now. Not when I'm trying to take care of my brother and his illegitimate offspring and Molly. My plate is fuller than ever before, and I need my men to trust me. I need them to believe I'm doing my best to take care of them, even if I'm doing it in a way different from my father.

"The Mazzeos?" Petr asks from the passenger seat. "Why don't I know about this?"

"Because I didn't want you to know," I say simply.

He nods in understanding.

"I didn't want to make the announcement that two of our men broke rank and attacked rival soldiers the same week another man was stealing from me," I admitted. "I will announce it once I've settled things with Mario and his son and have decided on a punishment. Until then, I don't want their insubordination to give anyone else ideas."

"Good idea," Petr says.

I sense he wants to say more, but he's hesitant.

"What?"

"Nothing," he says. But when I look at him out of the corner of my eyes, one eyebrow raised, he sighs. "You've been absent a lot. No one has seen you at the bar in a few weeks. They think your priorities are slipping."

"Today should show them that they aren't."

"There is more to being their leader than discipline," Petr says nervously. "They fear you, but they need to respect you and ... *like you*. That happens over a beer."

I know I should get out more, but the only reason I used to meet up with the men at the bars was to find a woman to spend the night with. Now, I don't need that. I have Molly.

I shake my head. I don't *have* Molly.

If anything, she has me.

If my men knew how head over ass I've fallen for a woman I'm supposed to murder, they'd overthrow me in a second. Hell, I'd overthrow me if I was them.

Are you really going to let a little pussy risk your rank? I can hear my dad's voice bark in my ear.

When we pull up to the agreed meeting spot, I realize I never responded to Petr. We drove the last few minutes in silence, and now there are more important matters at hand.

Mario and Rio Mazzeo have control of a small section of the city. Business between our families has always been tense, but respectful, and now some of my men have threatened that fragile coexistence. I've all but wiped out any real competition we had in the city, and now, rather than enjoying being on top, my soldiers are out starting fights with men from lesser families. *Idiots.*

"Leave your weapon," I tell Petr, motioning to the gun in his holster.

He frowns at me, but I nod to let him know I'm serious. "Mario will see it as a sign of trust between us. He's old school."

Petr does as I say, but asks what we'll do if they pull a gun on us.

I lean down and lift my pant leg, revealing a gun and a knife strapped to my calf. "I'm not going in unarmed."

Mario and Rio are like twins separated by twenty years. They have the same narrow shoulders, round middles, and thick heads of dark hair, though Mario's is graying around the temples and his face is considerably more creased.

They stand shoulder to shoulder against a brick wall between two buildings in the industrial district. Their car is parked at the end of the alley, blocking entrance on one side. The windows are too tinted to see if they've brought anyone else with them.

"Viktor," Mario says, nodding and holding out a hand.

I stop moving towards him and hold out an arm to stop Petr as well. I don't want to get too close and be penned in should they decide taking me and my second-in-command out would be good retribution.

I don't suspect the Mazzeos would be so foolish. They know that even without a leader, my Bratva could bring them to their knees. Plus, we've built a tenuous peace over the years, and no one has benefitted from that arrangement more than they have.

"Mario," I say, nodding to him and then his son. "Rio. Good to see you."

"Even under these circumstances," Mario says, running his tongue over his top teeth.

"Even under these circumstances," I echo. "I was sorry to hear about the fighting between our men."

"Were you?" Rio barks, leaning forward.

His father silences him with a glare, and Rio leans back against the wall, though his eyes are narrowed at me. Petr lays a hand on his hip out of instinct before remembering his gun is in the car and dropping it to his side.

"I was," I say coldly. "My attention has been split several ways these last few weeks, and I admit that some of my men took their new freedom to extremes. I hope no one was hurt."

"Hospitalized, but not dead," Mario says with a shrug. "Still, I thought it would be nice for us to get together. It has been a long time."

The last time I met with the Mazzeos, Fedor was at my side.

Mario has never liked Fedor, and he has never sought to make that fact a secret. He believes in respect and order and law—even if he prefers to be the one making the law—and Fedor cares for none of those things.

"I agree. It's good we see one another face-to-face every now and again."

Rio stands next to his father, looking like he'd rather be pummeling my face than looking at it.

Mario clasps his hands in front of his round stomach and sighs. "The story I'm being told is that your men walked into my territory and started a fight. They wanted to cause a war."

"Now, Mario," I say with a shrug. "A fight and a war are very different things. I don't think my men wanted—"

"They wanted to hurt my men and give us reason to fight," he says, cutting me off.

I press my lips together into a flat line, annoyed at his interruption, and wait for him to finish.

"If that's not the start of a war, then I don't know what is."

"Me declaring war is the start of a war," I say sharply. "Those men acted foolishly and without permission. They do not represent the wishes of me or my Bratva."

"How will they be dealt with?" Rio asks.

"That is for me to decide," I snap, pulling back my top lip in a snarl. "I came here because I respect your family and wanted to tell you that our relationship is, in my opinion, as strong as ever. I hope you won't allow the actions of two men to change your good opinion of me."

'Good opinion' is a stretch, and I can see that in Mario's face, even though he's more skilled at masking his emotions than his son.

"Assuming those men are dealt with," he says, lifting his chin and looking at me down the long hook of his nose, "then we can part as friends."

"That's great news."

"And I expect this won't be an issue for us moving forward."

"Nothing is an issue unless I say it is. And I say nothing is an issue. Are we clear?"

He nods stiffly. "We have had few problems this last year." *Since Fedor has been locked away,* he means. "But I do worry what will happen now."

"Now?" I ask, not following.

"Well, with the release of your brother. I suspect that is why your attention has been divided."

I frown in earnest now, drawing my brows together. "I don't—"

Mario interrupts me again, only this time I don't mind as much. Mostly because I'm trying to wrap my mind around what he's saying.

"I know Fedor is your family, and I would never wish to speak ill of him, but even you must admit he's impulsive," Mario says.

Rio snorts as though that's the kindest possible way of putting it, and he isn't wrong.

"Fedor is a risk to your authority, so in the spirit of our renewed friendship, I will help you keep an eye on him now that he's released."

Petr stiffens next to me, letting me know he doesn't know what Mario is talking about either.

Mario tilts his head to the side, studying me. Fuck. I have been too obvious. He senses a vulnerability. "Unless my intel is incorrect. I heard this afternoon that Fedor had been released. That lawyer your father kept employed all those years worked his magic and got him freed."

I didn't hear. Nobody called me. I visited Fedor just a few days ago. Kent wasn't there, and I found myself distracted with thoughts of Molly and what we'd done in bed the night before. Did he say something about being released? If he had, surely I would remember it.

I don't want Mario to know I'm out of the loop, though.

"I'm sure your intel is serving you well," I say as casually as I can.

He nods, still watching me carefully. Finally, he shrugs. "If you'd like, I can have my men keep an eye out for Fedor. We will let you know if he starts stepping out of bounds."

"I'm sure that won't be necessary."

"Ahh, I wouldn't be so sure," Mario says. "I'm sure you remember how he enjoys playing people against one another. I would hate for that to happen with us."

"My brother doesn't control who I am on good terms with, but I thank you for your concern."

Mario nods in understanding.

The conversation wraps up with the usual pleasantries, but by the time we get back in the car, I'm ready to peel out of there.

I need to get back home as soon as possible.

"Did you not know Fedor was out?" Petr asks. "Do you think it's true?"

"I don't know," I tell him truthfully. "But I intend to find out."

If Petr thinks me flying through the city to see my brother is curious, he doesn't mention it. He doesn't complain when I drop him off at the office, barely coming to a full stop to let him out of the car. The second the door is closed, I screech out of the lot and head for home.

If Fedor is out, my home is the first place he would go. He has his own key and he has always felt free to let himself in without warning.

If he really is out, he'll walk inside and see my tiny bubble of domesticated bliss inside.

He'll find Molly and Theo.

My heart feels like an ice block in my chest. Like it isn't even beating. Stuck in a terrified stasis while I rush to find out whether Molly and Theo are okay.

I pull out my phone and tap in the number that has grown familiar to me over the last few weeks. George has become an invaluable asset to me—an asset I wouldn't have had if I hadn't spared his life. When he begged me not to kill him the day I ambushed him in his liquor store, an instinct told me to spare him. He had been so grateful—shocked that a Kornilov was capable of mercy—that he all but volunteered to work for me.

I wonder what my father would think of this. If my father had shown up to assassinate a man who testified against the Bratva—especially one who testified against his own blood—my father wouldn't have hesitated to put a bullet between the man's eyes. Instead, I chose mercy. And that mercy has now given me a man I can trust more than my own brother.

I drum my finger against the sides of the phone as I tear through stop signs, desperate for the person on the other end to pick up.

I have to get to Molly and Theo now. I have to do what I can to protect them.

Pick up, pick up, pick up.

15

MOLLY

"Who are you?" Fedor asks.

His voice is similar to Viktor's, but where Viktor is direct and to the point, Fedor's voice has an amused lilt to it. Like a cat with a mouse dangling from its claw.

My back is pressed against the wall, and I can't seem to move or breathe.

It feels like I've been tossed into a horror movie, deposited in the middle of my worst nightmare. I'm tempted to pinch myself but that would require movement, which I'm incapable of.

Fedor tips his head to the side, and I finally look away, down to the coffee spilled on the floor.

"Such a mess," Fedor says, clicking his tongue. He doesn't sound disapproving or upset. Just a lazy observation. "I didn't mean to scare you."

He may not have meant to, but he's pleased nonetheless.

"But I would love to know who has the balls to speak to my brother like that." He takes a step to the side, trying to see my face better.

I turn and walk into the kitchen on numb legs and grab a towel hanging from the oven.

"A maid?" he asks, eyeing the towel.

I don't correct him as I bend down and sop up the coffee.

He doesn't recognize me. Fedor has absolutely no idea who I am.

The realization fills me with relief and rage. The two emotions mingle together in my stomach, a nauseating cocktail.

Fedor bends down, one arm thrown casually over his knee, and tries to catch my eye. I go so far as to look at his hand, but I don't dare meet his eyes.

Not yet. Not until I'm sure he won't recognize me. Not until I'm sure this house of cards won't come crumbling down with one solid look at my face.

He has letters and symbols scribbled in ink across the backs of his knuckles and his hands. The tattoos disappear beneath the sleeve of his black-collared shirt. Viktor doesn't have any.

"You were so talkative a minute ago," he says, trying to draw me out. "What happened? Are you stunned by my beauty?"

He's teasing me. If I didn't know any better, I'd think he was a nice guy. A charmer, for sure, but not dangerous.

Fortunately, I know better.

"Surprised," I admit quietly. "I was expecting Vi—Mr. Kornilov."

"You call him Viktor?" he asks.

I shrug and move back into the kitchen, desperate for the space the room provides. I can't stand in the narrow hallway with Fedor for another second. "Sometimes."

What is he doing here? If Viktor knew Fedor was getting out, I assume he would have told me. But then again, I don't know much of anything about Viktor's plans. I've been a bit too busy fucking him to ask any questions.

Stupid. Reckless. Horny.

I should have been plotting and planning. I shouldn't have allowed myself to become so comfortable in this house.

Then the idea hits me that this could all be a trick. Maybe Viktor told Fedor everything. Maybe Fedor knows exactly who I am, and he's here to play with his food before he eats it. Maybe Viktor is just outside the door, laughing, waiting until he can come in and they can both reveal the truth and finally get rid of me.

But does Fedor even want Theo?

From the little I know about him, he doesn't seem like the fatherly type. I would have said the same about Viktor, however, and he has proven me wrong. Theo loves Viktor.

"Call me Fedor," he says, shoving his hands in his pockets and slouching down into a comfortable stance. "I take it my brother isn't around, then?"

"He's out." The words are little more than a rasp. I wish Viktor was here, even if he's in on this scheme. I just want to know. I don't want to spend another second wondering when Fedor will reveal why he's here and what he has planned.

Fedor nods and then jumps up to sit on the countertop. "I can wait. I would have called, but the shitheads at the prison lost my phone."

I frown. So he got out legally. Somehow, he was released.

"Did you know I was locked up?" he asks. "Or does my brother not talk about his shameful little brother?"

"I knew."

He works his jaw from side to side. "I didn't tell him I was getting out today. It's a surprise."

Is he telling the truth? If so, Viktor will be just as shocked to find Fedor here when he gets home. I wish he'd given me his number at some point. I'd text him and warn him, ask him what I should do, where I should go.

Thank God Theo is sleeping upstairs. One less thing to worry about at the moment.

"He may not be home for a few hours," I say, checking the clock over the stove. "He usually doesn't get back until dinner."

"I can wait."

I stand in the kitchen, twisting the coffee-soaked rag around in my hands, unsure what to do. I could pretend I have work to get to and go clean, but I'm not even sure where the cleaning supplies are kept. I could probably find them, but if Fedor sees me searching high and low for window cleaner, he might pick up on the fact that I'm not who I say I am.

And what will he do when he finds out?

Kill me. That's what Viktor was supposed to do, after all. For Fedor's benefit, to boot. My death was supposed to help Fedor stay out of trouble.

But if he has been released, maybe it doesn't matter. Maybe we can forget this all happened and—

What?

I can't live with my rapist's brother. That's insane. I should be committed for even considering it.

"Especially when I have such beautiful company." Fedor arches his brow, and his electric green eyes pin me to the spot, wiping every other thought from my mind. I've been on the receiving end of that look before, and I know what it means. "I'm sure we can find a way to entertain ourselves."

I know his type. If I resist, it will make him try harder. It's easier to bend to his will, to give in and hope I can keep him placated until Viktor gets home.

But what if he really doesn't come back for hours?

Panic is simmering inside of me, threatening to turn into a full-on rolling boil, but I take a deep breath and smile.

"I'm sure we can." I toss the rag onto the counter and press my hip against the edge of the island, crossing my arms over my chest.

Fedor's eyes drop to my cleavage, and he touches his tongue to the center of his top lip, biting back a smile.

The only way to survive the encounter is to turn it all off. My emotions and my instincts. All of it goes dark, and I take on the role I'm supposed to be occupying.

I'm a maid. A flirtatious maid. A flirtatious maid talking with the brother of my employer. We've never met before.

It's scary how nice Fedor can be. It can't be counted as kindness since it's apparent he intends to see some form of return on his compliments. But it's still startling to realize how normal he looks. He doesn't seem like the kind of man who would drug and assault a woman. And yet.

Fedor likes to hear his own voice. He rambles on about his time on the inside and how long it has been since he has been with a woman. As he talks, I nod and smile and do my best not to hear a word. But then, he crosses the distance between us and drags a finger down my arm.

I can't help it. I flinch.

Something sparks in Fedor's eyes. "You don't have to be afraid of me. We're friends."

He hasn't even asked for my name. How can we possibly be friends?

Still, I nod and smile in agreement.

He adds, "Friends with benefits, I hope?" He quirks a brow.

The panic I've been pushing down for the last ten minutes rises again, and I look around the kitchen for an escape. An excuse.

Fedor leans down and if his lips connect with mine, I think I'll throw up.

His eyes flutter closed, and I note as he leans down towards me that he has the same long lashes as Theo.

Then, just before our lips can meet, I hear a key in the front door.

Fedor freezes and then pulls back and looks directly into my eyes. If there was a time he'd recognize me, this would be it. But he doesn't.

He sighs, disappointed. "Another time, I suppose."

He turns away from me but doesn't break contact. Fedor wraps his arm around my lower back, pressing me to his side, and I just stare straight ahead at the hallway.

Viktor rounds the corner, and I know immediately he had no idea this would happen.

His face is red and blotchy, and he's out of breath like he ran all the way here. As soon as he walks in, his eyes are wild and searching. When they land on me and Fedor, his brow wrinkles. What a sight we must be.

"Hello, brother," Fedor says, raising a hand. "Surprise."

Viktor rests back on his heels and gives his brother the barest of glances before he looks at me again. Then at Fedor's arm around my waist.

"Sorry," I say suddenly, jumping away from Fedor and grabbing the towel and half-filled coffee mug from the counter. "I should be working, but your brother arrived and distracted me."

I wave a hand at Fedor like I'm a Southern belle and he's some charming rascal, and he smiles smugly in return.

"Your staff has become much more friendly since the last time I was here," he says.

Finally, I see realization click into place for Viktor.

"Leave my maid alone," Viktor says playfully, crossing the room and pulling his brother into a hug.

"Have you laid claim to her?"

Laid claim. Like I'm some plot of land for him to stick his flag in. The analogy turns my stomach, and I realize that's what most women are to Fedor.

Viktor looks at me over his brother's shoulder, gesturing with his eyes for me to scram. "I lay claim to all of my employees. They're off-limits."

Fedor spins out of his brother's grasp and moves around the back of the island, approaching me from behind. My back tingles, my instincts warning me to flee. He tries to lay a hand on my waist, but I slip away before he can, moving closer to Viktor.

"Don't tempt me. You know I don't like being told no."

No shit, I think.

Viktor moves next to me and curls his arm protectively around my back, his fingers digging into my side. "You better get used to it if you plan to hang out around my house."

The brothers volley back and forth. Their tones are light, but their expressions are edged in something sharp.

I wonder if Viktor has had this trouble before. If Fedor has made it a habit to harass the women his brother employs.

Fedor takes in our position, the way Viktor has a hold on me, and the way I'm leaning into him—though he has no idea it's out of fear to him rather than a love for Viktor—and nods. "I see. You really have laid your claim."

Viktor pulls me closer. "Several times."

I feel my entire body blush. I want to slap him for talking about me like that to Fedor, and I want to do much worse to Fedor for many more reasons. But I also don't want to draw attention to myself. Fedor doesn't know who I am. He knows nothing about Theo. And Viktor seems like he wants to keep my secret. I shouldn't do anything to tip this very precarious boat I've found myself in.

Fedor whistles and runs his eyes down the length of my body. "Lucky man."

He moves towards us slowly, one foot in front of the other, his body swaggering from side to side like a drunk cowboy. When he stops in front of me, he's only two steps away. Fedor tilts his head to the side and pulls his mouth into a smirk. "I'd love to have this one working on her hands and knees for me."

He reaches out a hand to cradle my chin, but just before he can touch me, Viktor lashes out with lightning-fast reflexes and bats his hand away.

Rage flares in Fedor's eyes as he looks at his brother, but it dissipates quickly, replaced with a mild annoyance.

"Off. Limits." Viktor's annunciation is as crisp and clear as his meaning. But to bring the point home, he spins me around, putting himself between me and Fedor until I can't see anything beyond the silhouette of him.

I look up into Viktor's bright blue eyes, which are a much more natural shade than the electrifying green of his brother's, and he winks at me.

"Don't let us distract you from your work any longer," he says quietly, smoothing his hand up my side until his thumb is brushing against the curve of my breast. Even with Fedor standing two feet away, I feel my body light up under Viktor's touch. Heat warms my body, driving out the fear and confusion that has been eating away at me. "Stay out of the way until I need you."

If he'd spoken to me like this under any other circumstances, I'd stomp on his foot and knee him in his groin again. As it is, however, I understand the meaning. *Stay out of sight until Fedor is gone.*

I move my head to nod, but just as quickly as he swatted away Fedor's hand, Viktor reaches up and grabs my chin. His fingers are warm on my skin and his grip is velvety, but strong. He forces my face up to his, and a shaky breath slips between my lips.

Slowly, Viktor leans down and presses his mouth to mine.

His lips are soft and open. He curls his tongue up to flick at my top lip before sucking it into his mouth. Desire falls over me like a blanket, so thick and heavy I can't move. Can't think.

I stretch up onto my toes and slip my tongue against his, opening his mouth, and I feel his hand clench on my side. His thumb swipes over my body again, moving more solidly over my breast.

"I get it," Fedor sighs from behind him, reminding me of his presence. "You don't have to establish your dominance right here. She's off-limits."

Viktor pulls away slowly and looks down at me, his eyes dark and dangerous. By the time he turns back around to face his brother, he has situated his expression into a neutral mask.

I'm not as successful. I can feel warmth radiating off my face and neck, and I cross my arms over my chest to try and pull the desire inwards, to keep it contained.

Fedor raises an amused brow at me and tips his head to the side. "On second thought, dominate away. I'd like to watch."

The desire in my stomach turns to shame, and it's like someone threw a bucket of ice water on the flickering flame.

Viktor rolls his eyes and points Fedor in the direction of his office, but just before he follows his brother out of the kitchen, he gives me one more look over his shoulder. It's full of uncertainty, and I try to smile, to tell him it will be okay, but I'm not so sure it will be.

When I hear the office door close upstairs, I run upstairs and directly into Theo's room.

16

VIKTOR

I can see the tension in Fedor's shoulders as he walks into the office ahead of me and sits down at my desk. Usually, I'd order him out of my seat and give him a whack on the back of the head for being so bold, but today, I need him to stay calm.

"That seems like more than a fuck," he says, pressing his fingers together and rocking in the desk chair. "It almost seemed like you two are ... together."

If he knew who Molly really was, he would have said so downstairs. Fedor is not subtle. His strength—and the danger of him—comes from his rashness.

Still, I find myself wondering if this isn't some kind of game.

"She's my maid."

"That's what you keep saying." He purses his lips at me.

I sigh and drop down into the chair opposite the desk. The wood creaks under my weight. "Because you keep asking. She's my maid, and I don't want you touching her."

"No fun," he says, pouting his lip out. "She's more my type than yours, anyway. You like the models."

He isn't wrong. Fedor already chose Molly, though apparently he doesn't remember it. Beyond that, he always goes for the girl-next-door type. The innocent ones who never seem to know exactly how beautiful they are. I always found those girls to be boring in bed. I wanted a confident woman. Someone who knew how to use her body and, similarly, mine. The qualities I looked for in a woman didn't go beyond how good I thought she'd be to fuck. Shallow, but true.

Molly has proven my theories wrong.

She's a quiet kind of beautiful. She doesn't need makeup or skimpy clothes to prove she's sexy. I walked in and saw her in jeans and a sweater and felt my blood pressure rise. Though that also could have been because I saw my brother's arm around her waist.

"I like my maid."

My tone is harsh, and he lets out a sharp breath through his nose. "Fine. You called dibs. But please tell me when you're done with her. It has been a while since I've had the opportunity, and I have some pent-up energy to expend."

I want to wring his neck for even thinking about Molly like that. After everything he has done to her and Theo …

Theo is another important piece of this puzzle. The most important piece, perhaps.

If Fedor finds out that Theo is his, he will never leave Molly or Theo alone. It wouldn't even be out of a desire to be a father, but a desire to claim what is his. To control someone. Plus, regardless of how he disregards the other laws of the Bratva, Fedor cares about family. He believes in loyalty the same way I do, though he has a shitty way of showing it. If he found out Theo was his, he wouldn't stop until Molly had handed over custody, willingly or not.

Which is why they can't stay here.

Fedor thinks she's a maid now, but one day, he'll stop by the apartment and Theo will let the whole story slip. Four-year-olds are not known for their superior secret-keeping abilities, after all. It will be an accident, but Fedor will find out the truth. He'll learn that I didn't kill Molly like I claimed, and more than that, that I invited her into my home and kept his son from him. And once Fedor knows I lied to him, he will be impossible to control.

"How did you get out, anyway?" I ask, shifting the subject away from Molly. "And why the fuck didn't you tell me?"

"Surprise," he says, repeating what he said downstairs. "Kent has been working on something behind the scenes for a few months, and I told him not to tell you."

I shake my head. "Why do I go to those strategy meetings with the two of you if you're keeping things from me?"

Fedor frowns, a line forming between his brows. "Those weren't strategy meetings. They were visits."

If I'd known I was only there to keep Fedor company, I might have cut back on how often I visited. Maybe Fedor knew that, which is why he always made it sound like they were important.

"Good to know I took time away from work to gossip with you."

He dismisses me with a limp-wristed wave. "You're the leader. You don't have to work if you don't want to."

That goes to show how little Fedor actually knows about what it takes to run the Bratva. Being the leader requires even more work. More time and energy and organizing. But I don't have the desire or energy to try to prove that to him.

"What did Kent manage to work out for you? Last I heard, he was trying to lessen your charge to involuntary manslaughter, but even that wouldn't have gotten you released."

He leans forward across the desk, his mouth pulled up in a wicked smile, and whispers, "Bribery."

"With what money?" I bark. "I had to drop off money for you to buy new shower shoes. Who the fuck did you bribe with shower shoes?"

"Our money," he says, gesturing between us. "Kent named his price, and I said we'd pay it. I'm sure he'll call you to collect soon."

"Our money?" When our parents died, we each received an inheritance. Fedor, in typical fashion, blew through his in six months. He has no money. I gave him a high-ranking position in the Bratva and a salary, but I know for a fact he didn't save a thing. If anything, he's in debt due to all his legal troubles.

"Yes," he insists. "*Our* money. The Bratva is still a family business, isn't it? Aren't we all family here?"

"How much?"

He leans back in the chair and crosses his arms over his chest, his mouth sullen. "Fifty grand. Each."

I pinch the bridge of my nose and then run a hand through my hair, tugging on the roots. "To Kent and …"

"Some judge," he says, shrugging like it barely matters. "They got me out on parole."

I thought I'd be happy when Fedor was finally free. I wouldn't have to listen to him bitch about being locked up and how it was my fault. And, despite his ways, I thought I'd be happy to be able to spend time with my brother again somewhere that wasn't sitting across from a metal table.

But I don't feel happy. I feel overwhelmed.

"Okay, we'll pay the money."

"No shit we will," he says. "Unless you want me to get locked up again."

I hold up a hand to steady him. "Obviously we will. I'm just trying to formulate a plan right now. We'll pay the money, get you set up with your parole officer, and keep you away from the criminal elements of the business."

"No, throw me back in. I'm sick of sitting on the sidelines."

"Throw you back into what? You can't carry a weapon—parole violation. You can't get in a fight—parole violation. And you can't traffic drugs or weapons—parole violations. Our entire business will get you sent back inside."

"So I won't get caught."

"Like it's that easy," I say, rolling my eyes. "You've had a historically hard time not getting caught."

"Ease up," Fedor says, slamming his hands on the desk. "God, I thought you'd be happy to see me, but you act like I'm a burden."

If it looks like a duck and sounds like a duck ...

"Maybe I'd feel differently if you'd given me time to prepare," I snap back.

"Prepare for my triumphant return?" he asks. "I didn't assume my brother would need to work himself up to being pleased to see me a free man."

"You aren't a free man, Fedor. You're on parole. I'm trying to make sure you stay out of trouble and can actually be free one day."

"Semantics." The amusement has drained out of him, leaving only the caged frustration I saw when he was locked up. There is no telling what trouble he'll find when he leaves this room. "I'll stay free as long as no more fucking witnesses step up to the plate. This shit never used to happen."

"When Dad was in charge, you mean?" I ask, not bothering to hide my anger.

Fedor looks guilty for a second, and I see a glimpse of the brother I used to know. "I wasn't making any statement about your leadership," he says, sounding surprisingly respectful. "I'm just ... surprised there are so many people who want to put me away so badly they would risk their own lives."

We sit in silence for several seconds, the air thick as we each try to think of how to respond. Finally, Fedor breaks the silence.

"But I guess we sent them a message," he says with a smirk. "You took care of all of the witnesses, so unless someone else is stupid enough to step forward, I'm home free."

Any doubts I had about Fedor lying to me, about him actually recognizing Molly, disappear. He has no clue he just spoke to one of those witnesses downstairs. He doesn't remember her at all.

Then, the reality that Fedor can't recognize a woman he drugged and assaulted settles in.

Clearly, the incident wasn't as defining for him as it was for Molly. Clearly, she's not the only woman my baby brother has assaulted.

If he wasn't my brother, I'd kill him for what he did to Molly.

Part of me feels like I should do it anyway. I barely recognize the man sitting across from me.

A curious look crosses Fedor's face, and I worry for a second that he can somehow read my mind. That he can see the traitorous thoughts running through my head.

Then, I feel a small hand tap my arm. When I look down, Theo is standing next to me.

"Who is this?" Fedor asks, standing up and coming around the desk.

I thought Theo and Fedor were twins before, but seeing them in the same room at the same time ... the resemblance is uncanny.

Theo opens his mouth, ready to respond, and I scoop him up onto my lap and tickles his sides, stealing his breath and his words.

"Surprise," I say in the same tone Fedor used earlier. "You aren't the only one with secrets."

Fedor's green eyes go wide. "He's yours?"

I tickle Theo harder, hoping he will be too distracted to listen. "Yep. He's mine."

"When? How?"

"Well, you know how," I say, setting Theo on the floor and standing up, a hand on his back to lead him towards the door. "And four years ago, but I just found out."

The lies come to me easily. Smoothly.

Before Fedor can ask any more questions, Molly rushes in. "Sorry," she says, the horror painted on her face too real for the situation.

"It's fine," I say with a tight smile. "But occupy him until I'm done."

"He can stay," Fedor says around me, smiling down at Theo. "I'd like to meet my nephew."

Now it's Molly's turn to catch up with my lie. She does so immediately, nodding as if tucking the information away in her mind.

Our story is growing very complicated very quickly.

"You need to get going anyway," I say, looping my arm around Fedor's shoulders and dragging him towards the door.

He starts to protest, but I remind him about the money. "Kent will be looking for his pay now that you're free."

He groans. "He can wait. Fuck Kent."

"Language," I warn, pointing towards where Theo and Molly are disappearing back into his room.

"Is she the nanny, too?" Fedor asks.

"She takes on many roles." Very true. Molly is endlessly adaptable. She's a survivor.

I call Petr and tell him to get the money ready for Fedor to pick up, and send Fedor on his way in a matter of minutes. The second he's out the door, I pull out my phone and fire off a text.

He'll be at the office in fifteen. Be there. Follow him. Report to me.

Fedor has been out for a few hours and the shit has already hit the fan.

He has seen Theo. Before, I could have claimed to have fired the maid and had no clue where she was. Fedor probably wouldn't have even noticed her absence, to be honest.

But now, he's seen Theo. He thinks Theo is my kid.

I can't get rid of them so easily now, and I have no fucking idea what I'm going to do.

17

MOLLY

Theo is playing in the middle of his room, stacking blocks and knocking them down with a stuffed dinosaur toy, completely unaware of the danger we are now in.

How could I have let him out of my sight?

I walked into his room to check on him after Viktor and Fedor went into the office, and he was sleeping. I stayed in there for a few minutes, wanting to be there when he woke up, but then I had to go to the bathroom. I decided it would be better to go while he was sleeping, and then in the sixty seconds it took me to pee, Theo got out of bed and went to Viktor's office.

It has become his routine over the last few weeks. Whether Viktor is home or not, Theo wakes up from his nap and pads across the hall to see if he's there. He did that today and found much more than he bargained for.

His biological father. The sperm donor, as I've come to think of him.

Seeing the two of them in the same room made it obvious that there was some family relation, so I understand why Viktor said what he said. Why he claimed to be Theo's father. But the thought still twists my stomach.

Not because I don't like the idea of Viktor being Theo's father. I like the idea of Viktor being the dad much more than the truth. The nausea comes from the fact that Viktor has just tied himself to Theo forever.

Theo and I can't run and hide because Fedor will wonder what happened to Viktor's son.

I drop my face into my hands and try to take deep breaths to calm the rapid beat of my heart. I'm still in that position when I hear the bedroom door open and Theo jumps to his feet, giggling as he runs towards Viktor.

I slide across the floor and lean against the side of Theo's bed. I can see the exhaustion in Viktor's face, but he hides it well as he smiles at Theo and then sends him off to keep playing.

"We need to talk," he says quietly, tipping his head towards the hallway.

I'm about to say I don't want to leave Theo alone, but then his nanny returns, and I push myself to shaky legs and follow Viktor down the hall.

I expect him to lead me downstairs, but instead he pushes open the door to his office and steps inside.

I've never been invited in before. Even earlier when Theo ran inside, I hovered in the doorway, too nervous to step into Viktor's private space, especially when Fedor was inside as well.

Viktor ushers me in again, and I step inside. Circumstances have obviously changed now that Fedor is back. There is a lot to talk about, and we need privacy to do it.

The room is decorated in modern sweeps of white with warm wood accents. The wall of bookshelves to my right is full of books I can't imagine Viktor reading and dotted with pictures. I see one of Viktor as a teenager, standing next to a shiny black car, and next to him is a younger boy. It takes me a second to recognize that the boy in the photo is not Theo but Fedor.

They could be twins.

"I didn't know Fedor was getting out," he says, dropping down into his chair. "If that wasn't obvious. I found out and came home as soon as I heard, though it wasn't fast enough."

"How did he get out?" I ask the question with the smallest chance of crumbling the illusion of safety I've built for myself in this house.

Viktor leans back in the chair and runs a hand down his face, scraping his fingers across the stubble that coats his jaw. I haven't told him, but I think he would look good with a beard. The last time he came into my room I got a red patch on my inner thighs from his short beard. When I press my legs together, I can still feel it.

"Bribery," he says simply. "The lawyer was trying to get his charges lowered from murder to involuntary manslaughter, and when the legal system stopped working for them, they paid off a judge. He is on probation."

"Probation for murdering someone?" The argument of nature versus nurture pops into my mind. I remember discussing it briefly in my high school biology class, but now I wish I'd paid much closer attention. How much of Theo's personality will I be able to influence and how much will be genetic? Will he be impulsive and violent like his father?

"The situation was ... complicated." Viktor sighs. "The man was a business associate. He operated in the criminal world just like we did, and he disrespected Fedor. Or, at least, Fedor thought he did. He lost his temper."

"And murdered someone," I finish, nose wrinkled in disgust.

Viktor's eyes snap to me, frustration flaming there. "Like I said, it's complicated."

"Murder isn't complicated."

"You wouldn't know!" he snaps. "You don't know this world, so you don't know what it can be like."

"You do," I say softly. "You said you've murdered people."

He nods.

"And did they all deserve it?"

His jaw works from side to side. "I think so."

A flicker of fear I haven't felt since the first night Viktor and I met sparks to life inside of me. "What about the man Fedor killed? Would you have killed him too?"

His jaw works so hard I'm sure his teeth must be ground to dust. "Fedor grew up in my shadow. Our parents didn't care about him, and he didn't have a role in the Bratva. Or the family. It made him … reckless. He lashes out and sometimes … there are consequences."

"Deadly ones." Will he lash out at me or Theo when he finds out? He already wanted me dead and that was when he was thinking coolly, logically. I have to assume he'll be even more murderous when his anger spikes because I'm still alive and Theo has been kept from him for four years.

Viktor growls, a low sound deep in his throat. "You don't understand him. I know you have a … history with him, but—"

"Why are you defending him?" I don't mean the question to be accusatory, but it comes out that way, and I don't try to correct it. "You acted as though you were disgusted by what he did to me, but now you're trying to minimize it. Trying to minimize all his crimes. I thought—"

"That's the problem," he says, cutting me off. "You think you understand me, but you barely know me. Or my brother. You've seen one side of him."

"When someone shows you they're partly evil, the other sides don't matter."

"He isn't evil," Viktor says, jumping to his feet. He fists his hands at his side, flexing them like he wishes he could punch something. "Like you said, I've killed people too. Am I evil?"

I don't know if the question is meant to be rhetorical or not, but regardless, I don't have an answer. I've spent many nights since coming to live with Viktor wondering how I can reconcile the seemingly two different sides of him—the man who makes love to me and buys toys for my son, and the man who commands an army and kills his enemies.

"I can't turn my brother away without being a hypocrite," he says. "Plus he's my brother. He's blood."

"That doesn't mean you excuse his behavior."

Suddenly, Viktor rounds the corner of his desk. His blue eyes are sharp, piercing, and I swallow back my nervousness. "What would you do if Theo was ever accused of something like this?"

The thought makes me sick. Theo is a child. My baby boy. He is innocent and sweet and … part Fedor. I'd be foolish not to consider the possibility that I will one day have to deal with that side of him. That I will have to counteract his Fedor-like tendencies.

"He's just a kid," I say.

"So was Fedor. When I took care of him," Viktor says. "He wasn't always the monster you know. He was an innocent little kid who needed someone to guide him and help him, and I took on the task. I can't abandon him now."

My heart breaks. Not for Fedor, but for Viktor. For the pressure he has been put under, trying to maintain the Bratva while also take care of his brother. I never saw it before, but now I see the strain in him, the exhaustion. He has been taking care of Fedor since they were kids, and he doesn't know how to stop.

Viktor runs a hand through his hair. The dark strands are standing up in every direction like he has done that a lot today. He lets out a sigh, and it's the most vulnerability I've ever seen from him. His neutral mask is gone, and finally, I feel like I'm getting a peek beneath the surface. A glimpse into what it's like being inside Viktor's world.

"I will always care for Theo," I start. "No matter what. No matter what he does or what happens between us. But I won't condone him hurting innocent people."

Like me. At eighteen, I was innocent and naïve and excited about a future that I had no idea would be stripped away from me. Stolen by Fedor.

"If Theo did something like Fedor has done, I wouldn't sweep it under the rug. I would force him to suffer the consequences of his actions. It's the only way he would learn his lesson."

"Is that what you think I'm doing? Sweeping it under the rug?" Viktor asks.

This question is not rhetorical. I know he wants an answer, but I'm afraid to say anything. I'm afraid to say the truth.

Yes.

"I could have paid off a judge," he says. "Months ago. I could have paid someone to track down the witness and kill him before he could take the stand. People think the justice system is more powerful than money and power, but people are wrong. I could have had Fedor freed ... but I didn't."

"Why not?"

He leans back on the edge of his desk, his shoulders slumped forward, and I can see the weight of everything he has carried pressing down on him. Cast him in marble and he would make a lovely, somber statue.

"I think it's better if Fedor is behind bars," he admits softly. "For his safety, not to mention the safety of others. He has problems that I'm not sure how to solve. So, I didn't try to get him out, but now he is, and all I can do is make the best of it."

He has a point. He didn't know Fedor was being released. He didn't do anything to pursue that path aside from hunting me down, but considering he didn't follow through with the plan to murder me, I suppose I can't hold that against him. Unless ...

"Are you still going to kill me?" It has been a surprisingly long time since I've consciously considered that option, though it's always lingered somewhere in the back of my head. It was easier to pretend this fairytale of a life we'd built was real and free of complications. But now, Fedor has returned and everything is back on the table.

Viktor looks up at me, his dark brows raised in surprise and ... horror? His mouth falls open, and after a second of stunned silence, he shakes his head as if to clear his thoughts and clears his throat. "Is that really what you think of me after all the time you've spent in my house?"

"I'm not sure." It's the truth. I don't know, which is why I asked.

"No," he sighs. "I'm not going to kill you. I'm going to protect you. And Theo."

A weight I didn't realize I was carrying lifts off me. "How?"

Viktor slides from the corner of the desk to the center until he's standing in front of me. He reaches out, and I lay my hand in his without hesitation, grateful for the warmth of his fingers. Today has been crazy. I've experienced every emotion possible from panic and terror to relief, and here I am adding another to the list—desire.

Something about Viktor is magnetic. It draws me in and begs me to get close. Like a cat drawn to a heater, I want to curl into his body and take refuge there, if only for a few minutes.

I push the thoughts away and try to focus on his words. What he says is important. It will determine what the next phase of my life looks like. Of Theo's life. I don't have time to remember the brush of his fingers over my skin or the way his teeth feel when they bite into my flesh.

"Marry me."

My brain short circuits.

The gooey kind of warmth that had been flowing from my center, wrapping my limbs in need, draws inward in an instant, leaving me cold and frozen.

"What?" I try to play back the last few seconds and see if I missed something, if he said something else that gave this any context, but there is nothing. "What did you say?"

"Listen," he says, speaking plainly, his neutral mask back in place. "Fedor thinks Theo is my son. I had to tell him that so he wouldn't question the family resemblance. So, you two can't just disappear. He'll wonder what happened."

I'd already come to that conclusion on my own, so I nod in agreement.

"And I can't have Theo living here with you playing my maid. At some point, the truth would slip out. Fedor has to know that you're the mom, and I'm the dad, and that we're a family. So—marry me."

A family. I've always wanted a family. For me and for Theo.

But not like this.

I shake my head. "No."

18

VIKTOR

I never imagined proposing to a woman before. I never saw myself on bended knee with a ring extended, laying my heart on the line for a woman I loved.

More than that, I certainly never imagined being rejected.

"No?" I ask, making certain I heard her correctly.

"No," Molly says again. She crosses her arms over her chest, doing devastating things to her cleavage, and I pull my eyes away, blinking.

"I'm offering to marry you and protect you, and you're saying no?"

"I'm saying no." She runs her tongue over her lower lip. "I don't want to."

"And you think I do?" I say, letting out a humorless chuckle.

Molly stands up and walks around the chair, putting more space between us. "Wow. What a charmer you are. How could any woman resist such a sweet talker?"

I throw my hands up, letting them slap back against my legs. "This has absolutely nothing to do with how we feel about it or how nice I am to you. This is about survival."

"I've survived long enough without your help, thanks."

"Yeah, before Fedor knew Theo existed."

She flinches when I say my brother's name, and I wonder for the first time how hard it must have been to be close to him. To flirt with him in my kitchen to protect her identity.

"Now that Fedor knows about Theo, he has to be part of our lives. Theo is part of our family."

"Theo is *my* family!" She points to her chest and then places her palm over her heart and takes a deep breath. "My son. Not yours."

"One DNA test would prove you wrong," I say. "That's all it would take for Fedor to know the truth. For Fedor to realize who you are and who Theo is and what I didn't do. He would realize I didn't kill you like I said. He would turn his back on me and hunt you down and rip Theo from your arms."

Molly's eyes go glassy. I know I'm being harsh, but that is the reality. As much as I wanted to defend my baby brother earlier, I know what he's capable of. I know what he will do when he learns I betrayed him and finds out that Theo is his son.

"That DNA test would also be of great use to you in a court case," I continue. "You could take it to court and claim assault. That DNA test, along with your statement from all those years ago, could put Fedor back behind bars, and if you think he wouldn't do anything to keep that from happening, then you don't know Fedor very well. He *will* kill you if he finds out I didn't."

She turns away from me, facing the bookshelves, and I watch as her shoulders lift and fall with every deep breath. I wait in silence for her to speak, for her to agree with me. Because there is truly no other option.

I surprised myself when I voiced the proposal out loud, but I don't retract it because it's the only way I can make sure Fedor will leave her alone. If he thinks Theo is my son and Molly is my wife, he'll respect them as family, and he won't ask any questions. Everyone wins.

"No," Molly says finally, softly. "I won't do it."

"Goddammit!" I roar, slamming my hand on the table. "Why are you being so fucking stubborn?"

"Because this is my life," she says, spinning around and moving towards me. She jabs her finger into my chest like she did when she first arrived, the fire in her brown eyes sputtering and sparking. "Enough of it has been determined by other people. I'm not going to let a decision like this be made for me."

"And what will you do when Fedor finds out?" I ask flatly. "What will you do when he comes for you and for Theo?"

"Deal with it." Her teeth are gritted in stubbornness.

"Good luck dealing with the results of a DNA test. Good luck running away from him with no money and nowhere to go. Just ... good luck." I throw my hand up and turn away from her, frustrated. "If Fedor really did assault you, it's a wonder you aren't more afraid of him. Maybe you only came forward in the hopes you'd get a little money."

The words are spoken from anger and desperation, and I know the moment I turn around and see Molly's usually tan skin turn deathly pale that I've crossed a line.

I open my mouth to take it back, to try and talk sense into her, but she drops down into the chair opposite my desk and launches into her story before I can say anything.

"I'm only going to tell you this once because you don't deserve my explanation," she snaps. "I've never asked for a penny from you or from Fedor. If I was out to extort you, I would have told the world what happened to me. But I didn't. I retracted my statement to the police, I stayed quiet and hidden, and I raised a beautiful little boy all on my own without ever reaching out to you for help. *You* found *me*."

Her voice breaks when she talks about Theo, and I can feel the love she has for her son in every word. I want to stop her and take it back, tell her she doesn't have to keep going, but a morbid part of me is curious. I want to know what happened. What Fedor did. What Molly remembers.

"I was at the concert to celebrate my last few weeks at home. I was ready to go off to college and get a degree and start my life." She shakes her head as though the idea was idiotic. A pipe dream. "Then, a man kept bothering me. He was drunk and an asshole."

Fedor.

"And then Fedor arrived," she finishes, surprising me. "He pretended to be my boyfriend to frighten the guy away. He was … nice."

My eyes flick to the floor, alarmed by the similarities between me and my baby brother. Now, to protect her from Fedor, I want to pretend to be her husband. We've come full circle.

"I thought he was handsome and a gentleman, so when he offered to buy me a shot, I accepted. I didn't know he'd put anything in it."

"Molly," I say, changing my mind. I don't want to hear any more. I don't want to know what happened. "You don't have to—"

"I don't remember much after that," she continues. "Which I'm grateful for sometimes. Other times, I wonder what happened. I remember being placed in the passenger seat of a car. I remember hands under my knees, carrying me upstairs. I thought maybe someone was taking me home, but it's all a blur until the next morning. I woke up. Naked and uncovered. Fedor was still asleep next to me. Passed out, I guess, because he never stirred as I got dressed and left. That was only the second time I'd ever had sex."

My hands clench so hard my knuckles turn white, and I feel sick.

"I found out I was pregnant a few days before I was supposed to leave. I contemplated getting an abortion and going anyway. I wanted to forget it had all happened. But I couldn't. I don't know why. So, I dropped out. Then my parents kicked me out of the house when they found out, and I've been surviving on my own ever since."

"I'm sorry." The words are tense and tight, and I hate having to say them, but I can't think of anything else to say. "I didn't mean that."

She nods, acknowledging that she hears me, but doesn't respond. Doesn't accept my apology.

"My life was stolen from me that night, and I've spent years trying desperately to get back to it. To find a way to create a home for Theo. Stability." Her eyes go glassy, a tear escaping the corner of her eye, and I want to reach out and brush it away. "When Theo was born, I almost left him at a fire station, hoping someone would adopt him and love him, but I couldn't do it. I couldn't go through with it. Keeping him was my choice and raising him was my choice. I didn't get to make the choice to have sex, but I knew I could make the choices after that. I have, and no matter what you want, I will continue to make my own choices."

"It is your choice, Molly. I'm asking you to marry me, and you can choose to do that and protect yourself and Theo or—"

"Not," she finishes. "I know my options, and I choose not."

I let out a sharp breath through my nose.

This is all Fedor's fault. I knew that before, but I see the full scope of the damage he caused for the first time. Not only did he change Molly's life; he changed her view of the world. He took an eighteen-year-old, innocent girl, and made her calloused. He made her untrusting. Even now, as I'm extending a path to a better life for her, she can't take it.

For the first time, I truly want to kill Fedor. For what he did to Molly and Theo. He deserves the punishment. Just as much as any other Bratva member I've executed for similar crimes.

"And since we are clearly an inconvenience for you," Molly says, standing up and smoothing her hands down her jeans. "We'll leave now. Tell Fedor what you want about Theo. I don't care. Tell him the truth, even. I plan to be long gone before he starts looking for us."

She's walking towards the door, and faced with the reality that she's going to turn her back on me and take Theo and leave, I snap.

"You are welcome to go back to your old life living on the streets and begging for food, but you won't be taking Theo with you."

Molly spins around, the emotion in her eyes hardening to ice, sharp and clear. "He's my son."

"For now," I nod. "Like I said, one DNA test is all it will take."

"I'll tell the police he assaulted me," she counters. "My statement is already on file."

"Fedor will kill you for it. And if he doesn't, I have enough money to bribe every officer in the fucking city. Care to wager who will win that legal battle?"

She swallows and narrows her eyes at me.

"I'll prove that I'm his uncle and that you are an unfit mother."

The words feel like daggers leaving my lips, and they hit their mark. Molly flinches, and then before I can read anything else in her expression, she turns on her heel and walks away, slamming the door behind her.

19

VIKTOR

Three days out on the streets and Fedor is already causing chaos.

It's almost commendable how thoroughly he can fuck everything up in a matter of days. I want to ask him if he's trying to make my life miserable, but I don't want to give him any ideas.

"He ordered another soldier to be killed," Petr reports, reading from a list as long as my arm. "I stopped it from going through, and I think he was drunk, so I'm sure he won't even remember by the time he sobers up."

"If he sobers up," I say, running a hand down my face. "Why did he want this one dead?"

"He refused to kill another soldier Fedor wanted killed." Petr shrugs.

I lean back in my chair and stare up at the ceiling. I prefer my home office. The familiar smells and warm afternoon light that comes through the window. And until a couple days ago, the soft padding of Theo's feet up and down the hallway.

Molly has kept him away, however. It's hard to entirely separate us—my apartment is large but not palatial by any means—but she does her best. Theo has found me in a few quiet moments after a nap and before bed, but I haven't spoken to Molly since she left my office in a rage after our conversation.

After my threats.

I can't shake the feeling that I crossed a line. But every time I feel that, I remind myself that I draw the fucking lines. I define the rules. What Molly and I have is nothing more or less than what I say it is. What exactly that is, though… I'm still not sure. Is it a relationship? A partnership? Something more, different? I don't know. I don't fucking know.

What I do know is this: anyone who defies me is my enemy.

Molly and I are in a kind of war now, one that I intend to win.

"We are trying to keep an eye on him, but it's difficult," Petr admits. "Fedor moves fast. He doesn't keep a normal schedule. He's up at all hours of the night, and he can cause as much damage with his cell phone as he can walking the streets. He shot at a rival drug dealer last night. The soldiers with him pulled him away before anything could escalate, but it's getting bad. The only real solution is to lock him up."

"And we all know how well that worked out."

Petr is the only person I can be honest with. He understands my relationship with Fedor better than anyone else. He understands how complicated things are, and he has been there for some of Fedor's more epic meltdowns. The rest of the Bratva know he is unreliable and reckless, but they don't know the depths of his illness. They don't understand how unhinged he can become. I hope they never find out.

"There is talk that he's a liability. That you are to blame for—"

"Everything," I finish for him. "It was my fault that he was locked up and now it's my fault that he's free."

"That's the burden of being the leader."

I glower at Petr, and he wilts slightly, but shrugs as if to say, *What can you do?*

That's the question indeed.

What can I do?

~

Mario Mazzeo keeps an eye on Fedor and reports any interesting movements, but that ends the moment Fedor decides to touch Mario's daughter, Maria.

Maria is a beautiful woman. I would have been happy to bed her back when I was a single man. She trots around town in leather and low-cut tops without a single care in the world. She gives herself freely to men and is open about her sexual appetite. It drives her dad and brother crazy, but it drives a lot of men wild, too.

Now, however, my appetites have shifted.

"Your brother is dead," Rio says now over the phone. "Fucking dead."

For a second, I take him literally.

"He dropped Maria off at home last night," Rio says. "They stopped off at *his* place first, though. Maria told me nothing happened, but I know she's lying."

It was rumored for a while that the Mazzeos and Kornilovs were to form an alliance: Maria wed to a Kornilov son. But it was me who was to be married, not Fedor. Is this a cheap shot to get back at me? Fedor always wanted Maria, but Father forbade him from going after her. If any of his sons were to claim her, it was to be me. So now Fedor is laying claim to someone off-limits, just as he'd tried to do with Molly. Petty. Childish. Fucking reckless. It makes me even more desperate to keep Molly away from him.

"Our deal is over," Rio growls.

I bite the inside of my lip, swallowing back the litany of curse words I want to unleash on him. "Let's not make any rash decisions. Where's your father?"

"Sitting across the table from me," he says. "He told me to call. It's done. Your brother is your problem, but if he touches my sister again, he won't be anybody's problem anymore. He'll be dead."

"I'll talk to him. I'm sure there was a miscommunication. I respect your family, and—"

"If he touches my sister again," Rio repeated. "There will be war. Do you hear me?"

Mario Mazzeo is growing old, and Rio is poised to take over. I don't want to start my relationship with him off on bad terms. Not after the lengths my father went to to secure a peaceful alliance with the Mazzeos. I can't let Fedor's sex drive ruin that for me.

I try to arrange a meeting with Fedor, but he doesn't return my calls. I try to meet up with him at the bar, but he seems to disappear moments before I arrive.

He is dodging me, and we both know why. Because he doesn't want the leash I'm going to try to attach to him.

After my third visit to the bar in two days trying to find Fedor, I drop down into one of the vinyl-covered stools and order a scotch. It's the middle of the afternoon, but I've never needed a stiff drink more in my entire life.

If Molly is sticking to the usual schedule, Theo will be out at the park with the nanny, and she'll be sitting on the couch reading her design books. I haven't seen her for a few days, so I'm not sure if she's continuing on with things as normal or not.

I had the locks on the door changed the very night Fedor let himself into my apartment. For the sake of Molly and Theo, I couldn't let him have unfettered access to my private life. Thankfully, he hasn't come by the house and learned this fact for himself yet, but it will happen soon enough.

Curiosity getting the better of me, I pull out my phone and call the private guard I had put on Molly.

"Where is she?"

"Inside," he says. "Hasn't left all day. The boy left with the nanny half an hour ago."

So, business as usual.

"Good. Let me know if anything changes." I hang up and throw back the drink in one swallow.

My days are spent being Fedor's firefighter. Dousing the flames and destruction that trail in his wake, but as I toss back the drink and request another, I realize I can't do it anymore. I can't chase after him and clean up his messes. It's a pointless, tiring, and thankless job. I can't do it anymore, and I won't.

But before I deal with Fedor once and for all, I have to take steps to make sure Molly and Theo are protected.

I don't know what Fedor will do when I finally put my foot down and impose consequences for his actions, but I have to assume he'll come at me with everything he has. We are brothers, and I love him, but I know him well enough to be realistic. Fedor will come after me. And if he has any reason to believe my arrangement with Molly and Theo is strange, he'll look into it, and I'm honestly not sure what he will find. One conversation with Kent could bring the entire operation to the ground.

So, I need to marry Molly, change her last name, and adopt Theo. It's the only way I can think to avert suspicion and protect them from my brother.

When I get home, the drinks from the bar are buzzing beneath my skin, but my head is clear.

Molly is home alone, just like the guard said she would be. Theo is still at the park with his nanny and won't be home for another half hour—the perfect amount of time.

As soon as the door shuts behind me, I hear movement in the living room. The last few days when I've come home, Molly has retreated to her room immediately, avoiding any kind of confrontation.

Today, I cut her off at the stairs, extending my arm across the stairwell. She frowns but refuses to meet my eyes.

"Hey." My voice sounds more slurred than I think it should, and she must notice because she looks up at me, studying my face with hooded eyes.

"Are you drunk?"

I shake my head. "I had a drink, but I'm not drunk." *Maybe three or four drinks.*

"Several drinks by the smell of it," she says, waving her hand in front of her nose in two quick movements. "Get out of my way."

"Not until you talk to me."

"We've talked," she says. "I'm done talking to you. It's as productive as talking to a brick wall."

I shift so my body is between her and the stairs and my arms are crossed over my pecs. I flex. "Is that a compliment on my physique? If so, thank you."

She raises a brow at my flexed chest and rolls her eyes. "You've proven my point. Only an actual brick wall would think that was a compliment. Actually, that might be insulting to brick walls. Move."

Her fire is still there, burning brighter than ever. The Molly I've come to admire is still inside her, but now, rather than confiding in me, I'm the one dodging her flaming arrows.

I want her to smile at me the way she did before I fucked everything up. I want Molly to trust me again.

"We live here together, so we might as well try to get along."

"For now," Molly says. "The moment you stop having me guarded like an inmate, I'll get out of here."

And be killed.

I don't know how many ways I need to explain to Molly that she isn't safe. I was able to find her because Kent had a packet of information on her. Sources reported to him that Fedor had a witness floating around, and if Molly goes back on the streets, those same sources will report the same information. My house of lies will tumble down and Molly and Theo will be the ones trapped beneath the wreckage.

"You aren't being watched. There are still only two guards on duty. Just like before."

"I know you're lying. Just because I can't prove it doesn't mean I'm stupid."

Maybe I should just admit she has a private detail on her at all times. It might even make her realize how serious I am about her security.

Though, it also might be another example of me lying to her and make her hate me even more.

I clench my jaw and try to push down the frustration rising in my chest. "I know you aren't stupid, but that doesn't mean you can't make stupid choices."

"Enlighten me," she says, stepping forward, our bodies so close her chest nearly brushes mine. Molly looks up at me from beneath long lashes. Her long dark hair tickles my arm. "Tell me all the ways I've been stupid. Please. I'm dying to hear what a criminal thinks of me."

She spits the word "criminal" at me like a slur, and I reach out and grab her arm before I can stop myself. Maybe I am more drunk than I thought.

Molly's eyes go wide, but she doesn't relinquish an inch. She shapes her face back into an angry mask and continues to stare at me.

"First, you refuse to show fear when you should obviously be afraid," I say, gesturing with my eyes to where my hand is white-knuckled around her bicep.

"I'm not afraid of you," she growls.

I sigh. "You never keep your mouth shut."

"Fuck you," she says, lunging forward with every word, nearly spitting at my face.

"And," I say, pushing her back against the wall and caging her in with my arms. She gasps when her body thuds against the wall, and her breathing picks up, her chest rising and falling quickly. I catch myself staring down the front of her shirt and drag my eyes up to her face. "Worst of all, you refuse to accept help from powerful people who genuinely want what is best for you. And for Theo."

I want to kiss her.

It makes no sense. This woman is infuriating. She fights me at every turn, curses me, and refuses to respect my authority. And yet, I want her.

It has been days since I've touched Molly and being this close to her is muddying my thoughts more than the alcohol.

And maybe I really am drunk, or maybe she's looking up at me with something like desire in her eyes. I can't be sure, so I don't move an inch. I just hold my position, waiting for Molly to make the next move. Waiting for her to respond and tell me how to react.

She takes another long breath, her chest straining against the thin cotton V-neck of her shirt, and when I glance down to admire her, she seems to wake up.

Molly's hands are on my chest, pushing me back. "Stop pretending like you care about me. You care about what your brother will think when he finds out you lied to him, and you care about what I could do to your Bratva with the information I have. This isn't about me or Theo at all. This is about what's best for you."

Being separated from her body feels like being doused with a bucket of cold water, and I feel fully sober. I shake my head and sigh. "I wish you felt differently."

She crosses her arms over her chest. "Why? So I'd be easier to manage? So I could be like one of the soldiers you employ?"

"No," I say, reaching over her head to knock on the wall that separates the stairwell from the kitchen. In a matter of seconds, a man walks out of the kitchen, a folder pressed to his chest, and a gold cross hanging around his neck. "So you could marry me willingly rather than by force."

20

MOLLY

Despite my best efforts, I nearly get lost in the heady sensation of Viktor's hands on my body. His chest against mine. His arms blocking me in.

I hate him.

That's what I've told myself over and over the last few days. Every time I've caught myself sinking into the plush cushions of his couch and thinking what a good life it could be, I've reminded myself that all of it—the security and the comfort—comes at the cost of being near *him*.

He wants to lock me away and keep me as his pet. It seems like Viktor genuinely cares about Theo, but even that could simply be because of their blood relation. Regardless, he doesn't care about me, and I can't let myself forget that.

Except, I nearly have.

Even with alcohol on his breath, the woodsy scent of him is hard to ignore. Everything about him is intoxicating. As though Viktor was created in a lab with the express purpose of wooing the opposite sex and making them silly.

Silly is exactly how I feel until Viktor knocks on the wall above my head, signaling a man I don't know to walk through the door. Now, all I feel is dread.

The man is wearing a cross around his neck, and the first thing I think of is a funeral. *My* funeral. I'm dead.

Viktor said he wouldn't kill me, but he lied. He was keeping me around like a pig for slaughter, waiting for a convenient moment.

By the time I realize that theory is absurd, I've already shoved Viktor away again and slid further down the wall.

"So you could marry me willingly rather than by force."

Viktor's words are distant and unfocused, like I'm hearing them from underwater, but they hit me all at once.

"You want to get married?" Compared to death, I should be relieved that Viktor wants to marry me. Yet, somehow, the possibility is worse. It would make our current arrangement permanent. Viktor will be allowed to lock me up in his home, throw away the key, and raise Theo the way he would like.

The last four years of my life have been spent trying to find a foothold, trying to drag myself up out of the pit I allowed Fedor to bury me in. And now I'm supposed to tie myself to this man I barely know? To a man who is looking at me with glazed-over eyes like I'm for sale in a shop window?

Fuck. No.

I don't realize I've said the words out loud until the minister gasps out a startled breath and turns away.

I try to turn and run up the stairs, but Viktor's hand is back around my arm in an instant. He pulls me in front of him, crushing me against him until I have no choice but to look up at his face.

"I won't do it," I whisper, somehow ashamed of having the stranger overhear me. Whether he's an actual man of God or just a Bratva lackey with a minister's license, I don't know, but I still don't want him to judge me. "You can't make me."

"I can," Viktor says, nodding his head slowly. "But I don't want to. I want you to choose this. To choose me."

Choose me.

The words are shockingly tender, and I pull back slightly and study his face. All at once, Viktor blinks and shakes his head.

"Choose Theo, Molly. This is for him."

"Stop saying that," I plead, grabbing his shirtsleeve. "Stop saying this is about Theo when it's really about—"

"Theo," he repeats angrily. "This is about Theo, regardless of what you think."

The minister has wandered into the living room and is pretending to look out the windows. It's a remarkable view, but still, something about his posture lets me know he still has an ear trained towards us. I wonder what Viktor told the man to get him here.

"I think this is about you being a coward. You're a coward," I say.

Viktor snorts. "How am I a coward?"

I let go of his sleeve and let my hand slide over his chest and down his abs. Viktor arches into the touch, but I ignore the hard muscle beneath his clothes and grab the hem of his shirt, untucking it from his pants.

All at once, Viktor seems to realize what I'm doing, and he spins around and pins me against the wall, his hands around each of my wrists. Then he looks down to check his gun is still tucked in there.

My heart is racing in my throat, but I still manage a choked laugh. "Because you know you should have killed me, but you can't."

His eyes widen with raw vulnerability, allowing me a momentary, crystal clear glimpse behind the curtain that separates Viktor the man from *Viktor, the Bratva boss*. It's just a second, but it's enough for me to know I'm right.

"You can't do it," I repeat. "Even now that it would make everything easier for you, you won't do it. Instead of ending my life, now you want to ruin it."

"Ruin it?" he asks, releasing my hands and stepping away. "Is that what I'd be doing? Because from where I'm standing, it looks like I'm saving your life."

His jaw is clenched, and he reaches up and runs a hand through his dark waves. His hair has grown out since I first met him. The length on top is more unruly than normal. It makes him look younger.

"Fedor will kill you," Viktor says, his eyes cast down at the floor. "He will kill you, Molly. And the only way I can think to stop that is to make you my wife. Family is everything to Fedor. If you're my family, he won't touch you. He won't hurt you. If you take my last name, he will never know who you were before, and you and Theo will be safe."

"You'll take him from me." I wrap my arms around my stomach, doing my best to hold myself together. I can handle angry Viktor. And drunk Viktor. And seductive Viktor.

I can't handle honest Viktor.

"No, I won't." His eyes flare, and I feel myself drawn towards him like a stupid moth to a blisteringly hot and deadly flame. Even knowing everything I know, I want to trust him.

"Yes. Yes, you will." I shake my head and turn sideways, my shoulder leaning against the wall. I'm still in front of Viktor, but the position allows me some fresh air. It allows me to look somewhere other than directly at his annoyingly perfect face. "You will adopt Theo and change his name, and you won't need me. You'll steal him from me."

"Molly, I won't do that."

"You said you would!" I shout, pivoting towards him and rising on my toes. "You told me you'd have me declared an unfit mother. How do I know you won't marry me and then have me shipped off to an insane asylum somewhere? I'll probably be institutionalized, and Theo won't even know he ever had a mother. Or you'll finally get the balls to kill me like you promised."

"If I was going to kill you, believe me, I would have." Viktor's nostrils flare. "You are more than annoying enough to give me all the motivation I need. And still, I've taken care of you. I've helped you."

He has, but why?

If I've learned anything in my years fending for myself, it's that everyone has a price. No one does anything for free. If Viktor wants to marry me, it's because he will benefit somehow, and the only reason I can think of is that he would gain Theo.

And Theo would gain Viktor.

I drop down onto my flat feet and press my back against the wall. Suddenly, it feels like the wind has gone from my sails.

This isn't just about me and Viktor.

This is about Theo.

I've been so consumed with my own point of view that I haven't stopped to think about what would be best for Theo.

He would have a home. He would have clean clothes, home-cooked meals, and a cozy bed. The same bed every single night.

Me marrying Viktor would allow Theo to have everything I've ever wanted for him. And as much as I want to deny it, I would even be happy for Theo to have Viktor. To have a dad. A family.

I practically feel the color drain from my face. When I look up, Viktor's brows are pulled together, his forehead wrinkled. He lifts his hand, fingers extended towards my face, and then at the last second, he seems to think better of it. He curls his hand in a fist.

"What are you thinking?" he asks.

I look down at myself. At my thin cotton T-shirt, faded jeans, and socked feet. "I never imagined I'd get married with no shoes on."

Viktor takes a step back and places one hand on his hip. When he tilts his head to the side, I can't help but look up at him. He looks like an angel. I simply have to decide whether he's an angel of light or darkness.

"If I let you put shoes on, you're more liable to run away." Viktor turns to the side and extends his elbow to me. I know his other hand is resting on his gun. I know he could pull it out at any second and force me to walk over to the windows where the minister is waiting. And I know that there are two armed guards standing in the kitchen, listening in and witnessing the entire situation.

But none of those things are why I slide my arm through his and let him walk me down the proverbial aisle.

I do it because of Theo.

I picture Theo's round cheeks and pointed chin and brown eyes. I am doing this for him, for his future. Not for mine.

Staring out at the sun sinking down behind the skyline, I'm not sure I have much of a future anymore.

∼

I walk upstairs alone.

I try to get to my bedroom, but the emotion of the last ten minutes seems to wash over me all at once, and I have to fall back against the wall to keep my knees from buckling.

I'm married.

I'm a married woman.

I am Molly Kornilov.

The minister Viktor brought with him was clearly a hobbyist. There is no way he had ever done a wedding before. He stumbled through the words of a ceremony he printed out from the web, and Viktor spent half of the process circling his finger, trying to get the man to get on with it.

Because there was no sense in waxing poetic about love when we are not in love. There was no sense in telling us to cherish one another when we haven't even spoken in days. The minister would have been better served by making us promise not to kill one another. Because truthfully, I was less afraid Viktor would kill me when we weren't married. Now that we are, he could take out a hefty life insurance policy on my head and have me done away with. He has told me more than enough times that he can do what he likes in this city.

"Marinating in marital bliss?"

I start at Viktor's voice and jump away from the wall hastily.

Viktor continues like he doesn't notice my fear and holds out a flute of champagne. "To celebrate."

I take the glass with a shaky hand and tap it against his, but rather than a toast of celebration, it feels like an alcoholic send-off for my old life. As such, once I bring the glass to my lips, I can't seem to pull it away until the champagne is gone. I wipe my mouth with the back of my hand.

"That seems like a good sign," Viktor says sarcastically, taking my glass and setting it on a built-in bookshelf behind him.

"My drinking is not going to be what dooms this relationship." Relationship feels like such a heavy word for what Viktor and I are to one another.

What are we, anyway?

Viktor tosses back the rest of his drink, adding to what I know he already drank earlier in the afternoon. His cheeks are a bit pinker than normal, but he doesn't stumble as he takes a small step towards me. "What will be the reason, then?"

"Most likely?" I ask, screwing up my face in deep concentration. "Murder."

Viktor laughs, surprising us both, and with his white teeth sparkling, I can't help the way my heart leaps.

Our eyes meet, and his smile slips away like a wave being pulled back to sea. I want it to stay because things feel easier when he's smiling, but the emotion is lost to the depths of him. A flicker of happiness in the unknowable, churning chaos that is Viktor Kornilov.

He takes a deep breath and moves towards me another step. "The justice of the peace is gone. Everyone is gone. The house is empty."

"But the guards—" I start to say.

Viktor shakes his head. "Gone."

We're alone.

I've been alone with Viktor many times now. But this feels different. Vulnerable.

"Theo will be back soon, so—" I try to move past Viktor and go into Theo's room.

"He's staying with the nanny and a few guards until after dinner. He won't be back for hours. I just called and arranged it."

"We're married for less than an hour and you're already overstepping your boundaries with my son," I say. "Because he's still my son, Viktor."

"I know," he says, holding up his hands in a placating manner. "I don't mean to overstep, but considering the circumstances, I took a few liberties. I can call it off and have him brought back here immediately if you wish. But if I do, you won't know the reason why I've sent everyone away."

I can't say my curiosity isn't piqued. I wish it wasn't. I wish I could just be angry with him. Being angry with Viktor is so much easier.

He reaches out gently and curls his hand around my wrist, sliding down until his fingers are warm against my palm. I try to ignore it, but there is an electric zing that accompanies his touch.

Maybe the bubbles from the champagne have short-circuited my brain.

"You could be right. Maybe murder will be what ends us." Viktor's voice is low and gravelly, and I'm so distracted by the rumble of it that I can't even bother being afraid at his casual mention of murder. He leans down, stealing my air. "But whatever it is, it won't be a lack of chemistry."

I arch towards him out of instinct, proving him right. My body wants his. The feeling of him on my skin, between my legs. Even though I haven't missed Viktor's smug face, I've missed the warmth of him in my bed.

"No." I back away and shake my head. "You don't get to force me into this and then use me. I'm not someone you hired, and I'm certainly not your slave."

"As I recall," Viktor says, eyebrow raised, "you married me willingly. I didn't have to put you in a chokehold and drag you down the aisle. You wanted this. You chose this."

I bark out a laugh. "Most grooms wear a tux, not a gun."

"I didn't hold it to your head," Viktor says slowly, his eyes narrowing like he could imagine doing that very thing. Like, after all his promises, he might decide to press the gun to my forehead right now. "I didn't threaten you."

"You might as well have," I say between gritted teeth. "Don't get the idea I'm your blushing bride, Viktor. I'm not."

I move to walk around him, but Viktor throws out his arm just like he did downstairs to stop me from going upstairs. He plants his palm against the wall and then slides in front of me. "I'd have to be thick as the brick wall you think I am to believe you're happy about this arrangement." His head dips low, and his voice dips even lower. "However, you *are* blushing."

I turn towards the wall, trying to hide the evidence, but my entire body feels like it's radiating with warmth. Heat rolls down my back in waves and pools low in my belly.

"I just got married to a criminal. I'm allowed to be nervous." My defense is weak, and Viktor knows it.

He closes the distance between us and wraps his arm around my lower back. I push on his chest, but my arms feel like spaghetti.

"Nervousness could account for the fluttering you feel here," he says, pressing his finger against my temple before sliding it down my neck to rest above my heart. "And here."

My entire body is rigid like a cable. I want to pull away from him, but I'm afraid any stray movement of his hand over my body will cause me to snap.

Viktor circles his finger over my heart, each sweep growing wider until his finger brushes across the taut tip of my nipple straining against the fabric of my shirt. I gasp, and he grins.

"That, however, is usually caused by another emotion entirely."

His finger is frozen, and I'm unsure whether I should slap him or arch into his touch. My mind and body have never been more at war.

I hate this man. Don't I? That's what I've been telling myself anyway.

Yet, here I am, anxious for him in a way I've never experienced before. My insides feel molten, and although I know I should want to chop his finger off for what he just did, I can't ignore the part of me that desperately wants him to do it again.

As though reading my mind, Viktor flicks his finger upward, and I shiver against the sensation.

He flattens his palm against my chest, cupping my breast, and leans in, his breath warm on my skin. "Sorry to make you … *nervous.*"

He is taunting me, but I don't care.

My body collides with his with such force that Viktor actually stumbles backwards. I wrap my arms around his neck and slide my fingers through his dark hair, feeling the softness of it against my fingers. Then, I bring my mouth to his.

By the time our lips touch, he has found his footing. He slides his hands down my back and then cups my ass. I don't even have to jump into his arms. Viktor lifts me up, holding me like I weigh nothing at all, and I hate how attractive it is. I hate how much of a man he is, and how much it makes me want to be the gentle, fragile doll to his brute strength.

As an act of silent rebellion, I cup the back of his head and crush our mouths together. I kiss him until it hurts, until we are a mess of teeth and tongues and lips. Viktor growls against my mouth, the vibration sending a shock down my spine, and I arch my back against the shiver, inadvertently rolling my hips against him.

His excitement is obvious now, pressing against my inner thigh. It's like an optical illusion. Once you see it, you can't unsee it. Or, in this case, un-feel it.

There is no ignoring the press of him, and I can't help myself. I roll my hips against him again.

The contact draws another long growl from him, and then one of Viktor's hands slides from beneath me, tracing the curve of my waist up to my chest. I shudder when his palm brushes over my breast, and then, before I can compose myself, he grips the collar of my shirt and yanks it downward.

The material shreds, and I gasp in surprise and horror, forgetting for a moment that this isn't my only shirt. Forgetting that I have ten more like it hanging in my closet.

Old habits die hard, I suppose.

However, my thoughts are pulled from my spacious closet to the much more present matter of my breast being enveloped by Viktor's mouth.

His tongue swirls around me, flicking and teasing, urging small moans out of me. Then there is a sharp burst of pain. I cry out and raise my hand to slap Viktor and his teeth away from me, but before I can, his tongue eases the pain, replacing it with pleasure. I rest back against the wall, relaxing enough that I don't care at all when Viktor tears the scraps of T-shirt off my body with his one available hand and his teeth like he's a wild animal.

As much as I hate to admit it, Viktor is right. We have no lack of physical chemistry.

When my shirt is hanging from my shoulders in shreds, his hand smooths down my stomach and lower, fighting with the button on my jeans.

I want his hand there. I want his fingers inside of me more than I can describe, and that is exactly why I shove him away and unhook my legs from around his back.

Viktor's brow is furrowed in confusion, but I sink to my knees in front of him and watch it change to raw, primal desire as I unfasten his pants and wrap my hand around his length.

This is a consummation. But more than that, it's a surrender.

Clearly, Viktor planned for the house to be empty, for us to be alone to do this. If I give in without any fight, if I let him have me however he wants, then I'm giving up.

As I pull him free of his boxers and swirl my tongue around the very tip of him, however, I am claiming some kind of power. Viktor may have the money and the influence and the muscle, but I'm not entirely without recourse. I can make him pay where it counts. I can refuse to surrender here. Now.

I take him into my mouth inch by glorious inch until I can't take anymore. Viktor releases a long sigh and presses his hand against the wall for stability. I look up and see him watching me with hooded eyes. When I slide to the end of him and then back down to the base, his lids flutter closed and his mouth moves in a silent curse.

"Molly…" he groans, tipping his head back and thrusting softly against my lips.

My name in his mouth feels like a surrender, and I fight back a smile as I run my tongue along the rough edges of him. I move to take him in again, but suddenly he pulls away, leaving me falling slightly forward in anticipation.

Before I can right myself, Viktor falls to his knees in front of me and grabs my hair in his hand, wrapping it around his fingers. When his mouth lands on mine, it's hot and soft, and his tongue swirls between my lips, flicking the roof of my mouth.

My eyes blink closed, and I sigh, losing myself in the kiss. But just as I reach out to drag my fingers across his stubbled jaw, his mouth is gone.

Using my hair as a handhold, Viktor directs me to the floor. Usually,

I'd insist we find a bedroom lest someone from his staff find us in the hallway, but I know they're gone. Even if they weren't, the words feel far away. All words do.

Viktor's tongue draws a line down the center of my body while he deftly removes my pants and my panties in one go. With strong fingers, he peels the denim from my calves, his pinky dragging along the arch of my foot as I'm finally freed from the denim.

I open my legs immediately, letting my knees fall apart, and I smile at the stupefied look on Viktor's face. He studies my willing form for a long second as though memorizing it, and just when I think he's going to give in and dive between my legs, he wraps his hand around my left knee and rolls me to my side.

It feels like waves pushing against a helpless boat in the ocean as Viktor wraps his hands around my waist and drags my hips up, up, up.

No. Not like this.

He's meant to surrender to me. This is my war to win.

I open my mouth to complain, but then I feel the press of him between my legs. The warm hardness teases my opening, and any understanding I once had of the English language is gone. I know only want and desire and need.

I arch my back as he presses into me, sheathing himself entirely within my body in one stroke.

It is the killing blow. The one that undoes any willpower I may have had.

Viktor grips my hips harder, pulling me against him until I'm not sure where I end and he begins. His cheek rests on my back for a moment, and I feel his deep breath. As though this is the first breath of fresh air he has had in years. It is a quiet, tender moment that snaps the moment he lifts his head, drags himself out of me, and then plunges back in.

He sets a crushing pace that still isn't enough. I tilt my hips to ensure a deeper connection and reach behind me to grip his muscled thighs, to feel the way his body flexes and works with every thrust.

Our breathing grows more and more ragged with every thrust, and when I think I might pass out from the sheer lack of oxygen, Viktor slips his hand from my waist and finds my center. His fingers dip into my warmth and then flick across the sensitive bundle between my thighs.

I groan with breath I don't have.

He circles his fingers over me, pinching and massaging and coaxing until one word returns to my vocabulary.

"Yes."

Viktor stiffens behind me for a moment and then continues with renewed vigor. "Do you like that?"

"Yes," I repeat, closing my eyes and tipping my head back.

Viktor grabs my hair with his other hand, pulling until I'm looking up at the ceiling, and then flicks me with his finger at the same time he thrusts into me from behind. "Does that feel good?"

"Yes." God, yes. Fuck, yes. How many different ways can a woman scream that word? Because I want to say it in as many ways as possible.

Using my hair as leverage, Viktor pounds into me until the sound of our bodies slapping together drowns out almost everything else. His breathing is violently uneven when he speaks again. "Will you come for me?"

I clench my thighs, trying to hold off the inevitable. I wanted him to come first. I wanted him to surrender first, to be the weak one. It's where my power comes from.

Still, despite my best efforts, I feel the warmth building in my center. I feel my body climbing to new heights, desperate for the relief of tipping over the edge. Of free-falling.

Viktor flicks his finger over me, making it hard for me to focus on anything else. "Are you going to come for me?"

I bite my lip and try to pull away from him, to change the game. If I can get on top of him, then I can regain control. I can hold my own ending off until he has gone first. However, as soon as I try to separate our bodies even an inch, Viktor tightens his fist in my hair.

"Come," he commands.

The growl in his voice and the strength I feel in his thighs is so unbearably sexy that resistance is futile. Besides, even if I wanted to argue, I only know the one word.

"Yes." The word is a groan and a release and a surrender tied up in one.

Viktor releases his hold on my hair, and I drop my head as the orgasm moves through my body, sending my muscles into shuddering spasms.

"Yes." My body clenches onto his, drawing him deeper, begging him to stay. It's too much for Viktor, and I feel him finally give in as well. His hands drop to the floor on either side of my hips, holding himself up as he thrusts into my spent body.

When we are both finished, he pulls out of me and lies on the hallway floor next to me, one arm over his eyes. I watch him, studying him openly since I know he can't see me.

He is beautiful.

Frustrating and brutal ... and beautiful.

The lines of his face and his body are picturesque. They are art embodied. It's no wonder I gave in so easily.

Viktor sighs and pulls his arm from his eyes. I see his breath hitch in his chest, his lips open like he's going to say something, and I don't want it to be a taunt. I don't want him to boast about how he knew I was born to play the role of dutiful wife. I just want to console myself for my shameful forfeit.

So, before he can say anything, I hook my leg over his hips and press my lips to his. He starts for only a second before he grips my waist and sits up to better kiss me back.

There, in the hallway, with me straddling him, we consummate our loveless marriage again. And again.

21

MOLLY

At some point we move into his bedroom, and when I wake up in the middle of the night, I'm not sure where I am.

I sit up, not bothering to cover my naked body. Viktor has seen every inch of me over the course of the last few hours. Besides, the blankets are in a pile on the floor. There is nothing to cover up with.

I remember pushing the tangled blankets over the side, throwing Viktor down, and gripping the wooden post of the bed for leverage as I rode him. Heat floods my face and tingles down my arms. Who needs blankets when your skin is literally on fire?

I push the thought from my mind and look around the room.

It's darker than the rest of the house. The walls are a deep navy and the wood is all darkly stained and smooth. In the yellowish streetlight peeking through the curtains, I can make out that the room is lacking any real sense of décor. The rest of the house was clearly done professionally, but Viktor's room is just a bed, a dresser, and a closet. No personality, no sense of who he is.

Maybe that's why he only ever came to me in my room. Because he doesn't like his very much.

Viktor shifts slightly next to me, and I hold my breath. If he wakes up, I won't be able to help myself. Just like I couldn't help myself in the hallway.

Something about him calls to me. It makes it impossible to resist his touch and his warmth, and I find refuge there even though he's the person I most need refuge from. Him and his brother, anyway.

He settles back into his pillow, and his breathing evens out to a constant, deep slumber.

Like me, Viktor fell asleep without any blankets and naked. Entirely naked.

His chest is broad and muscles arch and dip down his midsection towards the deep cuts just above his hips. I let my eyes trail even lower and then wrench them up when a now familiar warmth sinks in my belly.

Viktor is sculpted. He is the embodiment of power and masculinity, and just the sight of his naked body next to mine makes me want to stay. It makes me want to lay my head on his chest and curl my body against his side and let him protect me.

Because that is what Viktor wants to do, right? Protect me and my son. That is what he has said.

My question, however, is: what does protection look like to Viktor?

I turn away from him and slide my feet off the side of the bed, stretching my arms over my head as my toes touch the floor. I fumble around for my T-shirt and jeans before I realize my shirt is shredded and my jeans are still lying in the hallway. So, I grab Viktor's white undershirt and pull it on. The hem just barely scrapes the tops of my thighs, but it's enough.

On my way out of the room, I notice a frame on the dresser. It's the only true decoration in the entire room, and it's a picture of Viktor.

Viktor is only four or five in the photo, but I recognize the blue of his eyes and the wide set of his jaw, noticeable even while wearing a childish grin with his arms wrapped around a chubby toddler sitting in his lap.

Fedor.

Viktor is grinning and squeezing his baby brother and there is true joy in his eyes. The same spark of joy I see whenever I look at Theo.

Innocence.

I look back towards the naked man on the bed, wondering how long it has been since he has smiled like that. Since he has been or felt innocent in the slightest.

The thought makes me want to crawl over him and kiss him awake. It makes me want to draw a smile out of him, to work and dig until I find the well of happiness he must keep buried deep inside.

It is that terrifying thought that eventually pulls me from the room.

I pad down to my own bedroom, lock the door behind me, and pull out my phone. It's four in the morning. Far too early to be calling anyone, but I have to speak to someone who knows Viktor. Someone who can help me.

"The hell?" a voice grumbles on the other end of the line. Matilda sounds like she answered the phone before she actually knew what she was doing and I immediately feel stupid for calling her.

"I'm sorry," I say softly, half to myself. "This is stupid. I'm sorry."

"Molly?" she asks.

I'm surprised the designer even remembers my name this early in the morning. We barely know one another, after all. One design project and a few shared meals do not make us friends. But she's the only person I can think of who knows Viktor but won't be afraid to tell me the truth about him.

"Yes, hi. I'm sorry," I repeat. "I shouldn't have called."

"Is this about the nursery?" she asks, clearly confused. "Because I don't usually take business calls this late. Or ... early, I suppose. I only answered because you called my personal phone."

"I thought it was your work phone," I say, as though that should excuse the odd time of the call.

"Viktor has my personal number. He's my best client," she explains. "Though, not this good of a client. Call me back in a few hours."

"Wait," I say, before she can hang up. "This isn't about the design. It's about ... Viktor."

I hear a rustling on the other end of the phone and then Matilda's voice comes through more clearly. "Is he okay?"

"Yes. Fine." *Exhausted*, I think. *But fine.* "It's just that ... well ... we just got married."

There is a long pause. "Oh. Congratulations."

"That isn't why I'm calling either," I say in a hurry. I lay a hand over my face, flushed with embarrassment even though Matilda can't see me. "I'm calling because I need to ask you something about him."

Matilda sighs. "Hurry. This conversation is the strangest I can remember having, but still, my patience is thin."

"How would you describe him? Is Viktor a ... a good man?"

"A good man?" Matilda asks. She clicks her tongue. "I do not make it a habit to become friends with my clients. For reasons much like this one right now. I don't want my personal life and business life intermingling."

"This is a one-time thing," I assure her. "I'll never call again."

"I'd rather you *did* call again. Though, next time, make it during business hours. And I want a floor-to-ceiling remodel. Give me another big job, and I'll forgive this indiscretion."

Negotiations. Again, it's no wonder Viktor is so loyal to Matilda. She's a shark.

"Deal."

She sighs again. "Okay, a good man. Hmmm. Well, Viktor is an honest man."

"Honest is not good," I say. "Racists can be honest, but their honest opinions are trash."

"Honest is good in business," she says. "Which, if you remember, is where I communicate with Viktor Kornilov. I know what rumors are spread about him, but I don't know anything about those. What I know is that he arrives to meetings on time, and he pays in full what he promises he will. He is honest, and that is good for business."

I don't know what I expected from Matilda. On some level, I think I expected her to reveal something about Viktor that would change my mind about him. Instead, she has simply convinced me that I can trust him.

"Thanks," I say softly. "I appreciate it."

Matilda huffs in annoyance and hangs up, and I drop the phone next to me in the bed and lower my face into my hands.

Viktor is honest. I can trust him.

He told me he would take Theo from me. He told me he would have me proven an unfit mother.

And Viktor always keeps his promises.

He has promised to keep me alive, but he didn't vow to honor and cherish me. He didn't vow to love me. We didn't even exchange vows.

Instead, Viktor promised to keep me alive, but what kind of life will I lead?

I attempted to resist him, to exert my own will over him, and I failed. Miserably. The moment he touched me, I folded like a bridge made of toothpicks.

If I stay in this house, my entire life will be like that. I will bow to his wishes and let my life be controlled by him until there is nothing left of me. Until I am broken down to the same scared, lonely, desperate girl I was when Theo was born. Except this time, I'll be surrounded by nice things.

That is no improvement.

I'd rather be destitute and still be myself than wear designer clothes and feel like a puppet. Like a ghost being forced through the motions.

If I allow myself to be lowered to that, I will be an unfit mother for Theo.

Not to mention, I'm the reason Theo is in danger at all.

It is my testimony that would make Fedor angry. And it is my identity that would make Fedor realize Theo is his son, not Viktor's.

But if I'm gone …

I'm grateful Theo isn't in the house. If he was, I'd never be able to leave.

After packing my bag, I would have stopped in to kiss his forehead one last time, and I never would have left. I would have collapsed in a crying heap next to his bed and been resigned to this life.

Since he isn't in his bed, however, I'm free to go.

I slip into some clothes and then pack the rest of the nice jeans and soft T-shirts and lacy underwear Viktor paid for. I also throw his white undershirt into the bag, though I can't entirely decide why. Then I go into Theo's nursery and pack the small picture frame Matilda hung up on the last day we worked the remodel together. It's a picture of the three of us standing on the balcony. Matilda insisted we needed a "family picture," and I didn't have the strength to argue. So, we took it, Matilda framed it, and I reluctantly hung it on Theo's bedroom wall.

Now, it will be the only printed picture I have of my baby boy.

In it, he's hugging a soccer ball and smiling up at Viktor. I'm standing next to them with my arm around Theo's shoulders, careful not to touch Viktor.

When I look at it, it will remind me that I did what was best for Theo. He loves Viktor, and I know Viktor will take care of him. Family is everything to the Bratva. He will look after Theo. He will make sure he's safe.

A tear rolls down my cheek, and I quickly wipe it away. I can't afford to let them start. If they do, I'm afraid they may never stop.

I try to come up with a lie to tell the guards so they will let me past. Something to convince them I need to leave and Viktor doesn't need to be alerted. But when I get downstairs, the guard on duty looks up sleepily from the couch and nods as I leave.

Viktor only cared about keeping Theo in.

And since Theo is staying at the nanny's house tonight, that's probably where all the guards have been stationed.

In some ways, this realization comforts me because I know Viktor is serious about protecting Theo. But in another, deeper way, it feels like a slap in the face.

Viktor doesn't care about my well-being. He only cared about me in terms of Theo. He will probably be glad to see me gone in the morning. Finally, Theo will be free from the inherent danger I brought into his life.

I walk out into the dark morning and march down the sidewalk, bag grasped firmly in my hand, without the faintest idea of where I will go.

I should leave the city, I know that. I should start over somewhere else.

But every step I take feels like jogging through sand. Like jogging through wet sand mixed with cement.

Every step is further away from Theo ... and Viktor.

I'm reluctant to tack his name on at the end, but I can't deny that I'm partially sad I won't see him again.

Viktor and I may have been married for less than twelve hours and under less than ideal circumstances, but I can't deny that part of me may have been falling for him.

A foolish part of me, no doubt. The part of me that trusted Fedor enough to take a drink from him at that concert. The part of me that accepted the free room Viktor offered me at the hotel.

I feel for Viktor despite all sense and logic screaming at me not to, and now I am escaping into the night, leaving my son behind.

I'm leaving him to a good life, I know that. A better life than I could ever provide for him. I'm leaving him to safety, and prosperity, and protection. Things that I can't give to either him or myself.

But leaving him feels like tearing my heart out. I tell myself again and again that this is what is best for him. In my head, I know that it is. I cannot do for Theo what Viktor can do for him. But it hurts worse than I could ever imagine. My heart is screaming at me that this is the wrong decision. *Go back,* it orders. But I let my footsteps carry me farther and farther into the night.

Finally, when I'm six blocks away from the apartment, the tears begin to fall and, like I predicted, there is no stopping them.

My cheeks are wet, the collar of my shirt is soaked, and I cry until there is no water left in my body. Until I am an empty, aching shell, seeking nothing but the essentials—food and shelter and warmth. Because if I let myself want anything else, there will only be disappointment.

22

VIKTOR

Crying.

So much crying.

I didn't know it was possible for a human being to shed this many tears without shriveling into a raisin, but Theo is still chubby and alive and ... crying.

"I cut the crusts off," I say helplessly. This is the third peanut butter and jelly sandwich I've made in ten minutes, and if I have to make another one, *I* might start crying.

Ask me to cut off a man's hand for stealing from my stash house? Done.

Ask me to cut off the crust of a four-year-old's sandwich for the third time, knowing he will only cry harder and ask for a new sandwich entirely? No way. I'm out. I can't handle it.

How did Molly handle it?

For the thousandth time since she left a day ago, I wonder how in the hell Molly did this on her own. Without a house or any help, even. It's unfathomable.

"There is shrimp stir-fry in the fridge," I say, snagging the plate before Theo can shove it onto the floor, adding it to the pile of food he has refused. "I can heat that up."

Do kids like shrimp? Or stir-fry? I need to ask the chef to make more kid-friendly meals. Molly never mentioned it being an issue before, but maybe she was handling Theo's meals on her own. Or, more likely, she was able to manage Theo. He probably ate fine when she was here.

"No!" he screams, testing the upper reaches of the sound barrier and making my splitting headache even worse.

When the nanny brought Theo home the morning after Molly and I were married, Theo went tearing through the house to find his mom. He ran in and out of nearly every room in the house calling her name. After I finally broke the news to him that I didn't know where his mother was, Theo plopped down in the middle of the floor, threw his head back, and wailed. I swear he hasn't stopped crying since. By the time I went in search of the nanny to ask for her help, she'd ducked out. If I hadn't felt so guilty about Molly disappearing in the middle of the night, I would have fired the nanny simply for running out on her charge before I'd given her permission to leave.

I toss the plate on the counter, letting it clatter into the sink, and drop my face into my hands.

Waking up in the morning to find Molly gone—to find her closet empty and her phone and purse missing—was one of the worst days of my life. That night, we'd been so close. Not just physically, but emotionally. At least, I thought so.

It felt like finally the walls between us were coming down, and I could imagine a future in which Molly and Theo were both safe. Safe from Fedor and the many obstacles she'd overcome in the last four years. We would be a family. Dysfunctional and untraditional and messy, but a family, nonetheless.

Theo crawls down from the table and runs into the living room. He flops onto the sofa and cries into the cushion, and I don't even have the energy to chase after him. Nothing I can say will make him feel better, anyway. He misses his mom.

I miss her too.

I'm not entirely sure when the idea of Molly actually being my wife became a hope of mine rather than a pragmatic solution to a problem, but there it is, regardless, burning a hole through the center of my chest.

I wanted her to stay and be happy and safe with me, but instead, she's gone. She chose to leave her son behind and run rather than be married to me.

I asked the guard on duty that night whether Molly said anything when she left, and he said no. In fact, he didn't ask her a single question. As soon as he realized she didn't have Theo with her, she was free to leave.

"But she left with luggage in the middle of the night. You didn't think that was worth mentioning?" I asked through clenched teeth.

He shrugged but had the good sense to look nervous. "You just said not to let Theo leave the house."

I nearly killed him for being the world's biggest idiot, but he was right. My command was to keep Theo from escaping because I never in a million years would have guessed Molly would leave without her son.

She probably knew the entire Bratva would be after her if she took Theo with her. Now that Fedor knows about Theo, he can't just disappear. It would raise too many questions. Questions I'm not prepared to answer. Molly also probably knew Theo would be safer with me. Still, it doesn't make it any easier to understand how she could leave. Theo was Molly's world. Her everything. How could she just give him up?

Theo kicks his feet and thrashes through his tenth temper tantrum of the day, knocking over an end table. He sends a stack of Molly's design books flying across the floor.

She gave up everything—her son and her dreams—and left. And for the first time, I let myself consider that I won't ever see her again.

Theo screams into the cushion, crying and raging, and I wish I could do the same. Instead, I run a hand down my face and walk over to the couch to try and comfort him. He is my responsibility now, and I have no idea what I'm doing.

∼

I talk to Theo until he finally falls asleep for his nap. The minute he does, I stumble across the hallway and collapse behind my desk.

I tip back in the chair and close my eyes, thinking I might actually fall asleep for a minute. The moment my mind starts to slip into unconsciousness, however, my phone starts to vibrate.

The sound surprises me, and I fumble for my phone in my pocket before I realize I don't even have it on me. I shuffle stacks of papers on the desk until I find it under the folder Kent gave me so many weeks ago. If I open it, I know I'll find information about Molly—where to find her, where she frequents, how to get in contact with her. I wish Kent would update it and give me some fucking idea of where she's gone now.

I push the folder aside and grab my phone.

"What?"

"Viktor?"

I don't recognize the voice at first, and I have to pull my phone away from my ear to read the name on the screen. Johnny Baranov.

He isn't part of the Bratva lifestyle per se, but he keeps his ear to the ground. I've always been able to rely on Johnny for good information for a reasonable price.

"Johnny. What's going on?"

"I've been calling you all morning," he says, sighing in relief. "Shit. Where have you been?"

"What's this about?" I don't owe him or anyone else an explanation. Even if I did, I sure as hell wouldn't tell him my new wife ran off in the night and left me in charge of a kid.

"Fedor," he says simply.

I close my eyes and hold back a groan. I'm in charge of two kids. How could I forget?

"What did he do?"

"It's bad, Vik. You need to talk to Petr. Your brother came around here earlier today to talk to me, but he didn't want to pay. I turned him away, and I thought he would pull his gun. Well, he did, just not on me."

"Who?" I ask, not actually wanting to know.

"Consiglieres. Two of them. For the Mazzeos."

"Shit." My knuckles go white around the phone, and I consider throwing it across the room. Good news rarely comes through the speaker. Perhaps a new phone would bring better reports.

"I'm good here," he says. "I'm still on your side. You know that. But you should get in touch with your brother."

"Bye, Johnny." When I hang up and the call screen disappears, I realize I've missed five calls from Petr and three texts from Fedor. I don't even read them.

Instead I call the nanny and demand she come back immediately and that I won't take no for an answer. Once she's confirmed that she'll be here within twenty minutes, I push away from my desk, grab my keys, and head for the door.

I stop before my guards out front and address the same idiot who had let Molly disappear into the night. "No one comes or goes except the nanny. Once she gets here, neither she nor Theo are to leave. Not even to the park. Got it? Disobey me and you won't live to regret it."

I stalk to my car without waiting for a reply, then head straight for the office downtown.

～

When I walk through the front door, there are men standing around in the lobby. They all look up as I enter and then look away just as quickly.

"Men." I tip my head.

There is a grumbled reply and then they all press against the walls, clearing the way for me to walk down the hallway. Clearly, they know why I'm here.

My office door is cracked open, and I hear Fedor's voice as I approach.

"Fucking careful, Petr. Can we call a doctor? We should have a damn doctor working around here. What did you all do while I was locked up?"

"We didn't get into random shootouts with our rivals," Petr says.

Fedor scoffs as though that is a ridiculous proposition, and his face is still screwed up in annoyance when I push open the door.

He rolls his eyes. "I see you called my big brother to bring me back in line. Thanks, *Pete*."

Petr is wrapping a bandage around Fedor's bloody bicep, but at the pointed nickname, he holds up his hands in surrender and walks away. "You're on your own, asshole."

Fedor narrows his eyes at him as he leaves and then turns to me. "This is why I should be your second-in-command. Petr is disrespectful. He's becoming too comfortable."

"He's our cousin," I remind him, pushing the door closed.

"And I'm your brother. Blood is thicker than water."

"That's not what that phrase even means," I say. "The full saying is 'the blood of the covenant is thicker than the water of the womb.' It means—"

"I'm not an idiot. I know what it means." Fedor ties a loose knot in the bandage and flops back in my chair. I can see there is blood smeared on the upholstery. "So family doesn't mean anything to you anymore? Is that it?"

"Of course not. Family is everything."

That has always been true for me, and I don't see it changing anytime soon. The question is, however, what does family mean now?

Molly feels more like my family than my little brother does, and Fedor is sitting directly across from me while I don't even know where Molly is.

"Good," Fedor says, wincing as he rolls his shoulder. "Then you need to help me kill some people. For our family."

Fedor leans back in my chair and tries to kick his feet up on the table, but he loses his balance and plants them quickly back on the floor. The falter reminds me of the clumsy kid who used to chase after me, tripping over his own feet. It is a flicker of the little boy I used to love and a stark juxtaposition against the wild man he has become.

"You need to remember whose office you're in," I say, hitching a thumb over my shoulder and walking around the desk. "Up."

He opens his mouth to argue, but I kick the base of the chair. It's already off balance because of his slouched posture, so he goes tumbling backwards, cursing.

"I just got shot, fuck head!" He grabs the bandage on his arm that's already soaking through with blood.

I ignore his name-calling and reclaim my chair. Fedor needs to be reminded who is in charge. He needs to understand that he does not call the shots. He may be the brother of the boss, but that does not make him the boss.

"So I heard. It seems you picked a fight."

He sits on the edge of my desk and rolls his eyes. "They started a fight with me. I was just trying to talk to Johnny."

"About what?"

Fedor's mouth tightens. "Nothing."

"He called and said you wouldn't pay. I'm not even going to bother asking what you were refusing to pay for. Tell me what happened."

"I don't have any fucking money." He jumps to his feet and paces in a small circle, reminding me of a caged animal. "My accounts are empty. I'm supposed to receive a check, but—"

"But you spent your last check and the next several paying off a judge so you could get out of jail," I remind him.

His mouth falls open. "That was for my freedom. You're really going to take it from my allowance like I'm some kid?"

I want to tell him he's acting like a kid. That I can't remember the last time I've seen him behave like an actual adult. But that would only make things worse. I cross my arms and nod.

"I can't show favoritism. The Bratva is a family. Every member is important. If I give you special treatment, it will breed resentment. Do you want your brothers to hate you?"

"Fuck my 'brothers,'" he says, throwing air quotes around the word. He points at me with his good arm. "I only care about one brother. My blood brother."

Fedor runs a hand through his dark hair and tips his head back. When he does, I see Theo's nose and sharp chin. He looks so much like his father.

Then I shake my head. I am Theo's father now. Not Fedor. I am all Theo has, and I have to get Fedor under control and back on track, otherwise I won't have the energy to split between the two.

"I was just talking to Johnny," Fedor says again. "The Mazzeos walked over to me. They made some cracks about me being the Crazy Kornilov. I had to defend our honor."

"You mean your honor."

Fedor turns to me, eyes narrowed. "My honor is our honor. We share the last name."

I sigh and try to come up with the words to explain to Fedor that he has to get his shit together or get lost, but before I can, my phone buzzes. I pull it out and see Rio Mazzeo's name on the screen.

"Who is it?" Fedor asks.

I ignore him and open the text.

"Are they more important than me?" he shouts. "Are you going to ignore me while I'm standing right in front of you now? Goddamn it! I don't know why I even got out of prison. Nothing has changed. You don't tell me shit."

I slam the phone down so hard I'm sure I just shattered the screen. "Shut the fuck up, Fedor."

My little brother opens his mouth and then closes it. His cheeks go red, and I'm surprised he's listening to me. I start talking before he changes his mind.

"The Mazzeos have responded."

He steps forward, jaw set. "What do they want?"

"You." I pinch the bridge of my nose.

Rio's text was only three words long. *Fedor or war.*

"They want to kill me?" he asks.

I nod. "In exchange for the men you killed."

Fedor is silent for a second and then barks out a loud laugh. "Ha. Those fucking pussies. What idiots. They have to know you would never turn me over to them. I guess we're going to war."

He whoops and hollers like he's excited about the prospect. Like he's happy to put our men at risk. When he realizes I'm not joining in, Fedor sits in the chair across from me with his brow furrowed. "We are going to war, right?"

"You fucked up a hard-fought alliance, Fedor. Dad worked with the Mazzeos for years, and I continued working with them in good faith. I kept the peace and in one stupid moment, you ruined it all."

He shoots out of his chair. "So you'll have me executed for it?"

"No!" I shake my head. "I don't know what I'm going to do. You haven't stopped talking long enough for me to think. I need a minute."

"A minute for what?" he challenges. "What is there to think about? You got two options: me or war. Is there seriously a question? You know I'd fight for you, Vik. You know I'd die for you."

My heart clenches at the sincerity in his voice. Fedor has made me question a lot of things in the last few years, but do I question his love for me? His loyalty?

Perhaps, if he knew everything I'd lied to him about, he'd change his mind. If he knew about Molly, he might want to go to war with *me*.

"I'd die for you too. But only if I had to. Only if it was the last chance to save you." I tap my finger hard against the desk and look up at him beneath my brows. "Will going to war save you?"

"Obviously. If you don't, they'll kill me."

"No." I wave a hand to stop him. "If I fight for you now, will you stop behaving like this? Will you respect my authority and the Bratva and stop killing people on impulse?"

The crazed, caged look in Fedor's eyes is gone. His bright green eyes are wide, and he looks down at the floor, ashamed. For the first time in a long time, I think I may have cracked through his crazy shell. I think I may have gotten to the Fedor hiding underneath it all. I may have finally found my little brother.

"Yeah," he says softly, sitting in the chair, his shoulders slouched forward. He shakes his head. "I'm sorry, Vik. This is all my fault. But yes, I'll be better. I'll follow your lead and be better. I swear it."

I stare at him for a second, trying to remember this moment. For a brief, miraculous moment, I think it may be a turning point in our relationship. A shift towards a brighter future.

So, I pick up my phone and text Rio back one word.

War.

23

MOLLY

"The coffee is cold and the creamer is warm."

A few weeks ago, I would have rolled my eyes at the annoying customer and pointed out that his coffee was still steaming. Now, I take the perfectly fine cup back to the counter, refill it, and return with fresh creamer. The man doesn't even say thank you.

It's so strange being back waitressing again. I planned to leave the city immediately and get as far away as I could, but money was an issue. So, with only a little cash to spend, I took a bus as far as it could take me—just a few hours—and then I went back to the only thing I knew I could do. The diner I walked into had needed someone right away, so I took up an apron and went back to work as though nothing had changed. Though everything has changed.

I tighten my apron around my waist and grab the mop from the back closet. A couple and their little boy came in for pancakes, and he spilled the entire bottle of syrup on the floor. I've been mopping the spot once an hour all evening and the floor is still sticky.

He looked like Theo.

Not really. His hair was darker, his skin lighter, and he laughed like a deranged bird. The boy didn't sound anything like my Theo.

But they were similar enough. Enough that I kept staring at him across the room, wondering what my son was eating for dinner. I lingered near their table, watching the mother fuss with his hair and tie a napkin around the boy's neck for a bib.

I miss doing those little things for Theo.

I miss my son.

"There is a dead fly in the windowsill," the man across the diner calls, waving his arm for my attention. "It's disgusting. Can you come take care of it?"

The man has been sitting in the booth for an hour, nursing scrambled eggs and coffee, and he has done nothing but complain. When he arrived, I had four other tables with multiple people, and he still occupied sixty percent of my time. Now that the diner is empty, he is even more demanding.

I grab a handful of napkins from the dispenser at the bar and scoop the fly up. The man holds his hands over his plate to protect his cold eggs, as though I might drop the fly in them. Honestly, I'm tempted.

His hair is buzzed short on the sides with a bald patch in the center, and his hands are white and clean. Usually, people who have had to do manual labor their entire lives are more understanding of the working class. It's the people with perfectly clean fingernails who make all the demands and refuse to tip because of a chipped coffee mug.

But this man makes even those people look reasonable.

"My fork is dirty. Can I have another?"

In your eye? I think, surprising myself with a bit of fire. I haven't felt very fiery since I left Viktor in bed and Theo behind. Compared to leaving my son with my husband—it's still bizarre to imagine that I have a husband somewhere in the world—nothing else matters. It's difficult to get a reaction out of me these days, but this man is close.

I drop a new fork on his table with a grimace and turn back to the counter.

Before, I was working myself to the bone for Theo. I was working to care for him and provide for him, and his little smile was all the motivation I needed in the world to work hard. Now I am working so I can get on a bus and leave him behind. Which isn't nearly as motivating.

Finally, the diner empties out save for the man, and after taking him more napkins, a new glass of water, and a third fork, he wipes his mouth, stands up, and leaves. I thank him for coming in, but he doesn't respond, and when I go to bus his table, I realize he left me a single dime as a tip.

"Jackass," I grumble.

"Hey!" I turn and the man is standing behind me. For a second, I worry he overheard me, but then he points outside. "My tire is flat."

I consider chucking the dime at his forehead and telling him to use that to cover the damages, but he would probably call for my manager, and I don't want to have to go into his office and interrupt him from whatever he's watching on his computer. "I'm sorry but we aren't liable for that."

"You are if the pothole in your parking lot caused the flat. I drove through a swimming pool getting into that space and it wrecked my back tire."

I sigh. "There are no potholes in our lot."

"Don't you work here? You must know that there is a pothole out there and that you are lying to my face right now," he says, his face going red. "Come see for yourself."

I glance towards the kitchen door, wondering if anyone in the back has overheard this buffoon and will come help me get rid of him, but the door doesn't swing open, so I sigh and follow him outside.

It's dark out and the lot is nearly empty, so it doesn't take long for me to walk past his car and see the perfectly smooth gravel behind it. "See? No pothole. Now, you didn't tip me at all, so I'm definitely not being paid enough to deal with this shit. So have a good night and please, fuck off."

"Language, language."

I jump at the unexpected voice and turn to see that the driver's side window is rolled down.

And looking up at me is Fedor.

He's holding a gun. For some reason, I'm not very surprised. It's like, deep down, I've been expecting something like this ever since I walked away. That doesn't make seeing him any less terrifying.

"You have a mouth on you." He grins. "But if you don't mind, I'd like it if you would get in the car without making a huge racket. I'd hate to have to shoot you."

The silky-smooth way he says it lets me know he would not have any trouble at all shooting me. In fact, he might even enjoy it.

I look up and the customer has a gun, too. His is held close to his jacket so it isn't obvious, but I know that any chance at escape would be met with a bullet in the back.

The man nods for me to walk around the back of the car, and I pivot and obey his orders. My legs shake as I open the passenger door and drop down into the seat.

"Thanks, Kent," Fedor says.

The other man—Kent, apparently—closes the door and then walks across the lot to his car parked a few stalls down. As soon as his back is turned, I reach for the handle. Maybe if I get out and run straight for the road, his distraction will allow me to escape. Maybe I can—

"Child lock," Fedor says when I pull on the handle and it flaps open with no resistance. "Wonderful invention. Besides," he says, laying a hand on my thigh and squeezing. "You can't leave just yet. I've got big plans for you."

∼

I feel like my chest is caving in. I can't breathe. Can't think. Can't move.

Fedor pulls out of the diner parking lot without checking his rearview mirror, and he floors the gas pedal, propelling us through traffic as though this is a race.

Is it?

If Fedor has captured me at gunpoint, I have to assume things between him and his brother are not great. Is he running from Viktor and trying to use me as bait? If so, someone should tell him Viktor only cares about Theo, not me.

If Fedor found out about our marriage, he might think Viktor actually loves me. He might think I'm really his wife.

"He doesn't love me," I say softly, trying to think of some way out of this. "The marriage was—"

"A sham, I know. My brother did it to get back at me."

My heart lurches. Does he know about Theo? Why else would Viktor marry me to get back at Fedor? It doesn't make any sense.

"I know more than you think I do," Fedor says over the roar of his engine, answering a question I haven't dared voice. "But I'd like to know what you know. Or rather, what you think I know." He takes his hands off the steering wheel, letting the car swerve dangerously over the yellow lines so he can clap in excitement before grabbing the wheel again. "Yes, this will be fun. Tell me why I kidnapped you."

I lick my lips but it doesn't do any good. My tongue is dry and my lips are cracked, and I feel seconds away from crumbling and blowing away in the wind. "Because you're mad at Viktor, and you thought kidnapping his wife would be good revenge."

He tucks his upper lip in and wavers back and forth on the road. "That's part of it. But why am I mad at Viktor?"

I don't want to tell Fedor anything he doesn't already know. I don't want to make things worse for myself.

Suddenly, Fedor slams his hand on the steering wheel and punches the gas. We fly around one car, cutting off a truck in the other lane. Angry honks rise up around us, and I grip the seat and squeeze my eyes closed. "Answer me!"

"Because he married me without telling you."

"That's weak, Molly," he says. "*Why?*"

"Because he didn't tell you about his son." I can't even bring myself to say Theo's name in front of Fedor.

"Ah yes, Theo." He smiles. "That is part of it, but you are still keeping your little secrets."

He knows everything. I can see it in the glimmer in his green eyes. Fedor knows everything, and he's delighting in this little game.

So, I decide to end it. I fold.

"Because Theo is your son, and Viktor protected both of us and lied to you about it."

The car slows down to a normal speed and Fedor waggles his finger like he's ringing a bell. "Ding, ding, ding!"

"What do you want?" I glare at him, relieved in a way that I can loathe him openly now. "I'm not going to testify. I was never going to. I just want you to leave me alone."

"This isn't about you," he says with a wicked laugh. "This is about Viktor."

"I have nothing to do with Viktor. He doesn't care about me. The marriage was just a scam to protect Theo. Viktor didn't want you—"

"To know my own son," Fedor finishes, his lip curling up in anger. "My brother wanted to keep my son from me. And more than that, he protected the whore who hid him from me."

My anger flares at the insult. "You didn't deserve to know Theo after what you did to me."

Fedor looks over, his eyebrows dancing. "You don't even remember what I did to you."

My stomach flips, and I look away. I hate that I've let him win this round, but if I maintained eye contact, I might have thrown up. Or yanked the wheel and killed us both in a wreck. It would almost be worth it to wipe Fedor from the planet.

"I recognized you the second I walked into his apartment that day. Did you know that?"

I didn't. Fedor acted the part perfectly. The memory of his hand on my waist, of the way he teased me and showed interest in me, pretending I was nothing more than a maid makes me feel dirty. He knew the entire time.

"Why didn't you say anything?"

"Because I wanted to see what my brother's intentions were. I wanted to know why he had locked my witness and my child away. I wanted to know what he had planned for you."

"Why would that change anything?"

Fedor flicks his tongue over his bottom lip. "Viktor has always looked out for me, protected me. When I saw you there, I thought maybe it was part of a plan he wasn't telling me about. That maybe he was going to dispose of you and keep me in the dark to protect me."

To protect him? The idea is laughable. What does Fedor need protecting from? Certainly not his feelings. I'm not sure he has any. Monsters usually don't.

"But he wasn't protecting me," he says, shaking his head. For a moment, he's quiet. Lost in thought. With a few fast blinks, he breaks out of it and sighs theatrically. "This is about more than you and Theo, though. This is about family and loyalty, two things my brother knows nothing about."

"Your brother did all of this to protect Theo—his family," I argue.

"I'm his family!" Fedor screams. "I've been his family for much longer, and he chose the two of you over me. But the final straw was him debating whether I was worth fighting for."

Fedor rolls his shoulders and it doesn't even seem like his attention is on me anymore. He is rambling, going on about choosing between family and a war, and he's talking so fast I can barely keep up.

"My brother's loyalty is flagging, so I'm going to show him what it means to turn on family. I'm going to show him what happens when you forget your blood."

"What does that mean?" I fold my hands in my lap, trying to hide the shaking.

Fedor looks over at me, a sick kind of hunger in his eyes. "First, I'm going to do what my brother should have done with you."

Kill me. That part of his plan is so obvious it doesn't even scare me. I simply nod, accepting the inevitable.

"And then?"

"Then," he says, pressing harder on the gas to make it through a yellow light and then swerving to change lanes and maneuver around a bus, "I'm going to claim the son who was stolen from me and raise him as my own. If my family can turn its back on me, I'll make my own."

The thought of my son being raised by this monster terrifies me far more than death. "Theo is innocent. He didn't do anything. Leave him alone."

Suddenly, Fedor reaches across the seat and strokes his rough hand across my cheek. I pull away but the car is too small to separate us, and he grips my chin roughly.

"I would never leave our son alone, Molly. He'll always be cared for. By me and the Bratva." He drops my face and grabs hold of the gun in his lap, driving with only one hand. "I'll raise him to understand loyalty. Don't you worry."

24

VIKTOR

The war has started, and Fedor is nowhere to be seen.

I've declared war in Fedor's name only because I have to display a united front. I can't let on that my brother is out of control, that I'm not powerful enough to keep my men in line. Besides, the Mazzeo consiglieres disrespected Fedor by calling him crazy. They didn't deserve to die for it, but I also can't let that kind of behavior slide. Not when my own men are doubting me more than ever.

Still, I initially expect Mario Mazzeo to come back with a counteroffer. His son has always been the more hotheaded of the two, and I expect Mario to balance Rio out. He has to know they don't have the manpower to overcome my Bratva. He has to know they will lose this war.

Maybe he does, but that doesn't change the fact that Rio Mazzeo has now attacked our office with every man he has, and we are now in a gunfight for our lives.

I call Fedor the moment the shooting starts. With his help, we can sandwich the Mazzeos between us and end this war before it can really even begin. Most of the men are inside the office with me, still reeling and strategizing for the possibility of the oncoming war, but Fedor could command the others on the outside and attack from both sides. But he doesn't answer my calls or my texts.

Petr holds the back entrance of the office with a few of the enforcers while a second team keeps the front doors clear. We are surrounded, but as long as they don't make it inside, I know we have the upper hand.

If worst comes to worst, we can barricade the basement, but that would feel an awful lot like defeat and it is my last option.

I decide to move to the second floor to assess the situation from above, trying to see where the weak points in the Mazzeo line are, but as soon as I reach the bottom of the stairs, there is a huge commotion from the back of the office.

The entire building shakes and dust falls from the ceiling.

"Bomb!" someone shouts from behind me, coughing as he stumbles forward. "We're breached."

I turn and find Petr stumbling out of a haze of smoke. He falls to his knees and then pushes himself to all fours, crawling out of the smoke. There is blood on his shirt, and I don't know if it's his or someone else's.

"Rio blew the back wall out," Petr says, grabbing my shoulder. "You have to go."

It's Petr's job to look out for me. To protect me. But I can't run away from this fight. If I do, it will only prove what many of my men already think of me—that I don't have their best interests at heart.

Maybe I don't.

I should have kicked Fedor out of the Bratva the moment he began acting out. I convinced myself I could help him though. I lied to myself and to Petr and everyone else and said that he just needed time to adjust.

But Fedor doesn't need time. He needs a fucking straitjacket.

He will always be my baby brother, but that doesn't mean I can continue to protect him forever. At some point, he has to figure his shit out on his own, and I have to do what is best for my men.

He is out of control, and now I've lost men and an entire wall of my office because of him.

"No," I say, grabbing Petr and moving him to the stairwell. "Stay here. I have to end this."

Petr might argue, but I run into the thick of the smoke and don't hear what he says. He also might have just collapsed back on the stairs and let me go. He knows better than anyone that my men will never forgive me if I sit back and let them die for Fedor.

The smoke is thick and dust is falling from the ceiling like rain. It feels like the apocalypse, but in the distance, I can hear a train whistle.

Beyond these walls, the world is still carrying on as though nothing has changed. It is a morbid kind of comfort as I pick my way through rubble and body parts, moving constantly towards the yellow glow of the streetlights.

The office is on the far edge of town in an industrial district that is always vacant this time of night. If anyone is close enough to hear the commotion, they'll think it's the sound of machinery or trucks being loaded. They won't pay us any mind, so I can't bank on the cops rushing in and scaring off Rio and his men.

I have to end this myself.

As soon as I get through enough of the smoke and dust to see a lone remaining window next to a gaping hole in the wall, I drop to my knees and crawl through glass and shards of metal to look through the window. I want to have a better idea of what I'm getting myself into before I charge out there and demand to talk to Rio.

There are fewer men than I would have thought. The Mazzeos have a smaller force than ours, but still formidable. It looks like they're operating with less than half of their normal men. Perhaps Mario did try to persuade his son not to fight but failed to control him the way I failed to control Fedor. If that's true, there's a chance I can end this without any more lives being lost.

My men inside have scrambled away from the wreckage of the wall. They listened to Petr's cries and retreated to take shelter somewhere else. So, with the absence of bullets raining down on them, I see Rio and a few of his men move from behind a car and start advancing on the building.

Rio lets his men move in front of him, clearing the way and checking that the coast is clear.

He's a coward. And it will work to my advantage.

I pull my gun from my waistband, make sure it's loaded, and watch as the soldiers grow closer to the hole in the wall.

The second they're out of my sight and only a few steps from moving inside the building, I catapult myself up and over the blown-out window.

I land hard on my left knee, but there isn't any time to recover. I push through the pain and stay low as I run the ten steps to where Rio is hiding behind his soldiers. He doesn't even turn to inspect the noise until I'm a foot behind him, my gun aimed at his head.

"What the—" he starts, but the words die in his mouth as I wrap an arm around his neck and press the muzzle of my gun to his temple.

His soldiers spin around, guns raised, but when they see the precarious situation their leader is in, they lower their weapons, looking around nervously.

"End this," I growl in his ear. "Call it off and let's talk."

Rio is pinned to my chest, but he turns his head as much as he can and spits. It misses me by a wide margin, but the move is still disrespectful, and I know there will be no negotiating with him.

So, I plow my knee into the back of his legs and force him to the ground, never lowering my weapon. I could kill him now. I could blow out his brains and claim this war as a victory, but it would spiral into more fighting and death. And for what? In the name of Fedor's short fuse.

No, I've always been the rational one. The thoughtful one. And that won't change now.

I call out for my men. Several of them move through the fog, guns raised, and force Rio's soldiers to drop their weapons. They comply.

"This fight is over." I send one of my men and one of Rio's men to spread the word. Then, I send for Petr.

He's injured and limping, but okay. His color has returned.

"Call Mario," I command. "Get him here now."

"You don't need to talk to my father," Rio argues. "Talk to me."

I press my foot into his spine and repeat the command. "We'll wait for the don of the Mazzeo family. In the meantime, if anyone fires another shot, they'll be killed on sight. And only I get to kill Rio."

I will kill him if it comes to that. I'll kill them all to save my men and myself. But not if I don't have to.

*

No one has said a word.

"We're all here because of your fucking brother," Rio spits after several minutes of tense silence.

"I've just let you move to a sitting position. Do you want to lie flat on your stomach again?" I ask.

Rio's shoulders tense, and he bristles at my show of power.

Rio hates Fedor, and I think it's because they're so much alike. Rio has a hot head and acts on instinct. Though, we both know he's right. Fedor started this. We wouldn't be here if it hadn't been for him.

"I don't know why my father insists on making nice with you," Rio continues. "Do you know our fathers wanted to try and convince you to marry my sister? They thought it would make a lasting alliance between our families."

"Yes," I said. "Unfortunately, it's too late for that. I'm a married man."

I feel married, even if I only spent one night with my "wife." Besides, I don't care about any other women right now. Maybe when this mess is over, I can focus on finding her.

Rio seems confused by my admission, but before the conversation can go any further, I hear several car doors slam shut at the front of the building. Then, figures round the corner.

Mario arrives like a president to a press event. He walks around the side of the building with four guards forming a square around him, each one armed and making up a corner of his security detail. I have no doubt they would throw themselves in front of him to save his life in an instant. Hopefully, that won't be necessary.

When he sees his son on the ground, Mario's mouth tightens into a frown. Then, it eases, and he focuses on me and the gun I have trained on his heir.

"I think we've had a misunderstanding," he says.

"I agree."

Mario glares down at his son one last time and then smiles at me. "I think we can all get rid of our weapons, right? No one else needs to die tonight."

I hesitate for only a second before I lower my weapon and step back.

Mario's security detail does the same and the word is spread that all soldiers are to fully stand down until further notice.

As soon as he's no longer under my gun, Rio jumps to his feet, shakes the dirt off his pants, and paces away with his chest puffed out. Mario rolls his eyes.

"I didn't want this fight," he admits softly. "I thought my son would handle the discussions on my behalf, but it seems he was incapable of communicating with words."

His admission is bold. It reveals his weakness, and I feel it's only right to repay him with one of my own. "My brother also chooses his weapon over his words. I'm sorry for the consiglieres you lost."

Mario shrugs. "It happens. Now, what is this about you taking a wife?"

I frown, wondering if the old man somehow overheard what I said to his son. "I have my own sources of information, and I don't tell my son everything."

"Your sources are correct. I took a wife."

"Congratulations," Mario says, though it doesn't feel genuine. "You know, I hoped you would be a good match for my daughter Maria. She requires a strong husband with a firm hand."

"You will have to find another firm hand, I'm afraid."

"Ah well," he sighs. "I suppose we will have to come to peace through different means."

Talking to Mario feels like talking to a sane person after a year of being trapped in an asylum. He doesn't want to fight. He doesn't want death. He wants peace and to be left alone.

I can relate.

"Your men disrespected my brother on contested territory. So, why not start there? The territory where the disagreement occurred belongs to my Bratva."

Mario's jaw tightens. "That would be fair except that your brother gunned down two of my men there. I don't think that kind of behavior should be rewarded."

"And it won't be," I assure him. "Fedor will be striped of responsibilities until he has earned back my trust. Another outburst, however, will result in being exiled from the Bratva."

Mario raises a brow. "You'd throw out your own family? Ruthless."

"When I need to be." It's a threat of sorts. A reminder that though we're being civil now, I am not afraid to do what needs to be done.

"That's a good start, but it's still not enough," Mario says. "If we give up that territory, we should get something in return. Perhaps one of your smaller stash houses?"

I cross my arms. "My men won't like that arrangement."

"Do you answer to your men or do they answer to you?" Mario asks.

I should fire a warning shot just for Mario's suggestion that I take orders from my own men, but I don't. Because it's not worth riling the still-simmering soldiers nearby who are eager to gun one another down. My actions would have a ripple effect that could be deadly.

"Partial control of the Twin Chandeliers," I suggest. "You're free to move product through there as you like and use the motel as a front. For the time being."

"That's not very concrete."

"It's temporary," I say. "Terms can be outlined later in an official meeting."

Mario is thinking, but I know he will take the deal. It's the best he can expect after his son blew a hole in my office building.

"Fine," he says after a long pause. "It will do ... for now."

Rio groans in the background and begins mumbling under his breath, but before I can catch what he's saying, an engine roars to life nearby. We all turn towards the sound and watch as a black car with deeply tinted windows rolls into the lot.

Mario's guards square up around him again, and he backs away from the car. I lift my gun again just as the driver's side door opens, and Fedor steps out.

Of course he shows up for *his* war after it's over.

As I watch him walk around the front of the car, I'm formulating the best thing to say to him—something that will both cow him and show Mario that I'm serious about discipling my out of control brother. But all thought flies out of my head as he opens the passenger door and Molly steps out, hands raised.

For one second, there's blinding relief.

She's here. She's alive. She's come back.

Then Fedor presses a gun to her head.

My vision goes red.

25

MOLLY

Theo isn't here.

As soon as I step out of the car, I scan the lot in search of my son, and am grateful he won't be here to see his mother shot and killed in front of him.

Then I see Viktor.

He looks shocked to see me. His mouth falls open, and he blinks at me like I just descended from the sky on a winged horse.

Then Fedor steps up behind me, and Viktor's eyes narrow.

"What is this, brother?" Viktor asks. His words are calm, but his voice shakes with anger. "What are you doing with my wife?"

"The same thing you're doing with my son," he says. "Holding a hostage."

Viktor's face goes white, and I know he understands what this means. Fedor knows everything. He knows about me and Theo. The game is up.

"You don't need to do this," Viktor says, stepping away from the armed men gathered to his right. I don't recognize any of them, but the old man nearby is being guarded like he's someone important. "You don't really want a child anyway. Be honest. I did you a favor. I took that responsibility for you."

"Don't act like you're a saint!" Fedor shakes with rage, and I squeeze my eyes shut, waiting for his hand to clench a bit too hard on the trigger. Waiting for the bullet to rocket through my brain and end everything for me.

Fedor takes a deep breath and then laughs, though it's devoid of humor. "You didn't keep Theo because you thought it was best for me. You thought it was best for you. A chance to settle down and be the family man you always wanted to be. Because, be honest, you've never been much of a don."

Viktor's spine straightens, and his jaw clenches. "You think you could have done better? Shooting any man who looks sideways at you and starting wars? That isn't how a leader operates."

"I had to do those things because you made the Kornilovs weak!" Fedor shouts back. "No one would have ever looked at me sideways if you hadn't let our good name fall in the dirt. And now, to add insult to injury, you marry my sloppy seconds and try to adopt my son?"

"She isn't your anything," Viktor growls. "What you did to her was wrong, and I, like always, cleaned up your mess."

The old man next to Viktor holds up his hands. "This is clearly a family matter that we have no part in. I think it would be best if we left and—"

"No," Fedor says suddenly, turning me in front of him like a human shield and facing the older man. As he does, another man joins the fray. He looks like the younger version of the other man, and I assume they are father and son. Another crime family by the looks of it. "I have business with you too. This isn't over." He laughs, and he sounds entirely unhinged. "I didn't expect you all to be in the same place, but this could really work out in my favor. Two birds, one stone and all that, you know?"

The older man glances at his son, looking uncertain, but Viktor claims control of the situation, stepping forward and holding his gun out to the side in a half surrender.

"Let Molly go," he says softly. "Please, Fedor. Just let her go, and we'll talk. We can fix all of this."

"I am fixing it. You, brother, are the one who broke it. In fact, I don't think you deserve the title of brother. Not after the way you've treated me."

"I went to war for you!" Viktor roars.

"Barely!"

Fedor's voice is so loud that my ear rings, and I try to pull away from him, but he tightens his arm around my neck, making it harder to breathe. "You had to think about it and that, on top of every other way you've betrayed me, is why we are here in this mess. Because you are a disloyal piece of shit who would rather dive headfirst into my secondhand pussy than support your own brother."

Viktor lifts his gun and surges forward several steps. His jaw is clenched tight. "Don't you dare disrespect my wife."

"See?" Fedor says, using his gun to gesture to everyone. "He is proving my point. My brother is loyal to his woman over his own blood, which is why his men are turning away from him."

Viktor's expression hardens. "They're turning away from me for not letting you rot away in prison. You ruin everything you touch. I'm done defending you."

Fedor snorts derisively. "That so? Then how do I have twenty Kornilov men ready and willing to leave your Bratva and join me in starting anew?"

I can see the disbelief in Viktor's face, and my heart breaks for him. I want to push away from Fedor and comfort him, which is a strange sensation in itself, given everything. I ran away from this man. Why do I only want to run toward him now?

Fedor turns back to the other don and his son. "We can strike a deal. We can unite and crush what is left of my brother's little family and rule this city like kings. I know that's what you've always wanted, Rio."

I look at Viktor again, waiting for him to shut this down. Waiting for him to fight, but he's staring at me, blinking. He looks like a man lost at sea, searching for the shore, and I want to open my arms and be his safe place to land.

It's the first time I realize the depth of my affection for him.

I want to protect Viktor. For weeks now, he has been trying to protect me and Theo, but somehow, I have grown to want to do the same for him.

His brother is a loose cannon and a danger, and I wish I could fix everything and let him keep what little bit of his family he has left, but I can't. And it breaks my heart.

"Viktor," I say softly.

Fedor tightens his hold on me, but the word has its hoped effect. Viktor flinches and then turns towards the men standing next to him.

"You admitted yourself, Rio, that we're all here because of Fedor," he says. "Fedor is the reason your men are dead and the reason we had to fight at all. You can't trust him."

Rio glares at Viktor and then turns to his father. They share a look that I can't decipher from this far away, and Fedor growls in frustration.

"He's crazy!" I yell, pulling away from Fedor as hard and fast as I can. If I die, I'm going to die doing my best to ruin Fedor's plans. "You can't trust him. He's delusional, and he'll turn on you just like he's turning on his brother."

Fedor curses and yanks me back, pressing the gun even harder against my temple. Hard enough that I cry out.

"If you hurt her, I swear to God, Fedor, I'll kill you myself!" Viktor shouts.

Everything is starting to dissolve, and I'm waiting for the first gunshot to go off. Because surely it will. Tensions are too high and there are too many weapons for someone not to end up dead. I simply hope it's me instead of Viktor.

The thought surprises me, but I realize it isn't entirely selfless. I left Theo with Viktor because I thought it was where he would be safest, and I still think that's true. If Viktor is killed, and I survive this, it will mean that Fedor escaped. And if Fedor is free, my son and I will never be safe. Viktor has to survive for Theo to have a future.

Fedor is struggling with me and still trying to talk to the don and his son, and I realize that he doesn't have enough arms or the attention span to do it all at once. Viktor is moving towards us, and Fedor hardly notices.

"He's a rapist," I scream, hoping my fight will distract Fedor long enough for Viktor to be able to help without getting me killed. I struggle against his hold, twisting towards the don and his son and away from Viktor. "Fedor is a rapist and a monster. You don't want to ally with him."

The two men look uncomfortable, but they have the good sense to stay quiet. Siding with either brother at this point could be a death sentence if the other comes out victorious.

Fedor digs his fingernails into my arm, and I cry out. "Stay put. I'm not done with you."

Goosebumps sprout along my neck and back, and I twist again, turning Fedor even more away from Viktor.

"You can barely control a single girl. How can you control the city?" Rio asks.

"I can't," Fedor says. "But *we* can. Together. I have information about the Bratva you would kill for. Except now, you don't have to. I'll give it to you for the price of your loyalty. For the price of partnering with me and my men."

Rio seems to be tossing the idea around in his mind, and his father is concerningly quiet. If they make a decision before Viktor can get to me, they may sic their men on Viktor and end his attempts to save me. And Viktor is still only able to creep forward. Any faster, and he will draw Fedor's attention.

I realize all at once that I don't have time to wait and be rescued. I have to do it myself.

"With my knowledge and your experience, we will own the game," Fedor says, his words dripping with passion and promise. I have no doubt he means every word he's saying. Though, based on what I've seen of him, he could change his mind within a minute. Fedor can't be trusted.

"What of Maria?" the older man says. "Would you want to take her as a wife to secure the connection or—"

Rio turns on his father, eyes ablaze, while Fedor bobs his head back and forth, considering it. I recognize it as my opportunity. Everyone is distracted.

So, with as much strength as I can muster, I twist in Fedor's arms and bring my knee to his groin the same way I did to Viktor the night I awoke to find Theo missing from the hotel room.

Fedor has the upper hand because of the gun, but I've also caught him off guard. He crumples immediately, momentarily forgetting the weapon in his hand, and I use the precious seconds I have to wrestle out of his hold and run towards Viktor.

I'm halfway across the parking lot when Rio breaks away from his father and moves towards me. The guards around him surge forward as well, following their leader's unspoken order, and Viktor spins and shoots. I can't tell if he hit his target or if he even had one, rather shooting blindly. The only thing I can think about is reaching him.

As soon as I reach Viktor, he shoves me behind him and moves backwards towards the building. He pushes me through a hole in the wall and then rushes back into the parking lot.

I call after him, but I don't follow. I don't have a weapon, and I know I would only be a distraction if I went with him. If he's going to fight his way out of this when the two men—Rio, at least—have decided to partner with Fedor, then he can't have a single distraction.

Shots are ringing out like crazy, and I stay hidden behind the wall, hoping and praying Viktor is safe. Though I don't see how he can escape unscathed.

I feel like I've only been hidden for a few seconds, but when I look back out at the parking lot, bodies litter the ground. Most of the guards for the other crime family are dead, and the older man has moved away from the bulk of the fighting. He has his gun pulled, but even in the gloom of the evening, I can see his hand is shaking. Really, this is between Rio, Viktor, and Fedor.

Viktor is outnumbered and now that there aren't so many other variables, I feel like I could help him. I look around for a weapon and see a bent metal pipe lying amongst the rubble from the fallen wall. I move on my hands and knees across the ground to grab it. As soon as my hand wraps around it, a shot rings out and a cloud of dust rises from the ground. I look over and see Fedor with his gun aimed at me.

I scramble back to my hiding spot, but not before Viktor roars in anger and charges at his brother.

Fedor fires off more shots, but he looks frantic as he scrambles backwards.

I know Viktor can take Fedor. He is much larger than his younger brother and more skilled, but there is Rio to worry about. He is more hesitant to shoot than Fedor, but I can see the hatred he harbors for Viktor in his eyes. I can't leave Viktor with his back unprotected.

So, I grip the pipe in my hands and charge out of my hiding spot.

I'm literally bringing a stick to a gunfight, but I have to do something.

Rio is so focused on where Fedor and Viktor are wrestling on the ground, no doubt trying to find an opening where he can shoot Viktor without also hitting Fedor, that he doesn't see me coming. I lift the pipe over my head, prepared to crush his skull with it, the consequences of killing a high-ranking mafia member be damned—

A long, loud horn breaks through the chaos.

Rio looks up for the source of the noise and sees me moving towards him. He jumps back. Even Fedor and Viktor stop their fighting.

Finally, a car moves around the edge of the building, rolling to a stop, and a man climbs out.

He should be shot on sight with how many men with guns there are in the area, but everyone is too stunned to do anything.

The man is middle-aged with a round middle, and he walks towards the scene like a frustrated parent sent to break up the kids. Then, suddenly, he pulls a gun from his hip and shoots at Rio. A split second later, he ducks behind the open door of his car as retaliatory shots are fired his way. He moves deftly for a man his size.

Rio yelps in surprise and scurries away from Viktor and Fedor, who have resumed fighting, this time with Viktor having the clear upper hand.

Whoever this new man is, he's clearly on our side.

With Rio in flight, the newcomer turns his attention to the brothers. He yells something to Viktor, and Viktor rolls off Fedor and stands up, crouched with his gun held in front of him.

Fedor reaches for something on the ground that I can't see and then flings an arm over his body, aiming wildly. But before he can, Viktor shoots.

Everything seems to be happening in slow motion and all at once. A gun falls from Fedor's hand and then he scrambles upright and runs away from the fighting. I can see blood flowing down Fedor's side, and I hope the wound is enough to kill him. I want him to drop to his knees in the parking lot, too weak to continue.

But he doesn't. He just disappears into the darkness beyond the parking lot.

Viktor turns to find me, his eyes searching, and I drop the pipe and run to him. I'm halfway across the lot when I notice the stain on his shirt. Then he drops to his knees.

"No," I breathe, slowing for only a second before speeding up.

Viktor tries to get back up, but he's wobbling. I reach him just before he collapses on the ground. We sink down to the pavement together as the older man pulls out his phone and makes a frantic call.

"It's okay," I whisper, smoothing back Viktor's sweaty hair. "It will all be okay."

26

MOLLY

I poke my head into Theo's nursery on my way downstairs. He is lying sideways in his bed, his legs tucked underneath him, butt high in the air. I smile and pull the door closed quietly.

Viktor keeps reminding me that the house is safe. Even though Fedor knows about Theo, and he has made his intentions regarding his son very clear, I don't need to worry about Theo's safety when he's inside this house.

Yet, my personal guard hasn't left the apartment in days.

I knew Viktor had someone keeping an eye on me even when he claimed he didn't, and I was proven right when that man came rolling into the parking lot that night. Now, I know his name is George and he's a surprisingly quiet and gentle man.

George is in the kitchen now with the newspaper and a steaming mug of coffee when I walk in. He tips his head to me and smiles, but doesn't let his eyes linger. He is nervous around me, even though I feel like I should be the one nervous around him. He was the one watching me.

"Viktor insists he's well enough to shower and work, but he can't make his own sandwiches," I tease as I pull out deli meat and cheese from the fridge. The chef made a week's worth of meals like normal, but Viktor insists the food tastes better when I make it. As soon as he's well again, I'll stop indulging him. But until then, I spread mustard on the bread and stack it high with meat.

"Thank God he had on the bulletproof vest," George says, folding his paper. "It could have been so much worse."

Even with the vest on, the impact of the bullets at such close range shattered a few of his ribs. His entire midsection is covered in bright purple and green bruises. It will be a while before he's at one hundred percent.

"Thank God you arrived when you did." It's the closest I've come to thanking George for what he did that day. I've been so busy tending to Viktor that I never found the time.

George shrugs. "He saved my life once."

I drop the butter knife in the sink and turn to him.

A small smile pulls at George's lips. "Like you, I was once a witness to Fedor's crimes. Viktor was meant to kill me, but he spared me instead."

My eyes widen in surprise.

"You thought you were his only exception?" George asks with a smile. "Believe me, I'm sure you're his favorite, but Viktor has extended his mercy to more people than even the two of us know, I'm sure. He is a good man, and I'm glad to work for him."

When I make it back upstairs with his sandwich, Viktor is out of bed and standing in front of the tall mirror in his closet, poking at his side.

"Sit your ass down!" I command, leaving no room for argument.

"How are you supposed to heal if you keep poking at your wound like a child picking a scab?"

Viktor wrinkles his nose and then wags his brows at the large sandwich I'm carrying. "Is that for me?"

"Only if you promise to be good," I say, narrowing my eyes.

His mouth pulls into a wicked smile. "Then I suppose I'll starve."

I roll my eyes and hand him the plate. He eats the entire thing in five bites, and I'm glad to see his appetite is back. When he was being looked at by the Bratva doctor, even as I was being assured his wounds would heal, I couldn't stop imagining him dying. I couldn't stop picturing what would happen if Viktor succumbed to his internal injuries and left me alone. Left Theo alone.

Fedor would come for us. He would kill me and take Theo and raise him to be a vicious, evil man.

And Viktor would be gone.

I watch him wipe his mouth and lay the plate on the bed next to him, shocked—not for the first time or the last—at the force of my feelings for him. Seeing him collapse in the parking lot has changed things for me in ways I am still grappling with.

I may have been forced into marrying Viktor, but I don't wish to be separated from him. Not now. Maybe not ever.

"How is Fedor?" I ask, distracting myself from the flurry of new emotions swirling in my chest.

Viktor's face falls, his eyes going dark. "Unconscious but guarded. If he wakes up, I'll know."

"What are your men going to do with him when he wakes up?" I ask.

Viktor is silent for a long time before he lies back on his pillows and sighs. "What needs to be done."

While he was on higher doses of pain medication, Viktor opened up to me. He was honest about his feelings towards Fedor.

He is conflicted, and I still see that, even if he's holding back now. Fedor is his brother, but Viktor has had to come to terms with the fact that his brother is irredeemable. His entire life has been spent saving Fedor, but finally, Fedor has proven himself to be beyond saving. The only thing Viktor can do now is mitigate the damage Fedor can cause and move on without him.

∽

A week after the fight, Viktor is well enough to leave the apartment, and he asks me to come with him.

I don't ask where we're going because I don't really care. Even if it makes me a fool, I trust Viktor. I trust that he won't hurt me.

We drive into the pink and orange of the sunset until we're on the outskirts of town. The buildings and industry give way to more open space, and I think we might be leaving the city altogether, when suddenly, Viktor pulls off on a narrow two-lane road into a park.

I can't imagine Viktor taking me on a walk through the park, but it's the only thing I can imagine until I see the metal archway that spans the road and the stone blips spread across the ground.

"The cemetery?" I ask.

He nods. "I have to do something, and I want you to come with me."

He opens my door for me, even though he's the one still recovering from wounds, and holds my hand as we walk across dry, crunchy grass to reach one large headstone spread across two graves.

I see George sitting in his car a long way off, sticking close enough to intervene should anything happen but giving Viktor and I space.

"Your parents," I say. Viktor doesn't respond because Kornilov is carved in large letters across the headstone. It's obvious. Then, I notice the dates. "They died on the same day?"

"They were killed. It is a brutal world I have chosen for myself."

I hold my breath. I don't know what to say.

"I'm sorry," Viktor says softly, and it takes me a moment to realize he isn't talking to me, but to them.

I move to pull away and give him space, but he holds my hand even more tightly and continues, his eyes never leaving the headstone.

"It was my duty to look after Fedor, and I tried. I really tried." His voice doesn't break or waver, but I can still hear the subtle changes in it. The sincerity and the sorrow. "But I can't anymore. I have a family of my own to protect now, and as much as I will always love Fedor, he isn't my top priority anymore. He can't be."

My heart races at his meaning.

He is talking about me and Theo. His family.

I wrap an arm around his elbow and tuck myself into his side, and Viktor responds by turning and kissing the top of my head. It's a tender moment I never would have expected, but now will never trade for anything in the world.

Viktor holds my hand the entire way home, glancing over occasionally to give me a nervous smile. I know he worries I'll leave again—maybe it's a fear he'll have for a long time. But I'm not going anywhere.

He sends George away to rest and leads me into the apartment and upstairs, one hand firmly pressed to my lower back.

I know where we're headed, and I do nothing to stop him.

Theo is out with the nanny, the house is empty, and it has been a long time. A couple weeks, almost. I've ached to be with him again, even though I tried to hide it.

He keeps the lights out as he leads me to his bedroom. To the place where we consummated our marriage and have been sleeping together for the last week. My phone charger is plugged in on the left side and my pajamas are folded in the top drawer ... and it seems easier to just stay here beside him than to move back to my own room.

As soon as the door is closed, I turn to him and wrap my arms around his neck. "You're still healing."

"I've heard love is the best medicine," he whispers, gripping my waist in his strong hands.

I freeze. He's never used that word before. I'm oddly worried I'll say the wrong thing and ruin the moment, so I say something more lighthearted instead. "That isn't what that phrase means."

He smiles and pushes me towards the bed. "I'm not sure we'll know until we try."

Viktor's arms are thick and strong as they wrap around my waist, and I fall back onto the mattress, comforted by the weight of him over me.

The last time we were together like this, I was angry. Angry with my circumstances and my life, angry with Viktor for forcing me into yet another situation I couldn't control. But more than anything, I was angry with myself for wanting him despite it all.

Part of that anger still lingers.

How can I want a man who has forced me to become his wife?

"Molly," he whispers.

I study his blue eyes and the creases in his forehead. "What? What's wrong?"

Viktor sighs and rolls off me, sitting on the edge of the bed. "I have to tell you something, and I'm not sure how you'll react."

My heart surges into my throat, blocking all air. "Tell me," I rasp.

He looks at me out of the corner of his eye. "Will you promise not to leave?"

"No." My answer is immediate and honest. If I've learned anything over the last four years, it's that even when you think you can trust someone, you have to be ready and willing to depend fully on yourself. And if Viktor told me something horrible, I would run. I'd leave and do what I had to do for myself and Theo. Because I'm never leaving my son again.

His mouth pulls up in a smirk. "I didn't think so."

"Tell me," I say, laying a hand on his shoulder. I curl my fingers, trying to hide their trembling.

He takes a deep breath, his shoulders rising and falling. Then he spits it out in a rush. "You're not really my wife."

I pull my hand back and stare at him, eyes wide. "What?"

He turns towards me, one leg folded on the bed. "The justice of the peace was real, but the papers we signed were fake. It was all fake. Just a show. I needed you to believe we were married so you would understand the lengths I would go to protect you. And so anyone paying close enough attention would understand those lengths as well."

My ring finger is still bare. We didn't exchange rings at the ceremony, but I still stare down at my hand as though it looks different all of a sudden. "I'm not your wife."

He shakes his head. "It was just a trick. A plan to try and—"

"Manipulate me," I say quietly.

His face falls. "No. I didn't want to force anything on you permanently. When everything calmed down, and we'd figured things out, I was going to tell you and let you make a decision. I just needed to keep you safe until Fedor moved on and forgot about you, but—"

"He knew the whole time," I say, cutting him off.

Viktor nods. "He played us both."

Somehow, I'm not as upset about this as I should be. I reach out and smooth a hand down his arm. I hate the way his brother's betrayal has affected him. Fedor was the only family Viktor had in the world, and now he's gone.

Except, no.

I rise up on my knees and crawl towards him, leaning against his arm. "Did you mean what you said today?"

"When?"

"About your family," I say softly. "About having a family of your own now."

It might be my imagination, but I think I notice his cheeks going pink. He nods. "I did. Every word."

I curl my finger under his chin and tip his face to mine. When I lean down, he meets me halfway, our lips pressing together.

Then, before I can even register that I initiated the contact, Viktor's arm is around my waist, and I am once again on the bed with his weight over me.

He smooths his hands down my waist and over my hips. He grabs the outsides of my thighs and works his way down my body, lifting my shirt to plant kisses to my stomach and lower still.

I lift my hips to help him remove my jeans and panties, and when he parts my legs and kisses his way towards my center, I grip his soft hair and open even wider for him.

His tongue is forceful and skilled, and my entire body shakes with pleasure as he has his way with me, licking sensuous circles across my most sensitive parts. But just before I tip over the edge, I tug on his hair. Viktor could do as he pleases. He could force me down and take what he wants. He could stay down there all day, knowing I'd be helpless to stop him. Yet, he yields to me.

I drag Viktor back up the length of my body, bringing his face to mine, and I swirl my tongue in his mouth, tasting myself on his lips.

When we first walked up the stairs, I thought our interaction would be sweet and slow, but I don't mind the frenzied act it has become.

Viktor pushes his pants down just far enough to free himself and then position his length at my opening. I lift my hips to take him in, and he pulls away, flicking his eyebrow up in amusement when I growl with impatience. I curl my legs around his lower back, hooking him against me, and his amusement fades to need. To desire.

He dives into me in one pulse and his pace never wavers. It is domineering and crushing, and I wonder if my cries of pleasure can be heard by the neighbors.

It doesn't take long for my body to be ready, for Viktor to get me back to the pinnacle of pleasure. I try to hold it off, to stay with him as long as I can, but when he nips at my earlobe with his teeth and whispers for me to surrender to him, I have no choice.

Viktor follows a second later, screwing his face up in beautiful torment.

When we finish, I lay my head on his chest and breathe in the woodsy, salty scent of him.

I'm angry with Viktor for lying to me. I'm angry with him for manipulating me rather than telling me the truth. Perhaps I always will be. Perhaps anger will be my default emotion with him. That might be the price I pay for being with this strong, stubborn, protective man.

He curls his arm around me and kisses the top of my head, sighing in contentment.

If it is, it seems like a fair price to pay.

27

VIKTOR

Molly never says it out loud, but I sense she's disappointed that our marriage was fake.

I'm not foolish enough to ever speak the idea out loud to her. She would never admit to it, but I catch her looking at her ring finger with a longing kind of look on her face more than once. And when I play with Theo on the living room floor after dinner, she smiles at us, but when I catch her eye, she looks away and knits her brows together.

I never considered marriage. Not really.

It was always a distant idea that seemed fine for some people, but not for me.

Then, I met Molly.

I've never wanted to protect someone this way before. Not even Fedor.

With Molly, my instincts feel primal, ingrained in my DNA. I want to be the person who holds her at night, I want to be the one she can confide in, and God forbid, if anyone comes for her or Theo, I want to be the man standing between her and danger.

If being her husband lets me do all of that, then so be it.

I think it might be too soon to have ideas like that. I've really only known her a couple of months and almost every second of that time has been spent putting out fires and solving problems. But now, Molly is looking into signing up for interior design courses, and the men who stayed by my side and didn't betray me for Fedor are willing to make our business more legitimate. We already have motels all around the city, so it isn't difficult to fix them up and, rather than treat them as fronts, use them as actual motels. With a great designer like Molly on my team, they could even turn into destinations in the city.

Even during this time of transition, we've found time for family dinners and date nights. Molly is eager to get into bed with me every night, and I have no desire to leave bed in the mornings. We're happy.

Molly, Theo, and I could have a real future together. One free of the dangers inherent in Bratva life.

It's that thought that propels me to pull into a parking space downtown and walk down the street lined with designer boutiques and hair salons. It's my hope for the future that convinces me to pull open the door and walk into the jewelry store.

∽

I leave Molly's ring in the car when I go into the Bratva's temporary office space.

The other building is being renovated because of the damage from the shootout, and we needed a more secure location to set up the infirmary.

Fedor is still in a coma. The wound to his stomach was a serious one, and he lost a great deal of blood. But the doctor suspects he will pull through.

"Any sign of the Mazzeos?" I ask Petr.

He has been acting as my head of security at the offices since half of our enforcers deserted to join what they thought would be Fedor's new Bratva. Unfortunately for them, that isn't going to happen now.

The moment Fedor wakes up and is well enough to understand what I'm saying to him, I'm going to kill him. I have to.

Petr has said many times that it doesn't make sense to keep him alive only to kill him, but I can't bring myself to kill my baby brother while he's unconscious. It seems wrong. Cowardly. I need to look him in the eye and face him when I do what must be done.

Part of me also has to admit that I want to give Fedor one last chance to correct his mistakes. I want to give him another chance at forgiveness. Even though I know it's too late for that. The day Fedor genuinely drops to his knees and asks for my forgiveness is the day the earth stops turning.

"Not a thing," Petr says. "Whatever hole they're hiding out in, it's a deep one."

"Good for them." The moment they show their faces, I'll kill them. I cannot trust them any longer.

"Fedor opened his eyes earlier this morning, but there hasn't been anything since," Petr says. "My guess is that as soon as we cut back on the painkillers, he'll come out of his stupor. Though, it might be better for him if he just stays this way. A coma has got to be better than where he's headed."

My anger matches Petr's. Honestly, it's probably greater. But I still can't bring myself to talk about my brother that way. Fighting with him in the parking lot, wrestling a gun from his hands to keep him from blowing my brains out, was one of the most horrific things I've ever done.

A lifetime of protecting Fedor disappeared in an instant. Suddenly, we were enemies, and I had to shoot him.

I haven't told anyone, but I pulled the shot at the last second. I could have hit him in the head as he ran. I probably should have.

But I couldn't.

I lowered my aim and hit him in the stomach. It still was nearly a fatal shot. He tried to run, but he did not get far. My men—those who remained loyal to me—found him half a dozen blocks away, bleeding out.

"Call me if he wakes up," I say simply. Even after his betrayal, seeing Fedor in a hospital bed is not pleasurable for me. Plus, I have other business to attend to.

~

"Theo did a cartwheel at gymnastics," Molly says, cutting off a piece of chicken and forking it into her mouth.

"Cool," I say, trying my best to sound enthusiastic.

She doesn't buy it and raises a brow at me. "Gymnastics is for boys and girls. I wish you wouldn't be so prehistoric about it."

"I didn't say anything!"

"You didn't have to. I can read your mind." She narrows her eyes at me, and I wink, making her smile.

If she could read my mind, she wouldn't be talking about gymnastics right now. The ring box sits uncomfortably in my back pocket, but I don't dare take it out. Not until the moment is right.

"Regardless of what you think you know, I'm happy for Theo. I'm glad he enjoys gymnastics."

I'm glad Theo and Molly are capable of enjoying anything, and I'm especially glad I can be the person who helps facilitate their happiness.

"Me too," Molly says, pushing food around her plate with a distracted smile on her face.

"What?" I ask.

She shakes her head, but I reach across the table and grab her hand. She drops her fork and smiles up at me.

"Tell me," I say.

"I'm happy." She shrugs like it's something simple. Like she hasn't had to work every day for the last five years for that happiness. "I'm just ... happy."

I really didn't think I'd be nervous, but now that the perfect moment has presented itself, my heart is pounding out of my chest. I drop her hand so she won't feel how hard I'm shaking and take a drink of water.

"I'm glad you're happy. I am, too."

"You are?" she asks.

I meet her eyes and lower my head, hoping she can see how much I mean it. "Of course I am, Molly. I'm so happy."

I swallow back nervousness and reach for the box in my pocket. "In fact, I'm so happy that I thought maybe we could talk about ways to continue it ... our happiness, I mean."

Molly's brows wrinkle and then shoot up. She must know what I'm saying.

I'm trying to remember the words I prepared beforehand, but they escape me, and I'm in the middle of stumbling through the most important moment of my life when my phone rings.

I thought I'd turned it to silent before dinner, so I reach for it, expecting to dismiss the call and continue on when I see Petr's name on the screen.

And the five text notifications underneath that.

"What is it?" Molly asks, reading the concern on my face.

I want to put down the phone and focus on her, but I can't ignore the nagging feeling in my stomach that something is wrong.

"I need to take this," I say, standing up and turning towards the balcony. "I'm sorry."

I answer before Molly can respond and immediately Petr's voice is shouting at me through the phone.

"Where the fuck have you been?" he screams. "We are fucked, Viktor! *Fucked!* Half of the guards are dead, I've been shot, and Fedor is gone."

I blink, waiting for Petr to tell me this is a bad prank, but there is nothing but silence on his end of the phone.

"What are you talking about?" I ask. "I was just there three hours ago."

"Yeah, well the Mazzeos were here ten minutes ago," he says. "They shot our guys and freed Fedor. I guess they liked the deal he was offering after all. Fuck!"

"Fedor was unconscious."

Molly can't hear Petr, but she can hear enough of my side of the conversation to know that something bad is going on. She stands up and moves behind me. "What is it?"

I stare into her brown eyes as Petr explains.

"I don't know if he was faking it or if it was impeccable timing, but he woke up. The Mazzeos helped him out of bed, and they fucking bounced."

I hear his phone buzz through the line at the same time mine does. I pull it away from my ear to read the message.

"Shit," Petr says sharply. "Shit. Fuck."

The message is from the manager of one of the hotels: *On fire. Bombing. Called 911.*

My phone buzzes again and again and each message seems to bring nothing but more bad news. All in all, four of the motels around the city have been attacked.

"What the fuck is going on?" Petr screams.

Molly repeats his question next to me, tugging on my arm to find out what is going on.

I sigh and respond to them both at the same time. "It's war."

28

MOLLY

I stare at the remainders of our romantic dinner—the flickering candles nearing the end of their wicks and the half-empty glasses of wine. Viktor was going to propose to me.

He was nervous, which he never is. That was my first clue.

My second was the bulge in his pocket. I spotted it when he led me to the terrace. It could have been anything—a wallet, a gun, a balled-up handkerchief—but I knew.

And I wanted it.

That is still the hardest thing to wrap my mind around. I wanted Viktor to propose. I was poised at the edge of my chair, desperate to accept him, to say yes and start a life with him.

And then the phone rang.

Just when I'd relaxed enough to think even for a second I could have a normal life, everything went to shit. Fedor is on the loose, the Mazzeos have resurfaced and are working in tandem with Fedor, and Viktor is gone.

I understand that he has to go and solve this issue. His business is literally burning, but I can't help but wonder if it will ever stop—the fighting and killing and burning. Will life ever be normal for us? Will there ever be an us?

I still think being with Viktor is the safest place for Theo, but how long will Viktor really want to put up with this drama? At some point, he'll get tired of protecting us. He'll decide to hand us over to Fedor and be done with it. I don't want to think that way about Viktor, but he's only human. We all have our limits. Except, I don't think Fedor does.

The insane don't understand limits.

He won't stop until he's killed Theo or has him. I thought he would be dead in a matter of days, but now he's free.

I press a hand to my chest and grip the railing of the balcony as an icy breeze slices through the warm air barrier provided by the outdoor heaters Viktor had installed.

He must feel so guilty. Viktor could have killed Fedor while he was unconscious, but he didn't want to. I supported him, and I still do, but if anything happens to anyone because of Fedor, Viktor will be riddled with guilt.

My fingers ache from how tightly I'm gripping the rail, so I release it and begin carrying dishes back inside. The maid will do it later, but I need something to keep me busy anyway. Theo is sleeping upstairs and the house is quiet. I'll be restless until Viktor gets home.

I scrape the food into the trash and take one last drink from my wine before pouring it down the sink. Then, I put the dishes in the dishwasher and lean back against the counter, frustrated that the task is over so quickly.

Suddenly, there is a loud bang.

I jump away from the counter, immediately searching the kitchen for a knife or anything heavy or sharp to defend myself with, but there isn't time. I see movement out of the corner of my eye, and Fedor is standing there. He has a walking cane in his hand.

It feels like a nightmare. I blink, expecting him to disappear, but he doesn't. He tips his head to the side and smiles. "Where the fuck is my son?" he snarls.

I run through the door to the right and straight for the stairs and the hallway that leads to Theo's room. I only realize the mistake I've made when hands reach out and yank me backwards, dragging me down to the floor.

Rio is standing over me. His face is twisted in anger, but it's easy to see that he's wavering. "Get what you need and let's go, Fedor."

"Your assistance is a condition of our deal," Fedor says, moving slowly and resting heavily on his cane. "Keep her here."

He walks past me, and I try to reach out and grab him, but Rio pins my arms to the ground with his knees.

Where are the guards? Where is George?

"Help!" I would usually be worried about waking Theo, but Fedor is going to do that anyway. "Help me!"

Rio's hand clamps down over my mouth. I try to bite his palm, and he backhands me across the face. "Don't do anything stupid."

I kick and thrash even harder. "Working with Fedor is stupid," I bite back, wrestling my face out from under his hand. "You're the idiot. He'll get you killed."

The fight drains out of me when I look up and see Theo in Fedor's arms.

They are mirrors of one another. The same pointed chins and wide-set cheekbones. The same wide eyes and dark hair and pale skin.

Seeing them together sends a chill down my spine. It is my worst nightmare come to life.

"Leave him alone." My voice is weak, but I'm afraid to raise it. I'm afraid for Theo to see me struggling and screaming. I don't want to scare him. I just want to appeal to whatever scrap of mercy Fedor might have left.

Then again, if I don't fight, this could be the last moment I ever see my son.

"Leave him alone," I repeat, my voice stronger.

Theo senses how upset I am and starts to wriggle in Fedor's grasp, his little confused face screwed up. "Get off my mom!"

Fedor grunts, trying to keep hold on the writhing little boy while trying not to succumb to the pain of his injuries. "Tell him to calm down or I'll calm him down myself. I don't have any problems carrying an unconscious kid out of here like a sack of potatoes."

My stomach roils and suddenly the fight drains out of me. "Theo," I say. "Theo, baby, it's okay. Just settle down, okay? These are friends of Viktor's."

The sound of Viktor's name settles him. That's when I realize Theo's been crying. Tears streak down his face and he wipes a balled-up fist under his runny nose. "What about you, Mom?"

"I'll be okay," I say, trying not to cry, too. Maybe if he cooperates, Fedor won't hurt him. But it will be harder for Theo to cooperate if I'm falling apart. My throat hurts from how hard I'm trying to keep my emotion in check.

Rio is still holding me down, but I do my best to remain what little dignity I have left as I shift my attention to Fedor. I have to try one more time. "Can't we talk about this? You don't want the responsibility. Believe me. We can share custody. You have a lawyer. Let's talk to him."

Fedor keeps his eyes on me as he tips his head towards Theo. "Take the kid, Rio. I don't want him to see her die."

My heart lurches. I want to grab for Theo, but if I do, Fedor will shoot me. And I don't want Theo to see that.

There is no way out.

My chest feels like it's being closed in a vise-like grip. I can't breathe, can't think.

Rio grabs Theo. My son reaches out for me, and I try to move towards him for one last goodbye—

"Don't," Fedor says. The crazed look in his eyes from the other night is gone now, replaced with something stable and dark. My hope of appealing to his merciful side vanishes. He has no merciful side.

Rio wrangles a struggling Theo and tries to move towards the door, but suddenly, he freezes.

I don't see anything, but we all hear it: the readying of a rifle.

Rio backs up into the living room and the person holding the rifle moves out of the shadows.

I could cry with relief when I see George. He is older than everyone in the room and less fit, but he has a bigger gun and much more training. Viktor told me he was in the military for most of his life. George has an arsenal of weapons that could rival most Bratva members.

As soon as George is in the room, he levels the gun at Fedor.

"Put your gun down or I'll kill her," Fedor says, waving the gun he has pointed at me.

"You'll kill her anyway," George says. "So, I'll keep my gun where it is, thanks."

I don't have any idea how George can be so calm, but I'm grateful for his presence. Especially as Fedor's eyes grow hard and distant.

"If killing her is inevitable, then why don't you turn and leave?" Fedor says. "Viktor will kill you when he realizes you failed to save her."

"Because I've wanted to kill you for a long time. If I have to die for it, so be it." George shrugs. "Kill her, and I'll kill you."

Fedor narrows his eyes in assessment.

"Are you doubting my honesty or my skill?" George asks. "Believe me, I'm an honorable man. If I tell you I'm going to kill you, I mean it. And if it is my skill that worries you, I served overseas for three tours. If you think I risked my life to come back to the States and let scum like you kill women and kidnap their babies, you're wrong."

"I don't have to kill her. We can compromise. Just let me take my son." Fedor reaches out a hand, gesturing for Rio to hand Theo over, but suddenly there is a loud, ear-splitting shot and the vase behind Fedor's hand explodes.

"You can't have the boy," George explains slowly. "If you want to walk out of here alive, leave the kid."

Rio drops his hold on Theo immediately, obviously taking George's threats seriously, and Theo runs to me.

I want to wrap him up in my arms, but with Fedor's gun still aimed in my direction, I can't risk it. I shove Theo behind my legs and take a step back.

The room is tense. Both men are in a stand-off, and I'm not sure if one of them is going to break or if they're going to shoot at the same time. Can George win this duel or will we once again be at Fedor's mercy once he lies dead on the floor?

I don't have to learn the answer to that question because Fedor finally lifts his gun into the air with his other hand. It's a lazy kind of surrender. A confident surrender, if such a thing is possible.

"Okay, okay," he says. "I'll leave ... but I'll be back."

Goosebumps bloom over my arms, and I grab Theo and haul him onto my hip. He buries his face in my neck and sobs.

"Don't cry, buddy," Fedor says softly. If I didn't know better, I'd think he actually cares about Theo. "I'll be back for you."

George moves between me and Fedor and gestures with his rifle. "Get out, Fedor."

He smiles, letting Rio flee the scene first before sauntering out behind him. He lifts one hand in a wave over his shoulder and then slams the door shut.

The moment the door closes, I collapse on shaky legs, press Theo against my chest like he's a baby, and sob.

29

VIKTOR

I thought I was putting out Fedor's fires before, but now I am literally putting out fires. My businesses are burning.

Four different motels that also operate as stash houses are on fire. Not only is it bad for business, but people are dying. Innocent people.

Three of the motels were mostly empty because they were under construction when Fedor and the Mazzeos struck, but one of them was half full and six people aren't accounted for yet.

This is all my fault. I should have killed Fedor when I had the chance. I shouldn't have let him live after what he did—kidnapping Molly, turning his back on me, and joining with the Mazzeos. He offered up information about my Bratva, and I let him live. I wanted to give him an honorable death.

Too bad he's not an honorable man.

One of the guards I had watching over Fedor at the hospital was a double agent. He pledged his loyalty to Fedor and then remained within my ranks as a mole. How many more men has Fedor turned? Who can I trust?

I run a hand down my face and turn back to the now-smoldering remains of the back half of the motel. Firefighters are digging through the remains in search of bodies, but they say it could take all night. Still, I don't want to leave. Not until I know how many are dead.

Molly will be okay at the apartment. She has George there and several guards.

Briefly, the idea that the guards stationed at the apartment could betray me crosses my mind, but I push it away. If something had happened at the apartment, I'd know by now. Molly would have called.

Unless she couldn't …

I tug on my hair and then press the heels of my hands into my eyes. An hour ago, I was about to propose. I was seconds away from dropping to one knee and asking Molly for her hand in marriage. And now?

My feelings are the same, but I can't propose to her on the same night my brother essentially has risen from the dead and brought me to my knees.

Fedor ruins fucking everything.

When my phone vibrates, I expect it to be Petr calling with news from the other motels, but instead it's George.

I answer calmly, hoping the rush of adrenaline I receive at the sight of his name is just an overreaction. A side effect of my overworked imagination.

"You need to come home," he says, voice low and serious. "It's not good."

I get enough information out of George to know that Fedor was in my house. He was in my house. With Theo and Molly.

He tried to hurt my family.

I don't start breathing again until I walk through the door—guarded by George and his rifle—and see Molly sitting on the couch.

"Molly!" I rush towards her. As I round the edge of the couch, I see the small leather bag at her feet ... and Theo sleeping next to her. He has his shoes on.

That stops me. I freeze and tilt my head to the side. "What is going on?"

"Fedor came here. He ..." She shakes her head and swallows down a sob. "He tried to take Theo. George scared him away."

"Shit, Molly." I drop to my knees next to her and grab her hand. "I'm so sorry I wasn't here. George said the guards watching the house were paid off. They deserted you, and I'm going to kill them for it. They won't live through the night."

"Were you going to propose to me tonight?" she asks suddenly.

The sudden question stuns me, keeping me silent for a moment. Then, I nod. There is no sense denying it. "I was. Just before the call came in."

She sighs, her lower lip trembling. "I thought so."

"We still can." I bring her fingers to my mouth and kiss her knuckles. "Fedor doesn't have to ruin everything. We can still be happy. Fuck him. Let's get married. For real. We can elope or have a big wedding or ... anything. *Anything.* I just want you and Theo. That's it."

I didn't think it made sense to propose to her before, but now it feels like this could be the perfect way to respond to Fedor's threats. He thinks he can waltz into my house and tear my family apart. Well, he can't. We will stay strong. Stay united. United against him.

As I'm talking, I realize Molly isn't moving. She's staring down at her lap, ignoring my breath on the back of her knuckles. My stomach flips.

"Were you going to say yes?" Maybe it's my own vanity, but I never considered she would refuse me.

Her brown eyes are wide and glassy with tears when her gaze meets mine. She nods. "I was."

I sigh with relief and grab her chin with my fingers, tilting her face towards mine.

She closes her eyes and leans into my kiss. Her hand fists in the front of my shirt, and I run my hands up her thighs, pushing her back into the cushions.

"I love you," I mumble against her mouth.

Molly goes stiff and pulls back.

I don't know how this could shock her, since she knows I was going to propose, but I say it again anyway. I look into her eyes and lay a hand across her smooth cheek. "I love you, Molly."

I can count on one hand the number of women I've said those words to, and I can count on one finger the number of times I've said it and meant it. I love Molly. More than I ever thought possible.

She's blinking up at me, dazed, and I expect her to break through the fog and return the sentiment, but instead, tears gather in the corners of her eyes, and she looks away.

I don't understand until my mind catches on the tense. *Was.* She *was* going to say yes.

"Molly?" I ask. "You want to marry me, right? You ..." *You love me?* The question hangs there, unspoken, too embarrassing to say out loud.

She nods. "I would have said yes, Viktor. I would have married you, but—"

"But nothing."

"But Fedor," she says passionately, before she remembers Theo at her side and lowers her voice. "It isn't safe for us here. I thought it would be safe with you, but I was wrong. This is the eye of the storm. Chaos and danger are swirling around us at all times as long as we're near you, and I need to get Theo out. I need to get him away from this mess."

"Where is *away* from this?" I challenge. "Do you think Fedor will give up? He won't. You are safest here where I can protect you."

"You couldn't protect us tonight," she whispers.

Rage snarls in my chest. "George saved you, and I hired George. That's a kind of protection. You won't have that anywhere else."

"We will start over somewhere new and change our names," she says. "It's the only way."

I shake my head. "No. You can't."

"We have to. You know that we aren't safe here. I have to do what's right for Theo, and as much as I want to stay, I can't."

"You can't," I repeat, biting out each word.

Her brows pinch together. "Excuse me?"

I stare at her, knowing she heard me. Knowing she understands what I mean.

"Are you telling me I can't go because you don't want me to or because you won't let me?"

Again, I stare at her.

She can't go. If I let Molly walk out of this house with Theo, I won't see her again. She'll be dead, and Theo will be … I don't even want to think about what Fedor has planned for Theo. I don't recognize Fedor anymore. I'm not sure what he's capable of.

"You can't keep me here," Molly says, standing up, towering over me since I'm still on my knees.

I rise to my full height and grab her hand. "I'm not trying to keep you here. I'm trying to keep you safe."

"That's the same thing," she says, her voice getting louder with every second. "You think you know what's best for me, so you don't care what I want."

"I know this world better than you do, Molly. You can't escape. If you go out there alone, you'll be killed. The safest place for your son is here. In my house. With me."

She doesn't say anything.

My fist tightens at my side. "I'm Theo's family, too. Don't I get a say? I want what's best for him, too."

She spins away from me and grabs her bag. "Then you'll let us leave."

Molly reaches for Theo to wake him up, but this conversation isn't over. She isn't thinking clearly.

I grab her hand and pull her back towards me, and she tries to draw it back, tries to pull away from me.

"Molly, stop."

"No!" she yells. "I won't. I'll never stop as long as I'm being held against my will."

Theo rolls over on the couch, blinking around the room. When he sees his mom, he runs to her and hugs her legs.

"Come on, baby," she says, patting the back of his head. "Grab your blanket. We're going."

Theo grabs the throw blanket and follows after her, and my vision goes black. It feels like I'm watching them leave through a television screen. Like I'm a helpless observer, screaming at the characters on the TV, begging them to make the right choice.

Molly is halfway across the room when I run to her and grab her arm.

"What are you doing?"

She tries to pull away from me, but I hold on tighter and pull her up the stairs. Theo follows sleepily behind us, taking the steps one at a time.

"Call it what you want—kidnapping or protection—but I can't let you leave. Not like this. Not tonight."

"Viktor!" Molly swings her arms, throwing her elbows at me, and I dodge.

"If you aren't careful, we'll fall down the stairs and land on Theo."

That stills her. Her shoulders go slack. "Viktor. Don't."

I pause outside her bedroom door. "Will you stay? Or will you run in the middle of the night like you did last time?"

Her silence is the only answer I need. I open the door and shove her inside.

The lock on the outside of the door is discreet. I realize Molly never even noticed when she's confused when she can't get the door open immediately. She tugs and twists on the handle but it doesn't budge.

"I'll talk to you in the morning," I yell through the door. "Get some sleep. Think about it."

She's still railing against the door when I put Theo to bed. He is confused, but exhausted enough that he falls asleep before I've even shut his bedroom door.

Once Molly quiets down, I walk downstairs and stumble into the kitchen. The wine I opened for our romantic dinner is on the counter, and I pull open the kitchen drawer and find the ring box under a pile of utensils.

I can't imagine Molly ever accepting this ring from me now. Not after I've literally locked her away.

"Fuck," I mumble, running my hands through my hair. I drop my elbows onto the counter and rest my head against my hands. "Fuck."

A few hours is all it took for Fedor to ruin everything. My business is in disarray, my relationship with Molly is over, and I have no idea what is going to happen next. Where will he strike? When?

My phone rings, and I'm embarrassed by how much the sound of it makes me jump. Then, I see Fedor's name on the screen. I answer the phone in a trance and lift it to my ear with numb hands.

I don't even say anything, but Fedor knows I'm listening.

"Sorry about all this fuss, brother." He almost sounds genuinely sorry. "You know how business can be."

"You came into my house. You touched my wife." He doesn't know the justice of the peace is a lie, and I don't intend to tell him. I suppose it doesn't matter that much anyways.

"You took my son," he counters lazily. "Like I said—business."

I grip the phone so hard I think it might crack in my hand. Red creeps into the edges of my vision. "You're right. It's business. Because you're not my brother. Not anymore. You came after my family—my real family—and that was a fucking mistake. I'm coming for you."

He chuckles. "Game on, brother."

~

The Kornilov Bratva duet concludes in Book 2, *TIL DEATH DO US PART*. Click here to start reading now!

ALSO BY NICOLE FOX

De Maggio Mafia Duet

Devil in a Suit (Book 1)

Devil at the Altar (Book 2)

Kornilov Bratva Duet

Married to the Don (Book 1)

Til Death Do Us Part (Book 2)

Volkov Bratva

Broken Vows (Book 1)

Broken Hope (Book 2)

Broken Sins *(standalone)*

Heirs to the Bratva Empire

Can be read in any order

Kostya

Maksim

Andrei

Tsezar Bratva

Nightfall (Book 1)

Daybreak (Book 2)

Russian Crime Brotherhood

Can be read in any order

Owned by the Mob Boss

Unprotected with the Mob Boss

Knocked Up by the Mob Boss

Sold to the Mob Boss

Stolen by the Mob Boss

Trapped with the Mob Boss

Other Standalones

Vin: A Mafia Romance

Box Sets

Bratva Mob Bosses (Russian Crime Brotherhood Books 1-6)

Tsezar Bratva (Tsezar Bratva Duet Books 1-2)

MAILING LIST

Sign up to my mailing list!
New subscribers receive a FREE steamy bad boy romance novel.

Click the link below to join.
http://bit.ly/NicoleFoxNewsletter

Printed in Great Britain
by Amazon